A Paris Affair

A PARIS AFFAIR

Book 1: The Hotel Baron Series

MARY OLDHAM

Kindle ISBN: 978-1-7377839-4-7
ePub ISBN: 978-1-7377839-6-1
Paperback ISBN: 978-1-7377839-5-4

Any references to historical events, real people, or real places are used fictitiously. Names, characters, and places are products of the author's imagination.

Story Editor
Edits by Sue, Sue Grimshaw

Cover Art by Lynn Andreozzi

Book design by Tamara Cribley at The Deliberate Page

Author Photo by Tanith Yates

Printed in the United States of America.

By-Creek-Ity Publishing
Portland, Oregon

First printing, 2021.

www.maryoldham.com

To MarySue Weekly Oldham, my sister from another mister. Thank you always for your love and unending support. You've always been my first proofreader and my first cheerleader. Love you!!!

CHAPTER ONE

PORTLAND

Pathetic much?

Daisy Miller stared at her cold coffee and wondered what her problem was. She was twenty-six, a smart, independent woman, but she'd been coming to this same little French café for two weeks and each and every day, Mr. Gorgeous appeared, and she'd turn into a lovesick teenager, one step away from puffing on an e-cigarette, in head-to-toe lululemon, parking an electric scooter on the sidewalk. *Pathetic.*

At 10:01 am, Mr. Gorgeous in t-shirt and jeans would walk into the French café, looking out of place in the busy little nod to Parisian elegance, that was until his eyes found hers and he would smile. Their smiles had become waves as he would slowly make his way to the counter where he would order a cappuccino and a chocolate croissant. Every freaking day, but today. It was her fault.

Daisy had blown it yesterday because she had changed the dynamic, taken charge, and ruined it. She hated to admit it, but aside from the upcoming interview she had next week, this was the only cherry on top of her life's sundae. The rest of everything was pathetic.

Yesterday, he'd looked at her, smiled, and what had she done? Did she smile and wave? No. Had she gone all stuck up and looked just past him? No. Had she ignored his twinkling emerald eyes as if every day a man looked so pointedly at her, and she couldn't be bothered? No. She had done something so much worse; she'd broken the pattern. She'd said, "Hello again, right on time."

And what had he done? He'd smiled, grabbed his coffee, and made a beeline for the door.

What the hell was wrong with her?

Yes, he came in every morning at ten like clockwork for the last fourteen days, including weekends. How did she know? Because she'd been stalking him for the past fourteen days.

She should be looking at her computer, trying to line up something else if this job at the Stark International Hotels didn't pan out. She took a moment and did the very equivalent of yoga breathing, only it was to keep herself from having a panic attack. Her life was imploding.

Her friend, Brigitte, had set her up with a few freelance marketing jobs, but they were coming to an end in a month or so. Severance from the job working for Satan was long gone. Heck, it had barely covered her legal fees when she sued him for sexual harassment and lost.

She had her third and final interview next week with Garrison Stark, the CEO of Stark International Hotels. The first two interviews with a sweet man named Don and his team had gone well. She had to get the job as the Associate Marketing Director for European Operations. It was a fancy way of saying work hard for little pay, but it was a wonderful resume builder. After a couple of years of hard work for Stark, she could write her ticket in the hospitality world and everything else that had happened with Satan would be forgotten.

Besides, if all she'd heard was true, she would finally get to travel a bit. So far, the team at Stark International Hotels seemed to like her, but she knew there was at least one other candidate, more likely two. Despite how well the first two interviews had gone, the CEO was the decision maker.

Thankfully, they hadn't questioned her resume too deeply, which was good because her last job, the reason for her departure, and the name of the company was all but omitted. Thankfully, Brigitte had provided an excellent reference and consulting line item. She was also a whiz at resume structure.

What really got to Daisy was that it wasn't her fault. What could she do? She hadn't asked for this. She had loved her job. The owner of the family business had fired her when he made a move on her that she didn't want to reciprocate. He was a married man, not that he cared. She'd taken the moral high ground, done the right thing, and it had gotten her fired.

She still remembered the way her boss of three years came onto her as they worked late one evening. "You know, Daisy, I think I've just about lost my willpower when it comes to you."

She remembered that she'd been confused by his words. What did he mean? He was attractive in a messy, young Brad Pitt kind of way, but he was married, and she didn't do married. She had met and liked his wife, Claire. In fact, she wondered why Claire was married to him. Now, she just felt sorry for the other woman. Daisy wondered if Claire knew she was married to Satan. That was how she thought of him now: the worst of the worst, destroyer of good people, especially women. He was evil and he deserved the nickname she had assigned him.

Daisy's mother hadn't allowed marriage to another woman to be a problem when she found her boss, Daisy's father, to be attractive and willing to embark on an affair that had lasted for decades, but that was another story and not one with a happy ending.

Her mother never let Daisy forget what happened when you gave your heart to the wrong person. It made her mother more than a little nuts. And wasn't Daisy the physical evidence of a bad decision? What a lovely moniker to always carry with you. The unwanted child. The result of a love affair that never should have happened.

Daisy's boss must have noticed she was confused because he looked at her and smiled before adding, "You drive me wild. I want to rip that suit off you and show you what I really do well. I could make you scream. One night with me, well, you'd never forget it. I'd ruin you for any other man. We could fuck each other's brains out. I know that is the kind of woman you are, you like to fuck and be fucked. I'm just the man for the job."

Her mouth had hung open for a good long time. Fly catcher, that is what her mother used to call it when something shocked Daisy so much she left her mouth gaping.

"I see I've surprised you. You've never seen this side of me before," her boss said, "but you've given me another idea. How would you like to taste me, call it an appetizer—"

He'd started unzipping his suit pants and she'd found her voice.

"What the hell do you think you're doing?" she asked as he presented his flaccid penis to her as if it were a gift like no other.

"I think it is time we moved this along. Enough of work, let's get to some pleasure. I think you've earned it. What do you think about taking our working relationship to the next level?"

Then he made the very, very wrong decision to take a step toward her and then another. Daisy perceived it as threatening. She let all the fight or flee responses kick in. Reaching down, she had picked up her red, Strathmore stapler from her desk. She threw it as hard as she could at her boss, watched it bounce off his forehead, saw the red smear of blood where it cut him, and she ran, ran until she was in her car with the doors locked.

Shivering herself back to reality, this was the time of day when she used to go for her mid-morning doppio (two shots of espresso from Starbucks), back when she used to dress in designer suits, her long, blonde hair worn up in an elaborate twist. That was when she'd been the marketing director for a chain of upscale restaurants. That was before she stood up to her boss when he suggested a little career advancement might be in order if only she would drop to her knees. When the president of the company asks for a blowjob and you report him for sexual harassment, chances are you might not win—especially when the business is family-owned and in the private sector.

Daisy still remembered what her lawyer told her when she showed him a copy of her personnel file, which had been artificially filled with violations and offenses that had never happened.

"Are you kidding? The boss basically grabbed your ass and asked for a little fun. You retaliated with force and then tattled to the HR manager who just happens to be his cousin? Kid, you're nuts. This

4

is the head cheese of a very large company you're messing with. Forget that social awareness, women's movement bullshit, this is 'he said, she said.' Women have finally moved forward, but there are still old family businesses that will never give you credit for just doing a great job. You can't win against power like that. Lick your wounds and move on," he'd advised, shaking his head in warning.

But she hadn't been able to let it go. A strong sense of right and wrong had her incensed. She wanted to sue. So, they did, and she'd lost. It had all come down to money: her boss had it and she did not. When Peter Crawley's lawyers made her an offer to keep the news of the lawsuit out of the paper, her lawyer hadn't advised her to do anything but settle. She still regretted the decision.

In the end, all she'd won was a black mark on her resume and three months of severance, of which her smarmy lawyer had taken half. She did have the third interview coming up and she hadn't yet decided how to spin what had happened if Garrison Stark started asking hard questions. It was starting to create real stress.

And what if she didn't get the job? What if she ran out of money, what would she do? Move in with her mother? Nope. Get a waitressing job? Well, she'd do what she had to do to make money as long as she could look herself in the mirror when she did it.

Her friends, many of whom worked with her in one way or another as coworkers or vendors associated with her previous employer, were forced to take sides. When it came to their employer or a large client who might actually be their largest client versus an outspoken young employee, it didn't take a rocket scientist to compute which side they'd choose. Their disloyal stampede away from Daisy's corner was not easily forgotten. She hadn't realized how much of her life was defined by her career. Aside from a few lifelong friends who had supported her like colorful Brigitte, and her passive-aggressive mother, she felt truly alone for the first time in her life.

Thinking of the humiliation and career suicide, not to mention the friends she'd lost or alienated, she shuddered and took a sip of the coffee which had turned cold about an hour earlier. She could not afford a refill. In fact, it was almost time for her to walk back to her apartment and watch television for a couple of hours, take a restless nap, and then defrosting something unremarkable and inexpensive for an early dinner. Ramen was her new food of choice. She had fallen a long way off the mark from the professional dynamo she had always envisioned for herself, and it still stung just as freshly as if it had happened yesterday. Heck, maybe it was time to admit defeat and start looking for a job in Seattle or San Francisco if the Stark job didn't happen. She'd been thinking that if that fell through, maybe a fresh start wasn't such a bad idea.

"I was wondering if this seat was taken?"

She looked up from her computer and into the emerald eyes of Mr. Gorgeous and felt her smile break out from ear to ear.

He was tall, a dark-haired man with broad shoulders that commanded the space around him. Dressed casually in a black silk t-shirt and khaki chinos today, he moved with the grace of a dancer, but had the build of a fighter. Every female with a heartbeat craned her neck to see if Daisy would let him join her. She had a feeling that if she didn't, Mr. Gorgeous would get a lot of other offers.

He was ten minutes late and she'd been woolgathering. He was holding two cappuccinos and two little bags of treats, which meant he'd come in, walked past her, and made purchases without her notice.

She was losing it.

"Hi there," he offered, smiling, and showing off a great set of dimples that transformed the hard angles of his face into something far more approachable. Not only was he handsome, but he was also cute. Dimples. Daisy liked dimples.

"Hel-oh," she managed, her voice cracking on the second syllable of her greeting.

"May I join you?" he repeated, as his luminescent emerald eyes lingered longer than they should, taking in every inch of her.

"Please do," she said and indicated to the chair across from her.

He had a great face. Stunning eyes, but it was his smile that held her attention. Okay, so the rest of him wasn't bad either. As nonchalantly as she could, she scrutinized him in much the same way he'd done to her. His arms were muscled without being overdone with a light coloring of tan that made her think of tropical beaches and faraway places. Powerful hands gripped the paper coffee cups. She glanced down at her half-eaten pastry and hoped she didn't have any stray crumbs sticking to her raspberry-red lipstick. She probably did, that would just be her luck.

"Thank you," he replied. Extending one of those tanned, powerful hands, the man across from her smiled and introduced himself. "I'm Alex. I've seen you here several mornings in a row. Almost feels like I know you, so I decided it was time that I did."

Warm, strong fingers engulfed the hand she'd automatically extended.

Swallowing hard, she whispered, "I'm Daisy. I've seen you here too."

"A pretty name for a pretty lady. Thank you for taking pity on me and letting me join you. I took a guess—well, the barista told me that you had the same order I did, so I brought you a fresh cappuccino and one of my favorites, a chocolate croissant." Picking up his coffee, he took a nervous sip and looked at her over the rim of his cup.

If there was someone taking pity, it wasn't her. Any woman in the café would have gladly freed up a chair for him.

"I'm happy for the company," she said wondering why he'd broken the pattern today. "Thank you so much for the coffee and croissant, that was very kind of you."

"Normally, I'd ask, if you come here often. But I know the answer, you're here each morning." The corner of his mouth curled upward.

"True, this has become a bit of a hangout since my job ended. It breaks up the day." Nothing like sounding like a total loser for the obviously gorgeous man.

"Their loss, I'm sure." But his smile faltered a degree. Now, she felt pathetic.

Running a hand nervously through her messy blonde hair, she smiled. "Thank you for that. It's been hard, breaking out of the pattern of going to an office every day. Boring actually. I like to work. And I like to be busy. To be honest, this is kind of torture, not having a job going somewhere, morphing into a career."

"What line of work?"

Wondering how to begin and hoping she wouldn't ruin this chance encounter, she offered, "I was the marketing director for an entertainment venue."

"I'm a little familiar with that line of work. Concerts and stuff? That sounds like it would be fun."

"Of course, it was a lot of fun," she replied. It was the most fun she'd ever had.

"What does a marketing director do for an entertainment venue? Book the talent?"

This was going off on the wrong direction. For each lie she told, she had to back it up with another lie. She worked for a restaurant chain for crap sake. This lie was taking on a life of its own.

"I handled all the advertising for twenty-eight venues, came up with the promotions, helped with the ad design and placement. In my last year, I took on the responsibility of a new venture. We decided to start promoting our ability to do large parties for weddings, anniversaries, and corporate events." She rambled on, watching as his lips curved into a warm smile. His rapt attention seemed to suck the intelligence right out of her. She didn't know what she sounded like, but she knew she should stop while she was ahead and shut up. She was pressing her luck.

"Listen to me. I'm saying 'we' as if I still work there. I'll stop talking now, so you can get a word in edgewise or escape, whichever is your preference."

"I like listening to you talk. I even like the sound of your voice," he observed between sips of cappuccino, almost sounding a bit surprised by the admission.

"You'll just have to believe me on this, I am capable of intelligent conversation." Even to her, her voice sounded unnaturally high. Was it him or the story she created? Either way, it was probably good rehearsal for the interview. She needed to calm down.

His head tilted to the side, then asked, "Am I making you nervous?"

Yes, handsome men, particularly *this* handsome man, made her nervous.

"No, I'm nervous about an interview I have next week, but I have seen you come in and out of the café and wondered if you work nearby?" Besides, he was good-looking and it wasn't easy to make eye contact with those emerald eyes. They looked through her. And there were women in the café who would kill for her chair.

"No, actually, I flew in about two weeks ago. I'm from New York. Tomorrow, I have a few meetings with my local client, but since I've never been here for any length of time, I thought I'd get the lay of the land. I was headed down to the waterfront a few days ago when I saw this place and decided to stop. The croissant and coffee were so good that I've been stopping here each morning."

How was it that for the first time in years she'd met someone who at first glance had everything she was looking for…drop-dead handsome, a brain in his head and a sense of humor, not to mention raw sex appeal…but he wasn't from Portland? Despite her efforts to improve her love life with the occasional date, her continued bad luck was alive and well, not skipping a beat. She supposed he was looking for a little short-term fun. Well buddy, you picked the wrong girl. Not only was she not interested in a quick fling, but she was also off her game for any kind of dating.

"What do you do?" she asked, her finger gently running along the white rim of the cappuccino cup he'd given her, pausing only briefly to wipe away a smudge of pinkish-red lipstick.

He took a sip of coffee and then offered vaguely, "I'm a glorified accountant. I go from place to place, solving problems. When I finish in one place, I'm on to the next. Home base is New York."

Even if the signals she was picking up were correct and he was as attracted to her as she was to him, he'd be leaving soon. She could hear her mother's embittered words: *The last thing you need is to get involved with someone who doesn't even live in the same city. He's probably married…He'll leave you brokenhearted!*

Daisy glanced at his left hand looking for the telltale indent of a wedding ring. No indent, but that didn't mean anything.

Could she allow herself to have some fun? Wasn't she a little tired of the job drama? This might be a fun distraction, if it didn't hurt her. She was a sensitive person, trying not to get hurt was like telling her it was okay to fall, but not okay to accidentally skin her knee. Things just happened.

She said, "That must be fun, living in New York…"

"Yes, when I'm home, which isn't often. I have a loft in Tribeca."

"Triangle below Canal Street."

"Very good, very few people know the actual area that makes up Tribeca," he said, looking impressed. "You've been to New York?"

"No, I'm not as well traveled as I'd like to be. But cities, geography, culture in general have always fascinated me. Kind of a hobby."

Aside from a trip to Mexico when she was sixteen and a couple of summer road trips to Victoria, BC, Daisy hadn't traveled anywhere remotely interesting. On the brighter side, if he wasn't from Portland, there would be no way he would have heard any of the stories about her ordeal with her Satan boss from Hell. That was good.

"Where does work take you besides Portland?" she asked trying to get more information out of him.

"I go all over. I've been spending a lot of time in Europe lately."

"That sounds like fun. I'd love to see Paris or Rome; even New York would feel like another country. I'm sorry, I must sound like a country bumpkin…"

"No, you don't. I'm lucky my job takes me all over. I predict you'll see all the places you want someday. Hopefully, you won't just be there for work, but you'll get to experience them as a tourist. Paris is the most romantic city in the world. This time of year, the blossoms are out, and the sky turns this incredible shade of pink at dusk. Everyone sits outside at cafés to people watch. The women are beautiful." He stared down at his cup and ran a fingertip over the rim, "You'd fit in perfectly."

Looking up from the hand touching his cup, she shyly met his eyes. He'd called her beautiful. The noise of the café dissolved. Taking a deep breath and releasing it slowly, she brought the world back into focus. Don't get drawn in. Don't let him think it is that easy to flatter you. Enjoy, but be careful! "Tell me more about Paris."

He did, and she was enchanted.

Daisy hadn't had a date in over a year and hadn't had sex since her last boyfriend a little over two years ago. It had been a downright pathetic experience at best. To be honest, her sexual history wasn't that great. A couple of boyfriends, neither of whom had rocked her world, nor were memorable for any reason that would matter. The man in front of her, well, he would be different. He wasn't some boy in his early twenties. Alex was a man, at least thirty-five, who looked quite capable of creating an earthquake that would knock her off her feet. It was the after effect that she worried about. She'd had a lot of those in the last few months, and she didn't need total devastation again. She could relegate this to just fun, couldn't she? As long as he didn't think she was easy.

Alex glanced at his watch and muttered a curse. "I'm so sorry, I need to be somewhere in ten minutes. But I have to tell you, this is the most enjoyable time I've had in a very long time, and I don't want it to end."

"Thank you, Alex, me too. It was lovely," Daisy said, and she meant it, giving him a tight-lipped smile. It had been glorious and now it was over. This would be a day she would not forget anytime soon.

"I'm leaving tomorrow, but I get to Portland fairly often. Would you like to have dinner with me tonight, maybe continue this great conversation?" he asked.

"Yes," she said, and smiled her biggest and best smile in a way she hadn't done in months. But what in the heck would she wear?

CHAPTER TWO

Garrison Alexander Stark sprinted back to the Stark International Hotel Portland. He was late for his meeting with the European and East Coast hotel managers. Well, they could wait. He hadn't been late in over two years, so it wasn't like he did it often or that he didn't respect their time. He just didn't think that he would spend so much time with the lovely Daisy. He was too late to change into a suit, so his team would see him in his casual wear—so what.

As he rode the elevator to the corporate offices on the fifteenth floor, he wondered, how long had it been since he'd been so enchanted with a woman? He couldn't remember. She was like no one he'd ever dated. She wasn't a model or actress, but with her looks she could be. No, she was a nice girl. That was a big change. Did he like nice girls? He didn't know. The only thing he could think about was her smile and the way she'd blushed. Who blushed anymore? None of his previous girlfriends ever blushed. His grandmother— now she used to blush.

The doors slid open, and he could see that his secretary was beside herself with concern.

"Oh, Mr. Stark, we were so worried. We tried your cell, and we could hear it ring in your office. Don was about to send out a security team to look for you—"

"Mrs. Cox, no worries. You haven't had me in Portland for too long, so please understand that I am unused to the city, and I got distracted. It will probably happen again, but at least next time I'll try to remember my cell, okay?"

"Yes, Mr. Stark."

A week ago, Alex had decided to stay a little longer in Portland. In fact, he was strongly considering moving his base of operation from New York to Portland. He could do that. He was the boss, and it wasn't like he didn't have a place to stay. Besides, one of his sisters and his best friend lived here. He could see Rebecca, and his friend, Peter, more often.

There would be a lot of whispering around the water cooler about his move. No one would ask him directly and that would be best because he didn't have a good reason. Well, he did have a good reason, but it made the hardened businessman look rather delicate if he was moving for a woman he'd had one conversation with who had intrigued him. When had enchanted become intrigued? Maybe that was a good way to think of it, that Daisy intrigued him. He'd like to say women intrigued him all the time, but something about her, this stranger, was so alluring like a fresh flower to a bee. He didn't want to think about it. He didn't want to think about Daisy. Now that he knew her name, it was much worse. He liked her name. It fit. Daisy. She really was a *Daisy*.

Alex stepped into the boardroom that was part of his office. "Sorry, I'm late, but I got distracted and lost track of time."

"What's her name?" Adam, his cousin in New York, asked from the zoom line that was projecting on the large screen. His smile was infectious, and everyone was soon smiling or smirking to keep their laughter at bay.

"None of your damn business, you little Runt," Alex said, affectionately, falling back on an old nickname they'd had when they were kids. Adam was now a handsome devil, a happily married husband and father. "What was your week like in New York?"

"Up 5 percent over last year," Adam said with a smile. Alex would tell him privately about Daisy.

"Nice, now let's hear from Paris, Rome, and London about the status on the anniversary parties," Alex answered and then pointed to a small cube on the screen that had a dark background. "Luis, an update from Paris please."

A well-tailored man's mouth began moving and Alex informed his employee, "Luis, you're still on mute."

Luis seemed to struggle with this problem, jabbing at buttons on his computer, finally calling over his equally befuddled assistant, Emile, who appeared on the screen talking excitedly to Luis.

"We will give you a minute," Alex said, and pointed to Maria in Roma. "How is Rome?"

"Bellissimo as always, Alex," Maria Medici answered through pouty lips as she examined her red fingernails. A Sophia Lauren lookalike, she was extremely temperamental, but one of his best managers. "Come see me, see for yourself."

"Yeah, I just might but I'm a little busy at the moment. How are you coming on the party? Still underbudget?"

Maria made a face and replied, "I'm not throwing a party for drunk American tourists in their stupid buses wanting little plaster replicas of the Colosseum. It is elegant. It is mysterious. It is Carnavale!"

"Watch your budget, please. Luis, are you on yet?"

"I'm here, Alex," the nervous man from Paris said.

"How is it going?" Alex asked, fearing his answer.

"The chef is working on a menu, the rooms are getting remodeled, and the chandelier was rewired yesterday."

Alex shook his head. He had a bad feeling about the Stark International Hotel Paris and also about Luis. Not only were they throwing a huge party, but they were also remodeling the hotel in the meantime.

"You're up, Benjamin." Benjamin Renwick was the manager of their operation in London. Alex despised him and was still toying with the idea of firing him for his constant insubordination.

"So, it is casual day in Yankland, I see," Benjamin began.

"When you're the CEO, they don't care if you dress casually. That is a perk of being the CEO," Alex said unnecessarily. He couldn't stand obnoxious and pretentious Benjamin Renwick. Not for the first time, he wondered why his father ever hired the man.

After the meeting, Alex watched everyone leave and then sat behind his desk that faced floor to ceiling windows. Portland, with the river running through it, was a beautiful city. It was so much smaller than his beloved New York, but where else could he be at the beach, the mountains, or the desert in an hour and a half? Yes, there was a lot to explore in the Pacific Northwest besides Daisy. However, all he could think about at the moment was Daisy.

His phone rang and he knew before answering who it would be.

"Her name is Daisy, okay," Alex said to his cousin Adam.

"And you met her how?" Adam asked.

"She goes to this French café every day at the same time. She's gorgeous. I'm intrigued. It is messing with me."

"It is about time. You've been all work and no play since you took over." Alex had taken over two years earlier when his father died unexpectedly. "Daisy, sweet name. What is her story?"

"Unemployed, works in the entertainment venue biz. More there, I feel it, but I'm not going to pry," Alex said.

"When is the next date?" Adam asked.

"First date is tonight."

"Don't do anything stupid. You did confirm she is single, didn't you?"

Alex hadn't asked. Now, the thought she might be married, or have some boyfriend consumed him. What if he showed up on their date and she brought some guy with her? Shit.

"I've got to go," Alex said.

"Naw, you're going to Google her, search her social media, try to figure out her details, but let me guess, you don't even know her last name?"

"Fuck off, Runt." But Alex was already considering hiring a private detective to find more information on his Daisy.

CHAPTER THREE

"Why is this so difficult?" Daisy asked her friend Brigitte as they stood in front of her closet in the apartment she rented in an old converted Victorian. "I have nothing to wear."

Brigitte smiled infectiously and said, "Well, you could do what I did last night. My man came over and I was on the dining room table totally naked except for the burgers and fries he likes from Red Robin. When you're naked, clothing doesn't matter. If he is as gorgeous as you say—"

"Stop. Seriously stop. I don't want to hear about it. It is our first date, of course I'm wearing clothes," Daisy said trying to get the image out of her head.

"Do you know how hard it was to keep fries warm?"

"La la la, we are going to Mother's Bistro, what should I wear?"

"I love the food there! So good!"

"And I should wear—"

"Those red silk undies you got when we went shopping at Nordstrom after work that night it snowed, remember?" Brigitte asked.

"You can leave now. I can figure it out on my own, My-Lady-Fucks-A-Lot."

"Oh, I kind of like that. My-Lady-Fucks-A-Lot."

"You would," Daisy said.

"Okay, let's use the red silk as a base and build on it. How about a black sweater, the cashmere one that shows a little cleavage, the dark jeans, and black suede boots or the black suede Gucci loafers you got at that fabulous Saks sale in Seattle?" Brigitte asked, pulling together the perfect outfit in moments.

"How long have you had this outfit sorted out?"

Brigitte smiled her Cheshire cat grin and said, "I thought about it on the drive over."

Alex had offered to drive her, but the slightly cautious side of Daisy declined. She drove her six-year-old gray Honda to 3rd Avenue and luckily found street parking almost in front of the restaurant.

As she started to use her cell phone to access Parking Kitty to pay for her parking, Alex appeared and shoved his credit card into the parking kiosk, adding in her license number and paying for her parking.

"You didn't need to do that," she said by way of greeting.

"I didn't need to, but I wanted to," he said as he pocketed his credit card, leaned toward her, and kissed her on the cheek. He then added, "See? Want and need, coming together. You look wonderful."

Where he kissed her, she tingled. So, it was going to be one of those kinds of evenings…

He was mesmerizing. It was all she could do to speak. "Thank you, I was hoping this wasn't too casual." He was in khaki trousers and a crisp white button-down shirt. His belt and shoes matched; they were faux crocodile in dark chocolate. She assumed faux because the thought they might be real…well, they could be, she didn't know how much he made, but if they were real, there was a real discrepancy between the two of them.

He offered and she took his hand as they walked the half block into the restaurant. He opened the door of Mother's Bistro and Bar and whistled.

"You haven't been here before?" she asked.

"No, it's gorgeous," he said. Sparkling chandeliers, high ceilings, gold-tin trim, and beautiful wainscoting along with subtle pastel upholstery made the restaurant feel like you'd entered a café in Paris, not to mention the little bouquets of roses on each table.

"Wait until you try the food," she said.

"What do you like to get?" he asked as they were shown to a table in a window seat reserved for "Alex."

Sitting on a cushion while Alex faced her, she said, "I like Mom's Meatloaf and Gravy." Besides, she didn't assume Alex was paying for dinner, but that, a cocktail, and tip would come in at under forty dollars, which she could afford, although not often.

The waiter arrived and inquired about a cocktail before dinner. Daisy was ready for a vodka and tonic. The one drink she'd be having that evening.

Alex looked at her and asked, "Do you like red wine?"

"Yes," she said, although it was the only liquor that had ever gotten her so drunk that she'd thrown up.

"Would it be okay if I ordered a bottle for the table?" he asked.

"Sure," she said and smiled. She liked this man.

He ordered something that was obviously expensive as the waiter smiled and nodded, then added, "Very good choice, sir."

A moment later the sommelier arrived and made a large production out of opening a bottle of something red from France. As Alex sniffed the cork, he winked at Daisy. Tasting the wine was as much for show as to impress the sommelier.

"Please allow her to be the taster," Alex said to the sommelier.

Daisy gave him a skeptical look. She didn't know about red wine, but once she took a small sip of the expensive ruby liquid she knew that money did buy happiness.

"This is amazing," she said truthfully.

Alex looked at the sommelier and said, "The lady likes it, so it stays."

She had her meatloaf, and Alex had a ribeye, which she knew was the most expensive thing on the menu. Ordering the meatloaf felt safe in case she needed to contribute to the bill, which being the modern woman she was, she would definitely do.

Pausing from her wine and food, she looked at the roses in a small vase on the table. This was a perfectly romantic evening.

"They are really perfect, aren't they?" Alex asked, following her eyes to the small arrangement. "If I could have made a rose to remind me of you this evening, it would be this rose."

"I think you just made me blush," she said, looking down.

As the waitress poured more wine, Alex asked, "Could you please find out what the name of the rose is in this bouquet?"

"I actually know," the woman answered. "I procure the flowers for the tables. This is the Blushing Lady."

Alex held out his arms as if to say he had guessed it right.

"Very good," Daisy said. "I love them."

They talked about Portland, the places he'd traveled, the places she wanted to go.

"Paris, Rome, London, New York, the Caribbean, someday," she said.

"Those are the short list?" he asked.

"Yes, but of course there is a second list and a third," she admitted. "Aside from Victoria, BC, Mexico when I was sixteen, and a trip to Disney when I was eight, I haven't been anywhere."

"Hawaii, Central America?" he asked.

"Priority list two," she admitted and wondered if she'd need to leave her car and take an Uber home. They were on the dregs of bottle one of wine and there were discussions of a bottle two.

"Did you like that wine?" he asked.

"Um, yes," she said.

"Good, let's order another bottle to drink with dessert."

Daisy thought of her credit card, if she had to split this meal with him, she could do it. She had about five-hundred dollars left on her credit card before it was maxed. She'd been saving the extra credit for an emergency, but what the hell?

"I'm so going to need to take an Uber home," she said.

"Don't worry about it. I'm having such a good time that I can't see an end to the evening."

"Neither can I," she said, surprising herself.

What had she learned about him? He'd grown up primarily in New York, but he'd been to Portland before because his mother's family lived here. He had a sister who lived in Lake Oswego, just south of the city. He'd gone to Wharton business school. She could almost smell the money and privilege, but Alex was unaffected. He was down to earth. And when he looked at her with those emerald eyes, there were moments when every rational, intelligent word left her. He'd kissed her cheek; she hadn't imagined that. And if she were a betting woman, she would be getting a good night kiss, maybe a few, which would be okay with her. The need to touch him, to be touched by him was strong.

He surprised her by asking, "You're not married or anything, are you?"

"No, I'm not married, and I don't have a boyfriend," she replied matter-of-factly. "You?"

"I don't have a boyfriend," he said with a straight face.

She playfully reached out and pinched his arm, as he grasped her hand in his across the table.

Bending close across the table, he whispered, "If I were with someone, I would never have asked to sit with you this morning or have dinner with you for that matter, okay?"

"You've got integrity," she said, with a smile.

His thumb rubbed over hers warming the skin beneath. "Well," he teased, "some."

Alex obviously liked dessert. He ordered that second bottle of wine and every dessert on the menu.

Daisy said, "Don't you just want to share some Crème Brûlée, as in one order?"

"We don't have to eat them all, but we have a full bottle of wine, so we might as well sample their full menu offerings."

When seven desserts including a crème brûlée showed up at the table, Daisy just shook her head. Her poor Visa card…it would take months to pay off this dinner.

But when the check arrived, Alex wouldn't let her pay for any of the dinner, part, half, Dutch, tip, anything. It was probably good because after they finished the second bottle of wine, she wasn't sure she remembered how to operate the zipper on her handbag.

They stepped outside Mother's and inhaled the night air.

"What is happening down by the waterfront?"

Smiling, she said, "It is May fifth tomorrow so that's the Cinco de Mayo celebration. It's a three-day event. Food, drink, and rides. It started this morning. I've been to it more times than I can remember. It's cheesy, but fun. A must-see if you've never been."

"It isn't your old employer, is it?" he asked.

"No," she said, "but I appreciate you asking."

"Shall we go check it out?" he asked.

She did not want the evening to end. So, when he held out his hand, she took it, and they began walking toward the bright lights and noise.

A loud knock awakened Daisy from her sleep. As she raised her head off the pillow, a dark web of confusion hung around her like a heavy black velvet curtain. Where was she?

"Oh my god," she said, recognizing a hotel room, but a little fuzzy on how she'd ended up there.

A knock thundered on the door, followed by a key turning in the lock.

"Housekeeping!" called a loud voice from the other room. A compact, dark-haired woman dressed in a black and white uniform stepped inside the suite's only bedroom hauling a large vacuum cleaner with her.

"I'm sorry," Daisy managed, as she covered herself with the sheet. "I...I just need a minute."

"It is one in the afternoon, well past check out time!" Daisy's head vibrated with each syllable.

"Just let me get up and then I'll leave." Was she in Alex's room? Where was she?

"Go. Now." The woman shook her finger at Daisy meaning business.

"I'll go," Daisy said.

Thankfully, she was still in her clothes and her purse sat on the highly polished surface of the desk.

What happened last night? Maybe she didn't want to know. Grabbing her things, she made a beeline for the door of the hotel room. Was she in Alex's room?

The maid gave her a dirty look, then began a verbal onslaught in a language Daisy did not understand.

Really, what happened last night? Where was Alex? And most importantly, what happened between them? Her brain was still under the dark veil of a hangover but started putting together the chain of events. They'd gone to the Cinco de Mayo celebration at the waterfront. They'd drank frozen margaritas that came out of machines. They'd ridden a rollercoaster. He'd kissed her on the Ferris wheel. More than once. The attendant had to kick them off, mid-kiss. And he hadn't been nice about it.

"Um, hello! The ride ended! Get off and get a room!"

They had giggled, really giggled, kissed more as they leaned against the walkway along the Willamette River. They ended up at the Stark hotel bar where Alex seemed to know the bartender.

After a cocktail or two…God, was it two? —at the hotel bar, Alex convinced her to go to his room. She remembered stupidly agreeing, knowing full well that she was setting in motion a night she might regret. When they'd entered the suite, a bottle of champagne was waiting in an ice bucket by the fireplace. Alex's cell phone rang midway through the bottle. He'd taken the call, then what?

Daisy found a mirror in the dark hallway outside the room she'd just been thrown out of and ran a comb through her hair, and to her dismay, noticed a pink stain on the front of her favorite jeans.

"Damn strawberry margarita." She'd spilled the second one she'd had. An alcoholic lightweight, she never had much more than a glass of wine. Last night, she'd been so caught up in being with Alex she'd thrown caution to the wind. They'd had two bottles of wine, a couple of margaritas, drinks at the bar, champagne in his room. It was amazing she was even vertical. Well, it was the early afternoon.

Pulling her hair back into a thick ponytail, she managed to apply her lipstick, the only cosmetic in her purse. She would not vomit in the large plant by the elevator, but she thought about it. Putting on her sunglasses to cut some of the painful light, she managed to punch the button for the elevator as her head pounded in anger. Fishing two aspirin from the bottom of her purse, she vowed to take them the moment she found a drinking fountain. With her luck, she'd only find a dog fountain, so popular these days in Portland.

She had awakened in a different room than the suite Alex had taken her to. Where the hell was he? She couldn't believe he'd checked out of the hotel and left her there. A quick check to her purse proved her wallet and cash were still inside. At least he hadn't robbed her. Great, she spent the night with a man she was worried might rob her? She was lucky to be alive with that kind of logic.

When she got to the lobby, it was all she could do not to break into a run. She wanted to get home and take the longest shower of her life. But instead, she headed toward the front desk to inquire after Alex. Had he already paid the bill? Pausing midway, she realized she didn't know his last name, hadn't looked at the room number when she left. How in the hell had she spent the entire evening with him and not known his last name?

As embarrassing as it was to admit, she needed to chalk this horrible situation up to pent up lust, a mariachi band, and way too much alcohol. Later, in the safety of her home, she'd kick herself in the butt for being so stupid and try to forget it ever happened.

Her cell phone, running on its last little bit of battery, displayed a text message as she found her car, with not one, but two parking tickets attached to its windshield.

WELL??? Brigitte.

I'M ALIVE. CAN YOU MEET FOR BREAKFAST? I NEED A DEBRIEF.

The response came back quickly, SWEETIE, IT IS THE AFTERNOON, I'LL COME TO YOUR PLACE WITH YUM BOWLS.

At the thought of a Yum Bowl with its yellowy sauce, Daisy opened the car door and wretched into the street.

"Fucking Luis in fucking Paris," Alex said after he hung up from his international call and downed three aspirin with a glass of ice water. He had a hangover. The first in several years. Then he glanced at the clock, called housekeeping, and then really let out a string of curse words.

After Daisy fell asleep while he was on a midnight call to Dubai the night before, he'd done the only gentlemanly thing he could think to do. He called the front desk and asked for a vacant suite near his own. Then, when the bellman delivered a keycard, he'd picked Daisy up in his arms and carried her to the suite. He'd laid her on the bed, removed her shoes, and covered her with a blanket.

He had done the right thing, although every cell in his body wanted to put her in his bed. Truth was, he didn't trust himself to do the right thing once she was in his bed. When he made love to Daisy, the moment had to be perfect.

He'd checked on her that morning as he'd made his way to his office. She was sound asleep. He'd checked on her two hours later, she was still out like a light. No wonder, they'd both gotten carried away, swept up in the moment. It was fun, and romantic. She was special, and he was a little more than intrigued, he was in lust. He couldn't wait to see her again, to kiss her, to feel her curvy body next to his own.

But the head of housekeeping had just informed him they had thrown her out. They weren't supposed to, in fact, he'd given instructions to inform her that he'd been called into a meeting and give her his contact info, his private cell, heck, his business card. It was time to be honest.

He should have left the card and a note on the bedside table. Why hadn't he left it? Because he trusted his staff to obey him. What did his father always say? "I don't pay you to think, I pay you to obey." Well, they had messed up and taken it upon themselves to think, and it would cost him dearly. No doubt she was extremely angry with him, and he couldn't blame her.

Now what?

CHAPTER FOUR

"One week, seven days, 168 tortuous hours and not a word have I heard," Daisy said as she mechanically looked over her suit for her Garrison Stark interview.

"Well, how could he get a hold of you?" Brigitte asked from where she sat on the corner of Daisy's bed.

"I don't know, I expected more I guess. It just feels unfinished, how we left it. How he left me. I mean couldn't he have slipped his business card into my handbag?"

"I think you are lucky because he could have been an international jewel thief or a hitman."

"He told me he was an accountant."

"What's he going to say, hey, I'm a jewel thief? Or I'm hired to kill people, but don't be scared."

"I get the sense he's a good guy."

"Why did you drink so much?" Brigitte, the usual life of the party who threw caution to the wind, asked.

"I was caught up in the moment and I trusted him. What is wrong with me?"

"You're too trusting."

"Yeah, I got that."

"It has been seven days, put it behind you and remember what is important," Brigitte said.

"My interview today with Garrison Stark at the scene of the crime."

"Your interview with Garrison Stark, end of story."

"You're right," Daisy said as she added a soft pink silk blouse to wear with her navy suit.

"What have you found out about the man you're interviewing with?" Brigitte asked.

"Garrison Stark. The Garrison Stark."

"'The Garrison Stark'?" she asked, frowning.

"I read an article in *Vanity Fair* from a couple of years ago. The title was 'Deep Cover: The Stark Family Secret Weapon'. They said he's a visionary. They also said he has a huge ego and is a total womanizer. He's been with a bunch of starlets and models, but never married, of course. He was a jet setting partier until his father died, then the family made him step in. There was a large concern he'd tank the business, but it has prospered despite his reputation."

"Sounds like a winner. What does he look like?" Brigitte asked.

"They showed him in shadow profile, but he was wrapped around this exotic-looking woman. I later heard she was one of his mistresses, whom he refused to marry. Can you believe they used the term mistress? I guess that is what rich people call their girlfriends. I was going to Google him but decided I can wait until the interview. I don't need to freak myself out. I don't think he'll want me for the job."

"Why would you say that?" Brigitte asked.

"Look at me, I look like a farmer's daughter, innocent and stupid."

"You are far from any of that, and we both know it."

"All I can say is that from what I've heard it is a good thing he has money, because he's had to pay his way out of a lot of bad boy behavior. The way he treats women, and with that ego, any decent woman would run for the hills. He'll think I'm a nun."

"Daisy, you don't look like a nun. Remember what Satan wanted you to do?"

"Yes, and that is what is scaring me. And, it wasn't just one article. It was several. He has a horrible reputation. Men like him use their power to their personal advantage. I read an interview with one of his ex-girlfriends. When he proposed to her, she thought he was asking for marriage, instead he was asking her to be his New York plaything. I have zero tolerance for men who objectify women like that."

"Excuse the pun, but what about the women who throw themselves at these kinds of men or bend the truth to sell a story to a tabloid?" Brigitte pointed out.

"They're pathetic, too. I bet if you could talk to one of Garrison Stark's women, she'd have the IQ of a gnat. Have they no respect? Don't they want to be known for their own merits?"

"Any photos of her?"

"No, she said he'd threatened to sue if they put in any photos, the jerk. And you are making an assumption. She might be the sane one who stood up for herself. In fact, to open herself up to such scrutiny, I bet she is the sane one."

"You know what they say about scorned lovers…"

"Stop defending him. They say he has crystal bowls of condoms on every table in his personal suites," she said as she held up two different shoes, one raw silk navy pump and the other a slingback.

"The silk pump," Brigitte advised.

"I've dealt with Garrison Stark's kind before. I refuse to let another skirt-chasing lothario stand in the way of my future."

"Lothario? Do people still say that? This is the twenty-first century, Daisy. Just keep an open mind. Just don't ruin the opportunity with preconceived ideas. Meet him, feel out the job, don't be hasty. I'd hate to think you wouldn't follow your dream because of one man. You don't know the whole story. Maybe he hasn't found the right woman yet. Maybe he regrets the past. Maybe he's searching for true love…Maybe he is just busy making the family business a success."

"Right, like that kind of man exists," Daisy replied, rolling her eyes.

"Alex was just a tease, let it go, not all men are like him. Who knows? You might find 'The Garrison Stark' attractive."

"Bite your tongue. Why did Alex have to be so damned perfect?" Daisy asked, still feeling a bit heartbroken over what had happened. Though she only had herself to blame. She knew he was in town a short while and in all of their conversation neither one thought to share last names. No, she needed to forget about that night and concentrate on getting this job.

"Trust me," Brigitte said, "men are like buses, there is always another one just around the corner."

After Brigitte left, Daisy finished getting ready for her interview with Garrison Stark. She was obsessed with thoughts of Alex. Angry that she couldn't get him out of her head, her lingering doubts grew legs of their own. She had to find a way to forget one of the best days of her life and stop trying to understand why he walked away. Correct that: abandoned her in a hotel suite! It hurt more because she was returning to the scene of the crime, the Stark International Hotel.

It had been over a week ago, why was she still thinking about Alex? Was she mad at him or herself? How could she have been so stupid as to go to a hotel room with a stranger? Well, actually she was damn lucky nothing happened. She was still a little fuzzy on how she ended up in a suite alone. Thankfully, she hadn't had sex with him. How much worse would it be if she had? Much, much worse. Then she wondered if he had indeed paid for the room and found a new depth for her guilt. What if he hadn't? Was the hotel going to come after one of them for stiffing the hotel on the bill?

For the next few hours, she had to focus on Garrison Stark. She couldn't have thoughts of Alex distracting her. They'd shared only a day together. She couldn't have fallen in love in those few hours. People didn't fall in love in just one day. But when she thought of their kisses and the way it felt to be in his arms, she wasn't sure. Even if he turned out to be an international jewel thief as Brigitte was sure he was, she couldn't deny they'd had chemistry. But he'd disappeared. So, to waste another moment on him was complete stupidity.

Shutting her eyes tightly, she clenched her hands into fists as she tried to drive thoughts of Alex from her mind. After a few deep breaths, she opened her eyes and checked her appearance in the mirror one last time. The navy suit with the pink silk shell looked good on her, as did matching midnight-blue, raw silk, high-heeled pumps and matching handbag. Good quality fake pearls at her ears and around her neck completed the look.

She took a moment to build up her confidence remembering her previous interviews. She'd sailed through the first two rounds. Everyone she'd met had been kind and made her feel welcome. Her dream job was an interview away. Unfortunately, there were two other final candidates in the same position. She had one chance to ace the interview with Garrison Stark.

"You can do it. You can do it!" She repeated the mantra until she felt the adrenaline start to course through her veins. Facing the mirror once more, she announced, "It's yours, girlfriend. This is your dream, your job. Now go prove to that playboy that he has to hire you!"

With renewed fervor, she grabbed her keys and marched out to her car, which waited in the parking lot behind the old, converted Victorian she lived in. Someday, she'd move out of her little apartment and get a real home. This job could make that dream come true.

Ten minutes later, she handed her keys to the valet at the Stark International Hotel. The bellman, dressed in a red wool jacket piped in gold, pulled open the door and bowed to her as she entered the cool hotel foyer.

The lobby was reminiscent of an elegant library in a large mansion. The rich walnut paneling set off the jewel tone accents of ruby and emerald. Low mahogany coffee tables surrounded by plush leather couches and oversized chairs hosted the afternoon tea service, in full swing at a little before two o'clock this precarious afternoon. It was a packed house just as it was when she fled the space a week earlier. Thankfully, there were also good memories that had nothing to do with being abandoned in the hotel.

Daisy had had everything on the afternoon tea's menu since the age of ten. The pomp and circumstance held sweet memories in her heart.

Purging the bad memory of a week earlier, she inhaled the rich air that hinted of worldly adventure and old money. The smell was always the same. Tea and lemon mixed with roses and a hint of Nepalese sandalwood.

On each of her birthdays, Daisy would come with her mother for afternoon tea. It was the one event they could enjoy together. They always started with a selection of tea sandwiches then moved on to honey crumpets and scones, finishing with petit fours. It was the one day each year she didn't feel like her mother's worst mistake.

Today, the smell of food made her stomach turn, her nerves raw and inconsolable as she made her way to the corporate elevator bay at the far corner of the lobby.

"Welcome Ms. Miller," the receptionist greeted, handing her the keycard that would grant her access to the executive floors. "Today, you're on fifteen for your meeting with Mr. Stark."

Daisy politely replied, "Thank you," as she accepted the keycard from the receptionist's outstretched hand.

Don Cooper, the Director of Marketing, was waiting for her when the elevator doors opened to the fifteenth floor.

"Welcome back, Daisy," he said, greeting her with a warm smile and an extended hand. Don, a silver-haired man in his late fifties had the demeanor of a favorite uncle. He would be her boss should she get the position, which was fine by her. She already liked him and knew he'd never feel the wrath of her stapler.

Taking in every detail of the opulent décor of the executive floor, she admired the deep, rich mahogany paneling and original art which adorned the walls. Her shoes sunk into plush Oriental rugs. What wasn't paneled in expensive wood was floor to ceiling glass, offering panoramic views of the city.

To her detriment, she had a very real, very debilitating problem with heights, struggling with the sense of vertigo since childhood. Sometimes it didn't bother her at all, like when she'd been with Alex riding the Ferris wheel at Cinco de Mayo. Maybe it had been the distracting company.

And sometimes, she was so incapacitated with the fear of falling she gripped onto anything solid around her and wouldn't let go until someone pried her fingers off the object in question.

"Thank you, Mr. Cooper. What a view." All the oxygen disappeared from the air around her as she tried to catch a breath.

"Please…Daisy, call me Don." The smile died on his face as an eyebrow rose in silent acknowledgment. "You're scared of heights." It was a statement, not a question.

Touching the paneled wall for reassurance, she admitted, "Maybe a little. This only bothers me because it looks like there is nothing between us and the ground below. The windows are just that clean."

"Our cleaning service would be happy to hear that. Would you like to sit down?"

"No, I should be fine in a minute. I wasn't expecting all the glass. It's like stepping into thin air."

He smiled and patted her shoulder. "The windows are strong. You could bounce against them, and nothing would happen."

She shuddered, her knees threatening to buckle under her weight. "Oh, let's not try that."

He laughed. "Don't feel bad, it happens to a surprising number of people when they step onto this floor."

"I'll pull it together in a moment or two." She wouldn't blow this interview because of a little fear.

"Then I'll try my best to distract you. Do you have any questions for me?"

"No, I'm just very excited about this opportunity."

"For what it's worth, I think you'd be great in this position."

"Thank you. That's very kind of you."

"I'm not just saying it. I think we'd be lucky to have you. Now, are you starting to feel even a little better?"

"Yes," she lied.

"Good, then let's not keep Mr. Stark waiting. We are very lucky, he told us this morning that he's decided to move his base operation from New York to Portland to be closer to his mother and sister. We will get to see him every day."

"Great." Something was making the fine hairs stand up on the back of her neck and it had nothing to do with the floor to ceiling windows.

"Just relax and be yourself. These interviews are very casual, informal chats really. We've told him a lot of good things about you already, so relax and enjoy yourself."

He made it sound like it was supposed to be fun. With trepidation, she followed Don through a labyrinth of hallways. They stopped in front of a set of double doors with an elaborate nameplate which read: *G. Alexander Stark*.

Alexander?

Alex.

Fear fluttered in her stomach with the strength of a thousand butterflies. Her *Alex* wasn't this *Alex*. But in the darkest recesses of her mind, she just knew they were one and the same person. Alex had been here all along. And he'd left her in the hotel room. *Alone.*

Don knocked and slowly opened the door, announcing, "Mr. Stark? I've got Deirdre Miller with me. Deirdre is her legal name, but she goes by Daisy. Are you ready for us?"

She heard a muffled response, then a brusque, "Daisy? Yes, come in."

The voice, the cadence…*no*! It *not* possible, no, no, no! It was like watching a horror film and knowing the heroine should run for her life, but she can't because she can't move her feet. *Run, you stupid girl! Run for your life!*

Smiling robotically, she followed Don into the largest office she'd ever seen. Positioned in the southwest corner of the building, the space caught both the morning light and afternoon sun. An oversized cordovan leather couch and chairs around a fireplace took up half of the room and a conference room table with twenty matching leather chairs occupied the rest. Garrison Stark had his back to them, staring out one of the floor-to-ceiling windows, but Daisy just knew it was him.

He was tall, imposing. His well-cut Italian black pinstripe suit fit like a glove, stretching across his expansive shoulders, framing his impressive physique. Yet, despite the fact he knew they were in his office, he had yet to turn around. It didn't matter. She'd have recognized him anywhere.

"Mr. Stark, I'd like to introduce you to our finalist, Daisy Miller…"

But it wasn't until he turned to face her that her body reacted and so did his.

Her tongue stuck to the roof of her mouth as her face flushed, radiating heat as those beautiful green eyes bore into her. Instead of the warmth and interest she'd seen in them a few days ago, now there was only cool detachment and absolute surprise. Garrison Alexander Stark. *Her Alex.* He hadn't known, but he was trying to cover it, she could see it.

She jerked back a step and tripped over the nonexistent elephant in the room, and heard her own gasp of surprise as she grabbed for the nearest thing she could to keep from falling. Don grabbed her arm, steadying her before she could make a complete fool of herself. Trying to speak, she found she had nothing to say. Nodding a silent thank you toward Don, she regained her balance.

Alex's eyes never left her as he stepped slowly toward her and extended his hand, then took hold of her palm in his much larger one. He held it a little longer than necessary, squeezed a little too hard. His palm was warm and dry, in contrast to her cool, clammy skin. It bothered her that he knew just how nervous she was by the contact alone. In a different place and time, this man had tenderly held her hand and kissed her as if she were the only woman in the world. Now what?

"Ms. Miller, why don't we sit down."

She had yet to utter a word, but her anger wanted to be heard. Was he kidding? He'd lied to her. A glorified accountant! Did he think she was completely stupid?

Don started toward the cluster of plush leather furniture by the fireplace, leading Daisy to where the other candidates had obviously sat during their informal chats.

"I prefer the table for this interview," Alex said and moved toward the conference table.

Confused, Don quickly guided her toward the imposing table next to the wall of windows. Alex headed for a chair closest to the glass and waited for Daisy to sit across from him, before seating himself. Don did the same, but sat next to her and offered, "Ms.

Miller is bit scared of heights. The windows are giving her some trouble today."

"Would you prefer not to be looking out?" Alex asked.

"No, I'm fine." She was anything but fine.

"You don't look fine, you look scared," Alex retorted, opening a strangely thick file that sat before him. She opened her mouth to tell him exactly what she thought of him, but before she could think of the appropriate snide comeback he said, "Let's get started. Would you consider yourself well traveled?"

He knew the answer. He knew of her desire to see Paris, and a myriad of other places.

"No, but as you already know, I'm well educated."

"What—" Don began.

Both Daisy and Alex said, "Shut up!" at the same time.

"Do you think you'd be able to handle the stress of international culture and travel when you've never done it before?" Not waiting for a response, he continued, "Stark International Hotels isn't Club Med. Your job won't be a dream vacation."

He had the nerve to be mad at her! She narrowed her eyes hoping he could feel the daggers she was shooting into him. He'd left her in a hotel room!

"I never thought this job would be a vacation. I thought you needed someone to help other people experience the luxury Stark International Hotels has to offer. My fresh perspective, as someone seeing everything for the first time will offer valuable insight."

She saw it then, his lips twitched as he stifled a contemptuous smile. He was just warming up. She wanted to lean across the table and slap that smile off his face.

"Do you worry you might lack the sophistication necessary that comes with exposure to other cultures through travel?"

That did it. She was going to take him down. Hard. Alex had lied to her and now he was just plain insulting. Beside her, Don shifting uncomfortably knowing he was in the middle of something but not sure what.

Bastard. He'd kissed her. She was going to stand up and let him have it. Just as she started to scoot back her chair, she realized it was what he wanted. He wanted to fluster her, get her admit their past so he wouldn't have to in front of Don.

"No, but I've studied every city where you have a hotel. I've learned about the areas and the local customs. I've spent the last two months preparing to work for this company. I highly doubt any of your other candidates have done the same. Nor could they list the forty-three cities where you have hotels. I can do it from memory. Hand me a pen and some paper. I'll prove it."

"Good answer, Daisy," Alex replied condescendingly and leaned back in his chair, close to the wall of glass.

Wincing, she drew his attention. "Does my proximity to the glass bother you?"

"Why should it?" The thought of his body hurling to the cement below was rather appealing.

"Just wondered if you have any concern for your potential boss's safety," he said, smiling smugly before he changed the subject. "What do you know about me?"

It was to be slow torture. Leave. Get up and walk out. "You?"

"Yes. What do you know about me?"

Lie. Tell the truth. What difference did it make? He was a bastard either way. "Only what I've read on the internet, in the Wall Street Journal, and Vanity Fair." He resembled the photos she'd seen online, but none of them had been clean-shaven. How stupid to have not recognized him, how dense could she be? *I'm just an accountant—*

"I'm curious to hear what conclusions you've come to..."

Narcissistic playboy. Egocentric jerk.

"...After all, we'll be working closely together, that is, should you get this position. Originally Don would've been your boss, but I've decided to make a few changes. I will oversee this position and the person who gets it will report directly to me."

Don stirred, kicked a table leg. Must be news to him, too. "Sir—"

"We'll talk about it later, Don," Alex said, still staring at Daisy.

"I want to make sure you'll be comfortable with that idea. I've quite a reputation as I know you've no doubt researched as you admitted." He smiled smugly.

"The internet is known for its inaccuracy." A thousand unsaid regrets filled her mind. If only she hadn't gone to that damn café last week. Then she wouldn't have met him, and damn if she still wasn't attracted. *But that attraction was to Alex, this is his alter-ego —*

It was then that she noticed a bowl of individually wrapped lollipops that bore a striking resemblance to colored condoms sitting conspicuously in the middle of the conference room table. Raising a single eyebrow, she glanced around the room and observed four other, similar crystal bowls adorning tabletops.

"What gives with the lollipops?" she asked, pulling the bowl toward her, and extracting an acid-green pop.

"I quit smoking two years ago, but I still like to keep my mouth occupied. Lollipops work well."

In that moment, she felt the heat wash over her. He was talking about their kisses, no doubt. She licked her lips slowly as she pushed the bowl back to the center of the table. If Don wasn't next to her, she wouldn't have trusted her next action, which might have been to leap across the table and kiss him—stupid, confused girl.

His mouth curved into a slight smile. "Don, do I have a reputation?"

"Yes, sir," Don replied.

"What is it?"

"You work us hard and demand our loyalty."

"He's right," Alex agreed, pointing at Don, but now looking at her. "Now Daisy, I'm going to be honest with you. Of the three candidates, you have the least amount of experience. I'm concerned, but you're the interview team's favorite. I'm left with a problem. I want to keep my team happy. But most of all, I want to be happy and after all, you'll be working with me."

Was he asking a question? Or was this merely a declaration? This ogre, inhabiting Alex's body didn't resemble the sweet man she'd met at all. How much worse would it have been if she'd actually had sex with him? Made love with this two-faced liar!

"Is your dilemma that you just don't like me, Alex, is that it?"

"That's Mr. Stark to you." He brought his hands together as if he were praying, leaning his chin against his fingertips in contemplation.

Tired of the conversation, tired of the jabs, she leaned forward and grabbed the lollipop off the table in front of her and ripped off the cellophane.

Alex smiled triumphantly causing Daisy's anger to find new depths.

Turning to Don, she asked, "I'm so sorry to ask this of you, but could I trouble you for a glass of water? I feel a tickle in my throat threatening to choke me."

Don looked to Alex, who waved his arm indifferently as he rocked in his chair, bumping against the glass window behind him. *Thump. Thump. Thump.*

"No problem, Daisy, I'll be back in a minute," Don said, looking pointedly at Alex.

"Make it a few minutes, Ms. Miller and I have to talk about a few things," Alex said, sounding bored. *Thump. Thump.*

Daisy stared down at the lollipop she twirled in her palm until she heard the door close. Pointing the candy at Alex, she snapped, "Stop the damn rocking."

"Bothering you?" *Thump. Thump.*

"Damn it, you know it is but why, I don't know. Maybe the thought of seeing you fall fifteen floors and crashing into a bloody pulp bothers me because I care what happens to you." Tossing the lollipop on the table, she added, "You're a bastard, you know that?"

He laughed then, his entire demeanor changing as he glanced toward the ceiling, smiling, his dimples showing as he resumed the rocking. "I'm so glad to know you care." *Thump.*

"Stop rocking and look at me, Alex."

He did. Staring at her with those penetrating green eyes.

"Don't do this to me. You lied to me. You didn't tell me who you really are. That's lying. You gave me the shock of my life, my heart almost stopped. How could you do that to me? How could you leave me in a strange hotel room like that? What is wrong with you?"

He leaned forward, his face turning serious. "One thing at a time. What could I have said about who I really am? Think about it. Is it too much to ask to see if a woman likes me for who I am, not the title I possess?"

"Oh please. You left me in a hotel room. You never intended on telling me the truth. You told me you didn't even live in Portland, but Don told me that you do. What a bunch of crap!"

"For the record, I've decided to stay in Portland on a little more permanent basis. My home base has always been New York, but I've always spent a significant amount of time in Portland. Recently, I decided to take a penthouse apartment in this hotel. And anyway, does any of it matter now? Nothing happened. But what the hell is wrong with you?"

"Excuse me?"

"How could you get that drunk with a stranger? Haven't you been warned about the bad things that can happen to a woman when she is incapacitated?"

"You were matching me drink for drink. How dare you question me like that? Double standards. Seriously, Alex, I'm disappointed in you."

He leaned closer. "I'm a lot bigger than you are. If I'd wanted, I could have violated you every which way I wanted. You weren't just asleep; you were passed out cold."

"Well thank you for not forcing yourself on me. That clearly would have been a mistake."

"I would agree, but I've never had to force myself on any woman. We would've been a horrible mistake." His words hit with stinging accuracy.

"Excuse me, Garrison *Alexander* Stark, I'm not the one who disappeared."

"It wasn't supposed to have happened that way. I'm still surprised you didn't recognize me with the supposed in-depth research you did for this interview. It's quite frankly a little disappointing, Daisy." He wagged his finger in disapproval.

"My mistake." Reaching down, she grabbed her handbag from the floor, then pushed back her chair and stood in one fluid movement.

"What? Are you terminating the interview?"

"Like you're going to hire me? I finally get the chance at a dream job and because you lied, I don't get it."

"You're so melodramatic. I mean, really...do you want this job? Can you handle working for someone who has bowls of condoms on every flat surface in his office?" He spread his hands wide to encompass all the bowls of lollipops scattered throughout the room.

"So, you read the *Vanity Fair* article, too, 'Stark's Secret Weapon'," she said.

"I'm in litigation to get a retraction. I've never had bowls of condoms in my home or office."

She placed the cellophane back on her green lollipop and dropped it into her open handbag. "I might as well enjoy the lollipop."

"Take the whole damn bowl for all I care."

Grabbing the crystal bowl, she poured the remaining lollipops into her bag. "Interesting for a man of your position to be filling bowls of candy because he can't get over a simple addiction to cancer sticks."

"I've cleaned up a lot since my partying days when getting photographed with a model seemed important. I cut my hair and shaved off my scruffy beard. Two years ago, I had a radical makeover because I had to. I had to grow up and take over this company because my father died. I traded my camouflage jackets and cigarettes for Armani suits and anything Gucci or Ferragamo I could buy. The only reminder of my past is the occasional urge for a cigarette. That is all the honesty you wanted, so I hope you feel better now," he said, his smile faltered, turning serious. "So, *Deirdre*, I'm sorry, *Daisy*, answer this question. Do you want the job?"

"Of course, I want it. It's mine and you know it. I'll find a way to work with you."

He had the nerve to laugh at her.

Alex couldn't believe it. Well, he could call off the private detective he'd hired. No wonder the man wasn't having any luck finding a Daisy with a gray Honda with a license plate that began with RT. It would be registered to Deirdre, not Daisy. He was about to accuse the man of being lazy and fire him. Well, that was a moot point now. Daisy, his Daisy, was in his office.

He needed to toughen up and find his edge or he was going to beg her for another date.

Turning serious, he said, "I'll only tell you this once, you get one chance and that's it. If you talk about me behind my back and I hear about it, I'll fire you. That *Vanity Fair* article was trash, and I won't have you spreading rumors. I'm fair and honest. I don't fuck around with my employees."

"To be fair, it was more than one article," she said, looking down at the empty crystal bowl absently running her fingertips along the serrated edge.

He was an idiot. This was a colossal mistake. And he'd said fuck. He never said fuck. Especially not to employees.

"That is exactly what I'm talking about. I don't care if there were three hundred articles. I'm your boss. From this day forward, the past is the past." Who was he trying to convince? Taking a deep breath, he said, "Our relationship is one of employer and employee. The moment I hire you, you are off limits to me and vice versa, despite what has happened in the past. You'll respect my position, or you'll walk away. Conversely, I'll respect you and give you space."

"You know I'll be good in the position," she surmised.

"You didn't answer my question. What's it going to be?"

She worked hard to contain herself. Like a lid atop a boiling pot, she wanted to explode. He could see it in her eyes and in how she raised her chin defiantly.

"Despite how much I hate you for lying to me and the fact that you left me alone in a hotel room, I want this job a lot more than I ever wanted you, so I will make you proud, Mr. Stark, very proud."

In that moment, he couldn't meet her eyes. The thought of her lush body had kept him awake for the last week for a host of reasons. Everything she'd done since stepping in his office had been well-orchestrated foreplay. Heck, if she had smiled at him the way she had the night of their dinner, he'd have taken her in his arms and kissed her, apologized for leaving her, and explain that he'd never hurt her again. He couldn't do that.

This wasn't going to end well. He could feel a host of bad things headed right for him. And all of them had one thing in common: *Daisy.*

"And despite that I know I'm making a huge mistake by taking you on, I can't help myself."

"Why would you say that?"

"You lack experience, aren't well traveled and quite frankly, you scare me a little."

Those aquamarine eyes narrowed, sparkling as she announced, "Within six months you'll wonder how you made it without me."

"That's highly unlikely, but six months is the exact length of your probation."

Boldly, she held up a green lollipop and twirled it in her fingers. "You're already impressed."

He swore under his breath. Damn it, she could read him. He loved her fire.

"Do I have an office?" she asked.

"Smallest one on the floor and close so I can keep an eye on you."

"What, like next door to yours?"

Leaning back, he smiled, it sounded like a fine idea to him. There was an available space, and it was right next door. "What do you think?"

"I know it is."

"It will teach you a lesson, so I suggest you come to terms with your fear of heights. You have floor to ceiling windows as well, but your office is the size of a broom closet." Literally, there was a maintenance closet next door with a wonderful view, he'd thought about knocking out a wall, remodeling it, and expanding his office. Now, it would be Daisy's.

"Lovely," she replied, but he didn't think her ego had suffered as he'd intended. She appeared fine with his lack of interest.

"You know what they say…Keep your friends close and your enemies closer. It will be interesting to see which one you are. You start on Monday. Come at nine and be ready to work."

Daisy, *his Daisy,* was now his new employee.

CHAPTER FIVE

O n Monday morning, Daisy unsuccessfully ignored the butterflies in her stomach as she stepped onto the fifteenth floor
of the Stark International Hotel to face her first day. She'd
been to Human Resources, received her photo ID and keycard.
When she signed her contracts and received a report of her bene-
fits and salary, she'd almost asked if there was some sort of mistake.

Her new position, Associate Marketing Director for European
Operations, came with a 50 percent raise over her last position.
Her $6,000 clothing allowance came with a deep discount at all
the hotel's boutiques.

What would she do with all the money? After she paid off
her student loans, she could eventually buy a little house. It would
have to be low maintenance, because she would be traveling so she
might opt for a condo or townhouse. What would she have to do
to prove she was worthy of such a generous salary?

When she'd left Alex's office the previous Friday, he'd told her
nothing of what she would be doing on her first day. All weekend
long, her emotions ran to extremes. Dressed in a new plum-colored,
brushed-silk suit with matching suede shoes and subtle gold jewelry,
her hair up in a twist, her makeup complementary but subdued—
on the inside she was trembling with fear.

No one waited to greet her. In fact, it was very quiet on the fifteenth floor and for a moment, she worried she was at the wrong
place. She made her way to Alex's office with the knowledge she
belonged next door. Each office she passed was empty, adding to her

fear. Ignoring her insecurities and the massive walls of windows, she looked for the double doors with the nameplate bearing Alex's name.

After a few twists and turns down the quiet hallways, she saw the double doors ajar just ahead. To the right of Alex's door, she found another bearing her name. How had they managed to get it done so quickly? Was it already on the door Friday when she'd interviewed? Running her fingers over the engraved brass plate, she felt the smooth grooves spelling out her name. This made it real.

"Good morning."

Startled at the interruption in the silence, she spun around and rammed into Alex, hitting him so hard he took a step back to regain his balance.

"Whoa," he exclaimed, righting himself.

"I'm sorry," she said, taking a step away from him. "Did I hurt you?"

"Hardly. I see you found your office."

"Yes, but I haven't been inside yet. It…it seems very quiet. Where is everyone?"

"Staff meeting on the fourteenth floor. When you're in town, your attendance will be required. Today, we both get a reprieve because we have business to discuss. Get settled and come to my office." Without waiting for a reply, he headed back to his office leaving her in the empty hallway.

Her office was one-tenth the size of her boss's. It wouldn't have surprised her if he'd purposely refigured the walls to make the space overtly smaller to prove a point. Had it not been for the view or the high-end furnishings, she would've called it a closet, but she could smell fresh paint, which made her all kinds of suspicious.

There was a small desk with two chairs facing the floor to ceiling windows. Taking up their own fair share of the space were half a dozen waist-high, leafy green potted plants with excessive foliage that had been thoughtfully arranged along the base of the windows, creating a barrier between her and the glass. She made a mental note to thank Don for being so considerate.

Don had never reappeared on Friday. She figured he would have a lot of questions for her. What was she to say?

In such a small space, she had to fight with the encroaching green leaves just to put her purse in a drawer, as she looked for a pad and pen. A moment later, she knocked on Alex's door and waited to be invited inside.

"Come in, Daisy."

When she saw his glowing smile she thought it was for her, only to realize he was in the middle of a phone call. It was the first time since their day together that he looked like himself with a natural smile and friendly tone. Sitting in one of the plush leather chairs in front of his desk, she tried not to listen, but was helpless to avoid his end of the conversation.

"I know. I had a lot of fun, too." He pointedly glanced at her as if she were intruding. "Okay sweetie, I'll see you tonight. We will do anything you want. Just try to contain yourself until six." He chuckled at whatever the caller said in response and hung up.

'Try to contain yourself...' What an ego! She let out a small growl as she gritted her teeth and uncapped her pen. She'd been the one to dodge a bullet. No other way to look at it. She was lucky. Damn lucky she hadn't slept with him. Egomaniac. Skirt chasing playboy! Had she jumped from the fat to the fire? First her Satan boss, now Alexander Stark. She supposed she'd have to get used to seeing him with his girlfriends. That would not be easy. A part of her, well a rather large part of her, felt that she'd missed a very large opportunity at happiness by being with Alex. Her heart still hurt.

"My niece," he explained with a shrug.

She didn't dignify his explanation with a response. She'd bet her new salary his 'niece' was probably a blonde bimbo he'd met at the hotel bar the night before, but it wasn't her business. And at least, he'd made himself clear...He wasn't interested in her. Theirs was a business relationship. She forced her anger into a tight-lipped smile and stared him down.

Losing the smile he'd had for his caller, he got serious. "All right, let me tell you about your first project."

After witnessing his phone etiquette, civility would be hard, and jealousy would have to be dealt with.

Oblivious to her personal conflict, he began, "As you know, the Stark International Hotels chain is celebrating our one hundredth year in business. In a couple of months, we're hosting an anniversary party to be held at our hotels in Rome, London, and Paris. We've invited some of our most loyal guests, which include a few celebrities from Hollywood and Europe, a handful of royalty, and several heads of state. We'll start in Rome, move on to London, and end up in Paris for the grand finale six days later. Guests will spend two nights in each city, and we'll pamper the hell out of them. During the day, we'll offer exclusive experiences, something very special and unique in each city. For example, in Rome there will be a private Vatican tour and undiscovered treasures of Pompeii, and so on. These aren't run of the mill tourist events. No tour buses—only limousines. The second night in each city will have a party hosted by each hotel. Each party will offer something unusual. We are well underway with plans, but I have concerns.

"Mrs. Lindstrom, our former Marketing Director, came up with the idea. As you might have heard from Don, she has chosen to stay at home with her new baby. We'd hoped she'd be able to continue as a consultant, but with a newborn and the travel involved, it's too challenging. She put together a report on the progress at each hotel before she left. I've been following up, but we have a deep concern about one of the hotels being ready in time. The Stark International Hotel Paris is about finished with a full-scale renovation. The manager is Luis Gardot. From my communications with Gardot over the last few days, I think Mrs. Lindstrom's concerns were well founded. Not only is he being extremely vague about his plans, but he lacks the confidence I need from him to carry them off."

Raising an eyebrow, she waited as he leaned back in his chair and sighed. Speaking more to himself than to her, he said, "The Paris party must be the best of all. Not only is it the finale, but it's also the grand reopening of Stark International Hotel Paris. I think Gardot's in over his head and too scared or stupid to ask for help."

He pushed back his chair and stood, walking over to the wall of windows, his hand casually in his trouser pocket as he stared out at the view. Looking over his shoulder, he met her eyes and said,

"I can't be everywhere, and I need someone I trust to oversee the operation, answer questions, make decisions. I've decided you'll fly to Paris and be that person."

Her head snapped up in surprise, eliciting a small smile from him. "After you meet with Gardot, I want you to assess the situation and call me. I'm trusting you'll find the problems and solve them before they get too out of hand. I don't want this to blow up in our faces."

She wasn't sure if she was more surprised that he considered her worthy of such responsibility or that he trusted her.

"Do you have any questions?"

"What are your areas of concern and how long will I be gone?"

"I want you to spend at least a week with Gardot. Have him show you around the hotel, check out the rooms, meet the staff, and see if they're trained. Check on the renovations, make a note of where they're falling behind, and get him to tell you about the party. Get into the details. Go over the menu and décor. Look into the excursions for the VIP guests and confirm all the details pertaining to them. Most of all, make sure everything will be ready on time."

It was a daunting list. "All of that in just a week?"

"If you don't have a handle on it in seven days, we will reevaluate."

That sounded a bit threatening. "Does he know I'm coming?"

"Yes, and he's nervous. I think he's hiding something from me. You need to find out what it is."

"Kind of sounds like I'm a spy."

"You are a spy. You're my spy." Walking toward her, he sat on the corner of his desk, looming over her to emphasize his next words. "You answer only to me. Your loyalty is only to me. If Gardot gives you any trouble or tries to tell you anything in confidence, I want to know about it. Understand?"

"Yes, sir."

"Good. Now, the party specs, guest list, and everything else is on your desk. Take the rest of the day and learn them. You're leaving tomorrow afternoon. That is why we asked about your passport at the first interview."

"My passport is good for another seven years," she said, trying not to react. Tomorrow she would be flying to Paris! "Thank you, sir, anything else?"

Looking irritated, he added, "Call me Alex. Hearing you call me 'Mr. Stark' and 'sir' just isn't right."

Seeing a glimpse of the man she'd once fallen for, she replied, "Thank you, Alex."

With a sad smile, he dismissed her, "Have a good first day, Daisy."

So, they weren't going to discuss what happened anymore? It was over, a part of the past. Part of Daisy felt bereft and wanted to cry.

A steady stream of people stopped by her office to introduce themselves and wish her well.

When Don arrived, she thanked him for the potted plants.

"It was very kind of you," she offered a bit shyly. "They're absolutely beautiful. It really makes being in this office tolerable. I feel like I'm in a tropical rainforest."

A peculiar look crossed his face. Glancing cautiously toward the hall, he whispered, "It wasn't me. They weren't here the last time I was in your office."

"Then who?"

He pointed to the office next door. "I'm not sure, but I heard they were delivered on Saturday, and he was seen arranging them Saturday afternoon after the paint dried."

"Alex?"

He nodded.

"Should I thank him?"

"Absolutely not. If he wanted you to know it was him, you would know. By the way, I take it you'd met before the interview. You both looked shocked."

"It's complicated, was only one date, and it is over, so I now know. I guess I need a job much more than a boyfriend."

"Absolutely his loss," Don said is a quiet whisper.

"Thank you," she said, and fought the urge to cry. "They look so expensive, the plants. Why would he do this?"

"Trust me on this. Let it go. Maybe someday he will tell you."

"Pathetic as it is, I hope so."

"Me too, but put it out of your mind," he said.

She tried. But for the rest of the day, each time she brushed a shiny green leaf she thought of Alex, not the hotel baron next door, but the man who'd kissed her one magical evening.

CHAPTER SIX

PARIS
TWO DAYS LATER

Standing in the lobby of the Stark International Hotel Paris with her luggage beside her, Daisy walked in a slow circle, taking in every angle of opulence the twelve-story balconied space offered. Workers walked past her carrying large bolts of carpet, pieces of molding, and cans of paint. Not yet open to the public, the red and gold space was beginning to take shape but had a long way to go in a few short weeks. The floor was covered in debris, the large lobby devoid of furniture. Listening as voices wafted softly in French around her, she heard machines whirring and nails being pounded into wood as a strong sense of unease overtook her. How could this space possibly be ready in time?

Luis Gardot, the elegantly dressed hotel manager, hurried through the chaos to greet her. She thought he had the boyish look of a young Matt Damon as he shook her hand delicately. Wary, nervous blue eyes assessed her. He had to be in his early forties, but he felt more like a peer to her twenty-six-year-old self.

"Welcome, Mademoiselle Miller. It's so nice to meet you. Welcome to our beautiful hotel," he offered, extending his arms wide for emphasis.

"Please call me Daisy."

"Merci. I'm Luis. After you've had a chance to relax in the Executive Suite, I thought we would have a late lunch and talk. I know Alex—, Monsieur Stark is anxious to hear about our progress and plans for the celebration. He tells me you're quite a valuable asset to have at my disposal."

She watched a huge crystal chandelier being tentatively hung five stories above her head, the soft sound of chimes ringing musically as hundreds of glass prisms brushed against each other. She took several protective steps back, wishing to steer clear of imminent danger.

"That was uncharacteristically generous of him," she said, her eyes never leaving the crystal chandelier overhead.

Following her gaze, he studied the dangling, two-story crystal structure and gave her a wide smile, "Do not worry, they know what they're doing."

"Before I go to the suite, why don't you give me a brief summary of where things currently stand so I can be thinking about how I might help you while I freshen up."

He shrugged dismissively, "We've been anticipating our reopening for a year and a half. Then we were asked to be ready for the anniversary celebration. It's our chance to reintroduce ourselves. We have the extra challenge of both events happening at the same time."

"How is your timeline coming along?"

Luis sighed, "I left the anniversary celebration largely to our former chef. He planned the menu, put in the order for everything we would need and then, two weeks ago, he was hired away by the Ritz-Carlton—"

"We don't have a chef?" she asked, her voice rising over the loud hammering.

With a shrug, he said, "Oui, but do not worry. Through a very accomplished culinary acquaintance, I was able to hire someone else quite quickly, but he has his own ideas. We've been trying to integrate the two very different visions as best we can."

She was suspicious of a chef who was easy to get on short notice. Maybe Alex would be willing to lend them another chef from one of the other Stark hotels.

"Two different visions…tell me about that," she said, fleshing out something that he didn't want her to know.

"Well…"

"What is it? Is there a theme?"

"Oui."

"It's something European I assume. Parisian?" Her mind went to the world of Toulouse Lautrec or Marie Antoinette, but she was ill prepared for Luis's next words.

"It is something American."

"American? As in something like Pacific Northwest cuisine?" she asked, familiar with Pacific Northwest cuisine. It tended toward an Asian influence. It could be elegant and tasteful at the same time. They could swing it to be a little more French, a kind of French-Japanese fusion. The décor could have Japanese lanterns and beautifully prepared plates of sushi. It could be spectacular.

He shook his head and unease settled like fog around Daisy as he uttered the word of her sure downfall.

"Barbeque."

"What?" she asked, no longer caring about the chandelier overhead. "You're telling me that Alexander Stark approved a theme of American barbeque?"

"Not exactly. It was the chef's inspiration. I must admit, some of the items that are arriving are quite unique and I'm now second guessing his vision..."

"I bet," she agreed, thinking that Luis had a big reason to be nervous. "What has arrived?"

"A mechanical bull, bales of hay, cowboy hats, cases of Jack Daniels..."

They were in Paris, one of the oldest cities in the world, and the man who was responsible for the largest party the company had ever thrown was talking about a barbeque. Images of rich Europeans in elegant gowns and tuxedos trying to eat beef ribs and potato salad flooded her mind. It was Busters BBQ meets the Versailles. It would be horrific. Calming her voice, trying to hide the impending doom, she asked, "Is it too late to change? Maybe consider the whole Pacific Northwest idea..."

"We've completely spent our budget. The previous chef figured many of the guests coming from America would be tired of the rich, European faire by the end of the week of parties and chose the idea."

"Mrs. Lindstrom, the woman on maternity leave, did she know about this?"

"No, it was decided after she left," he offered and then, "May I suggest we show you to the Executive Suite and allow you to freshen up?"

"I have a couple of things to share with you before I freshen up, my friend. Two thoughts: First, we're going to be the laughing-stock of Paris. Second, Alexander Stark is going to blame you for this idea and me for not finding a way to save us from complete humiliation. When he's done, we are both going to be his former employees. Understand? Comprende vous?"

"It would appear that you understand the situation quite clearly," he said, before snapping his fingers for a bellboy to fetch her bags.

Daisy fumed all the way to the Executive Suite as an inexperienced bellboy showed her to the top floor. She tipped him with a ten Euro note, part of the traveling package delivered to her home along with her first-class airline ticket the night before she left.

Stepping inside the suite, she allowed herself a moment to forget Luis and his Parisian barbeque. She dropped her purse and wrinkled suit jacket on the nearest surface and walked slowly to the window, savoring the magnificent postcard before her.

The Eiffel Tower was framed perfectly against the Seine River in the center window. Despite whatever happened with her job, she would always have this moment. Not even the powerful Garrison Alexander Stark could take this away from her. She stared at the breathtaking monument for several minutes in disbelief. She reached out and touched the thick, ornate window frame, it gave her comfort, helped with how high up she was. Eventually, she scanned the rest of the space, taking in each lovely detail.

Decorated in cream and gold Louis XVI furnishings, the two-bedroom, two-bath space was huge. She chose the mauve and cream bedroom with a complimentary pink marble bath. Everything looked new. This renovation on this suite had gone well. The sheer opulence flooded her senses. For one person, the space was enormous. Catching a glimpse of her reflection in the mirror, her raccoon-like, mascara-smeared eyes looked huge, and filled with awe. No wonder Luis suggested she freshen up. After shedding her travel weary clothing, she stepped into the pink marble shower, adjusted the temperature to her satisfaction and dunked under the spray. Alex no doubt had stood in the very spot. She doubted he'd been alone. One of the articles she'd read talked about a tall, dark-haired European mistress. Thinking about him and wondering about the other women in his life was pure torture. She had to forget about Garrison Alexander Stark and his extensive sex life. Neither item had anything to do with her. He was her boss, nothing more, nothing less.

They'd shared an evening…one glorious, over the top, never to be forgotten experience. They hadn't been lovers. But when she thought of the kiss they'd shared, the intimacy of his lips on hers, she had to lean against the cool marble wall for support.

Remembering the phone call she'd eavesdropped on, she felt the regret burn deep. Despite how much he protested to the contrary about looking for the love of his life, he hadn't let any grass grow under his feet. After he left her in the hotel suite, he moved on, easily.

But wasn't this better? Wasn't a dream job better than a dream man any day? Turning off the shower, she decided it was best not to think about it anymore. She had bigger, more important things on her plate.

Hurrying to get ready for lunch, she used the supplied hair dryer, reapplied her makeup, and then dressed in a pair of cream linen trousers, matching silk blouse and burnt orange suede jacket. She added a strand of oversized fake pearls. Knowing she still looked like an American straight out of a Nordstrom catalog, she turned up the collar of her blouse trying to add a bit of style. At some point, she would be hitting the Chanel boutique just around the corner from the hotel. She wanted to treat herself to a pair of sunglasses or a blouse. Anything Chanel would make her feel more Parisian and with the salary Alex was paying her, she could afford it.

Luis waited for her, nonchalantly leaning against the highly polished mahogany front desk. He did a double take as she approached, standing up straighter, his eyes scanning her appreciatively from head to foot.

"Ah, you look refreshed. Are you ready for lunch?"

Ignoring his roving gaze, she answered, "I am, thank you." Holding up a yellow legal pad, she added, "And we can get started on the situation at hand."

He led her out to the front of the hotel where a shiny black BMW sedan waited. As they sped through the streets of Paris, Daisy absorbed the marvelous views. Picking up on her interest, Luis acted as tour guide.

"See up on the hill?" he asked, pointing to a large white church.

"Is that Sacré-Coeur?"

"Yes, first time in Paris, Daisy?"

"Does it show?"

"Oui, everything delights you."

She offered him a weary smile. "Your city is beautiful."

"Wait until dark. The view from your balcony is lovely. You're in the front row for the Eiffel Tower light show."

"How often does that happen?"

"Every night. You cannot miss it."

The car stopped too soon at the café Les Deux Magots. She'd heard of the café, knew it was in the Saint-Germain-des-Prés district, rich with high-end fashion and known for being the literary heart of Paris. It wasn't easy, controlling her tourist excitement as they were seated under a large green awning along the sidewalk. She might be in Paris, sitting at a sidewalk café in the middle of a warm, summer afternoon, but she was in the middle of a mess and in over her head.

"Would you allow me to order for you?" Luis asked, smiling over the menu, which was entirely in French.

"Anything but snails or tartare."

"Ah, but they are both delicacies," he sniffed indignantly.

"Take pity on the American, okay? I don't eat snails or raw meat."

With indifference, he ordered them a lunch of Salade niçoise and a bottle of champagne. If he were going to try and get her drunk to distract her from the task at hand, he was sadly mistaken. The waiter filled her glass with Perrier-Jouët, but she ignored it. Time to let him know she meant business.

Leaning toward him, she smiled, drawing him closer and then she asked, "How long have you been hiding this barbeque thing from Alex?"

Two hours later, Daisy used the last of the champagne to chase three aspirin. She'd filled sheet after sheet on her tablet with notes and ideas carefully illustrated in her tiny, precise script. The Perrier-Jouët bottle was upside down in the ice bucket next to their table and clouds were forming in the sky above them, a definite omen of things to come.

"There has to be a way to switch up the menu," she said, trying to create a miracle out of a mess.

"We've already spent 1.5 million euros on specialty food items, decorations, and equipment," Luis said, wiping his brow with his linen napkin. "Mr. Stark will fire me for sure."

"Probably. Let's go over it again. What exactly did you buy with all that money?"

"I signed the invoices, but I have a feeling things were ordered without my approval at the discretion of our previous chef. Each day now I get deliveries of things I didn't approve. Yesterday, twenty buckets of BBQ sauce arrived from Texas, USA. I got a confirmation email that Angus beef from the state of Montana is arriving two days before the party. Real tumbleweeds from Arizona arrived last week and are in our basement floor waiting to be used as decoration."

She wanted to strangle him with her bare hands. The postage alone on tumbleweeds probably cost thousands of dollars.

Frustrated, she asked, "How, just tell me, how did you let this happen?"

"I was a little distracted with the renovation. The choices I make will last for years. The party only happens one night. Our chef was bored, waiting for the reopening and wanting something to do. I thought everything was getting handled."

Arguing with him wouldn't get them anywhere so she'd keep her cool no matter how much she wanted to blast him. Then another agenda item entered her mind. "What about the staff? Are they hired? Are they outfitted?"

"Yes, they will start in a month for training. I have cowboy hats from Texas, Levi's blue jeans, and western shirts for the party."

Daisy shook her head and filed away the idea of the uniform cost. "I want to see the event space. I want to see your vision for the décor. Then you can walk me through how you think we might save this thing."

"I'm trying to cancel the country band."

"Are they coming from the States?" she asked, cringing.

"Yes."

"Of course," she replied, thinking of the expense. "I know I've only been here a couple of hours, but I have to say…we've so many problems to solve in such a short period of time, I don't know where to start. Please tell me you're concerned."

Rolling his shoulders, but not meeting her glare, he answered, "Oui, it is deep merde."

"No, we are in deep merde," Daisy corrected.

Back at the hotel, Daisy retired to her suite vowing not to resurface until the next morning. Tired and slightly nauseous from the jetlag and champagne, she tried not to let her frustration with Luis and the situation get the better of her. On some level, she liked him. Sitting at the well-appointed desk in the corner of the living room, she compiled a list of her concerns. Her thoughts had to be organized before she made her obligatory call to Alex.

Confident as she was going to get, she phoned using the private number he'd given her on her first day.

"Alex Stark," he answered gruffly on the second ring.

"Hello…Mr. Stark, it's Daisy Miller…"

Even though she was in another continent, she could hear him sigh, "I thought we were past the name game…Daisy."

Putting a smile into her voice, she tried again. "Hi there, Alex, it's Daisy calling from Paris."

"What's going on over there?"

Trying to sound calm, she removed all emotion from her voice as she brought him up to speed on her meeting with Luis and their plans for the following day.

"A barbeque? I sure as hell didn't approve a barbeque," he said, his anger easily crossing the miles that separated them.

"From what I've been able to gather, it was suggested and handled by the previous chef."

"We have a new chef. What the hell?"

"You really didn't know about the Ritz stealing our chef?" she asked.

"Obviously, I didn't know."

"It might be for the best. Luis hired someone new. I'll meet him tomorrow, but I was thinking maybe we should consider borrowing someone from another hotel for the party."

"That would be problematic for more reasons than I care to explain. Meet the new chef and get back to me. Forget that outrageous menu. I want it changed. It's Paris for God's sake. We are serving French cuisine."

Wanting to tell him not to shoot the messenger, she paused and composed her words carefully. "I'll tell Luis, but he has already spent a substantial amount of money on supplies, which are non-refundable."

"How much?"

"One point five million euros."

He swore loudly. "Not only should I get rid of this incredibly stupid idea, but I should also get rid of him."

Not wanting to be responsible for Luis getting fired, she said, "Please don't do anything yet. From what I can see the staff that's here likes him and respects him. I fear the company is in too deep to make any sort of change right now. I'll look at the setup tomorrow and try to get a feel for Luis' vision. I'll let you know if I think it's truly feasible."

"You're probably right."

Had he just agreed with her?

Unaware of her surprise, he continued, "We're in too deep. The head count is up to two hundred. I don't want anyone to get wind of any unrest within the company. If I fired him now it would make the papers."

"Undoubtedly," she agreed.

"How's the renovation look?" he asked.

"Coming along, but if the lobby is any indication, there's a long way to go."

"Will the rest of the hotel be ready in time?"

"I'll have a better idea tomorrow after I have a look around."

"Check in tomorrow, Daisy." He hung up without so much as a goodbye.

CHAPTER SEVEN

Daisy awoke early on her first full day in Paris and ordered a continental breakfast from room service. She nibbled on a mouth-watering croissant as she applied her makeup. The chef knew his pastry. Dressing in a long black skirt and pale pink duchess satin silk blouse, she added a strand of her signature large fake pearls before heading for the lobby. It was early enough she could take her own private tour of the hotel.

She started in the impressively large Grand Ballroom. It was stripped down to the studs in some places. She hoped it would be a magnificent space one day, but it would take more days than they had. Luis better have a plan.

Ten minutes later, she spotted Luis with a man in his early twenties. He introduced his assistant Emile, a cute, sandy-haired apprentice who smiled at her shyly, speaking carefully in a mix of French and English. They took a tour of the hotel from the basement to the guest suites. About a third of the guestrooms were finished, which gave her some peace of mind.

Over the next few days, she and Luis worked closely with Emile. They covered everything from the promotion of the grand opening to the anniversary celebration. Despite their rocky start, Luis was enthusiastic and listened to her suggestions. For his part, he took pride in showing her the ins and outs of running a hotel as large and grand as the Stark International Hotel Paris. She caught him watching her when he didn't think she was aware of his scrutiny. Several times he offered to show her the Parisian nightlife at the end of a long day, but she feigned exhaustion and politely refused. Alex was still the first thing she thought of in the morning and the last thing at night before she fell asleep. This was a complication she didn't need but was helpless to let go of—the memory of the dinner they'd shared from his wink to his kiss, she was still messed up over her boss.

With Luis and Emile's help, they sorted out every detail from what kind of welcome gift they would have for their guests upon arrival to the events they were hosting outside the hotel. Language proved to be only a slight problem, but Daisy wondered why Alex hired her, knowing she could only speak Spanish. She was learning French with a language course she'd downloaded on her iPhone, but she wasn't learning it as fast as she needed to. It would take time, something she didn't have.

The guest excursions they'd planned were over the top. There was a private tour of the Palace of Versailles with a distant relative of Marie Antoinette's, a champagne tasting at Veuve Clicquot Ponsardin in Reims with the Cellar Master conducting a lesson in how to saber a magnum of champagne and an exclusive tour of the Louvre just to name a few. All the transportation and contacts had to be confirmed. Security accommodations and concessions had to be arranged for those who needed it. A press release had to be completed and sent to Le Monde and Paris Match. Hopefully, the entire anniversary tour would get a photo spread in Paris Match. It was the exact magazine in Paris where they needed to be.

With Alex's permission, her week stretched to ten days. Luis and Emile were becoming her friends and with each day she felt better about what the American party theme had morphed into. She spent time with the new chef, having recognized him from one of her favorite restaurants in, of all places, Seattle, which further built her confidence.

They might just pull this off after all.

CHAPTER EIGHT

Alex paced in his office, tears running down his cheeks. The phone on his desk buzzed quietly and he picked up the receiver. His sister, Rebecca, sounded broken on the other end of the line. She'd been crying, her voice sounded wrong, husky and off. This was bad.

"It is true then," Alex said. For the last hour he'd been hoping for the rumors that were coming out of New York not to have been true. Messages had trickled to him that his cousin, Adam Black, had been in a horrific car accident with his lovely wife Melinda, and their son, Adam Jr., or A.J. for short. A.J. looked like both Adam and Alex. He was dark-haired and already a handsome boy. Alex had a special fondness for the little guy who was his only godchild. When he was in New York, he'd spent a substantial amount of time with Adam, Miranda, and A.J.

"It is worse if that can even be true. Melinda and Adam Jr., they didn't make it. Adam is in the hospital, and he doesn't know yet." At this, his sister had to stop and take a breath. "He has a bunch of broken bones and they've put him in a coma to heal. Alex, he doesn't know about Melinda and A.J. They were his world. Who is going to tell him? How could this have happened?"

"Shit, I don't know," Alex said. "Do you have any idea what happened?"

"Adam told the police who were first on the scene that a car crossed the center line and hit them. It was and still is, storming in New York. The rain is awful, which contributed to the accident. They don't know if the driver got confused by the rain or was impaired. They took him in, and I'm sure they will test him. He wasn't hurt. The bastard who did this wasn't hurt. He could have been drunk for all we know. He didn't get injured, but Melinda and A.J., they didn't even have a chance. They died on impact."

"Are you okay? I'm worried about you," he asked his sister knowing that she was especially close to Melinda. She had introduced Adam and Melinda.

"No, I'm a fucking wreck," she said. "Mitch and your niece are scared shitless that there is something really wrong with me. I can't stop thinking about it or crying. Are you going to New York?"

"Yes," Alex said, thinking of how close he was to Adam, how they had all but grown up together. Adam was like a little brother to him. "I'm taking the plane in about an hour. He shouldn't be alone. I want to be there for him; however he needs me."

"Her family is there," Rebecca said. "Money grubbing whores that they are."

"For that reason, it isn't the same as us being there. They will have their own grief to deal with. Besides, Adam isn't a huge fan of Melinda's family, especially her sister, Tess. I think he nicknamed her 'the succubus' in better times."

"If I was ready in an hour, could I go, too?" Rebecca asked.

"I'll send a car for you. I don't want you driving right now."

"Funny, neither does Mitch."

"He's a good husband, I'm glad you found each other."

An hour later, they were on the plane. Five hours after that, they were in New York where they stayed in the corporate suite at the family hotel.

On the flight, Alex remembered everything he could about the big moments in Adam's life. His wedding to Melinda, how he'd told Alex that he was going to propose. Alex had helped him pick out the ring. A large oval diamond with a heart shaped diamond on each side, because Adam was sentimental. Alex had been his best man when Adam married Melinda. As a wedding gift, he'd given them a honeymoon to Fiji. They had gotten pregnant almost immediately and Alex had been happy for them. Then they'd had A.J.

and asked him to be the godfather. Alex was honored and slightly jealous of their happiness. Adam had confided that Melinda had been acting strangely and he thought she might be pregnant again, but he thought she was waiting to tell him on their anniversary. It wasn't something everyone knew. Rebecca didn't know and Alex didn't intend on telling her.

Alex had been so happy for Adam and Melinda feeling like they were two people who should have been together, who added so much to each other's lives, he could no longer remember a time when they weren't together. Their love story had been one that he'd gone back to time and again. How did you know when you'd met the one person you were meant to spend the rest of your life with? Adam had told him it was quite simple. When you know, you know.

It was five am in Paris when Alex called Daisy. He needed to hear her voice. He needed her. She was still in bed and her reaction didn't disappoint.

"Alex," she said sleepily, her voice husky. "What can I do for you? I don't think anyone else is awake yet, but I am."

"How are things going in Paris?" he asked, ignoring that he'd awakened her but trying to make his voice soft. He hated to admit it, but he missed her. He wished he was there with her, holding her in his arms, kissing her like he had at the Cinco de Mayo celebration and back in his room. It was time to acknowledge how much she meant to him. It wouldn't happen right away, because she was hurt, but he'd do it. And she would be his.

"No differently than they were seven hours ago when we spoke," she said.

"What time is it there?" he asked, masking surprise.

"It is five in the morning. I don't remember requesting a wakeup call, but I don't mind getting an early start. I like talking to you." Alex surmised the last phrase was bullshit, but how he wished it was true.

"I know, I'm sorry, I just needed to check in with you," Alex said.

"You can call me anytime you want. Is everything all right?" she asked, her voice softening, intimate in a way it hadn't been a moment earlier.

"No, nothing is," he admitted. "Something very bad happened to my cousin, his wife, and their son."

He heard the sheets rustling, knew she wasn't going back to bed, but sitting up, rearranging the pillows so she could settle in.

"Talk to me, tell me everything," she ordered. "I might be in Paris, but I'm here and I care, Alex."

"Adam is more like a brother to me. Something awful happened last night, and I guess I just needed to talk…to you…" Which was true, but really Alex just needed to hear her voice.

Daisy cried in the shower. The story Alex had shared with her an hour earlier had broken her heart. There was a man in a hospital bed who wasn't awake, who would awaken to discover his world was over. Her heart went out to this man, this stranger, who Alex had said was more of a brother than a cousin. She felt sick, hurt, and wanted to hold Alex. It made no sense, but he had reached out and she wanted to reach back. She was glad he was there for his cousin, and she wondered when she could be there for Alex.

Her work at the hotel stretched out another few days. The terrible news about Alex's cousin made its way to Paris, laying a sadness over the planning. Daisy continued to update Alex each evening and although she didn't ask, she could hear the sadness in his voice. His cousin had awakened two days after the accident and Daisy could hear the grief in Alex's voice, knowing that his cousin had lost everything he cared about. She knew Alex was staying with him in New York, helping him to make the necessary arrangements. It was a grim task, and she could tell Alex didn't want to talk about it, so she didn't ask.

This different side of Alex was yet another layer in the mystery that was Garrison Alexander Stark, not that it would change their relationship in anyway. She hoped it would, but she had to be prepared.

"I have an idea for you, Daisy," Luis announced the day before she was to fly home.

"Bring it on," she replied happily, uncapping her pen, and finding a clean sheet of paper. They sat with Emile around a small table in Luis' office eating a quick breakfast of croissants and café au lait as they went over the plans for the day.

"You fly back tomorrow, but you've seen so little of Paris. I think it's time you got out and explored."

Despite their budding friendship, she didn't want to spend a day with Luis touring the most romantic city in the world.

"Why don't you take the rest of today off and enjoy?" Luis suggested.

Meeting his warm blue eyes with a smile, she realized she'd misunderstood. He wanted her to explore by herself. A little embarrassed, she said, "I'll be back in a couple of weeks. I can do some sightseeing then."

"Nonsense. Emile and I have everything covered and if you look through the window one more time at Sacré-Coeur, it will break my heart."

"What about the Fashion Tour for the ladies?"

"We can handle it. Emile will confirm which fashion houses will open for us and make the arrangements."

Emile nodded and winked as he pulled a map from his pocket. "You could stop by the Louvre on your way to Sacré-Coeur." He pointed to each place and then circled them with his pen.

"I sense a bit of a conspiracy," she said, but smiled as she added, "I might want to start at the Eiffel Tower."

Emile smiled and added another circle to the map.

"It's still early in the morning, you can see all three," Luis suggested.

"And what if Alex calls?"

He had started doing a lot of that. Calling her instead of waiting for her to call. She knew it had to do with his cousin. She was a lifeline away from the pain.

"I'll tell him you're out working on the arrangements. Don't worry about him," Luis said dismissively.

"He's my boss. I'm still new. The man is going through a lot with his cousin in New York."

"You see, he is distracted, he will not mind," Luis said offhandedly.

"I think he will. Adam is like a brother to him," She said. Alex might have forty-two other hotels to focus on, but for some reason the Stark International Hotel Paris was firmly in his radar. When he wasn't with his cousin, he was checking up on Daisy.

"I think you underestimate his…um…confidence in you," Luis offered. "I've seen him with his cousins and siblings, he doesn't call or waste a moment unless he wants to. Everything he does is calculated."

"He can barely tolerate me. I'm firmly in his crosshairs." Since that first phone call that she would only describe as tender, he questioned her relentlessly with each subsequent call. Was he making up for his vulnerability? Maybe. There were uncomfortable silences when neither of them said a word. On more than one occasion she'd wanted to ask him if he regretted hiring her but came to her senses in the nick of time. He was a man out of his element. She gave him a break with each call.

Ignoring her objection, Luis said, "Emile will type up a sheet of our progress. He will slip it under the door to your suite so that it's waiting for your return. They're laying carpet in the lobby today. Hopefully it will be finished by the time you're back from your adventure."

As he said the last word, she felt a twinge of foreboding. If Alex knew she'd snuck away, he could accuse her of all sorts of things, which amounted to stealing from the company.

"This job isn't a vacation. This isn't Club Med Paris."

"Daisy," Luis said, his accent heavier as he placed his hand atop hers, "You've worked very hard to help us. You've put in sixteen-hour days. Mr. Stark will be proud of you when I tell him…And yes, I do intend to tell him, mon ami."

When she didn't say anything, he suggested, "Call it a tour to familiarize yourself with the city. I just wish I could go with you to see you experience the joys of Paris for the first time…Now go and enjoy."

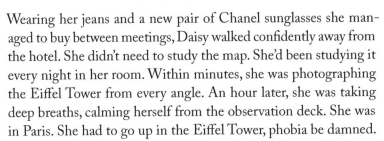

Wearing her jeans and a new pair of Chanel sunglasses she managed to buy between meetings, Daisy walked confidently away from the hotel. She didn't need to study the map. She'd been studying it every night in her room. Within minutes, she was photographing the Eiffel Tower from every angle. An hour later, she was taking deep breaths, calming herself from the observation deck. She was in Paris. She had to go up in the Eiffel Tower, phobia be damned.

Finding the Stark International Hotel in the skyline, she felt a thrill remembering back to the last time she'd been this happy. Her day with Alex. They hadn't been looking at well-known landmarks or walking around a famous city. They hadn't needed either distraction. Their company and discovery of each other was enough. Quickly calculating the time difference, she thought of him asleep in his plush suite at the Stark International Hotel Portland. Or was he still in New York? It was none of her business, but she was able to admit that she missed him. Bittersweet resentment burned deep within her as she left the Eiffel Tower in hopes of other distractions.

"Get over it," she murmured to herself.

At the Louvre she moved efficiently, having plotted a quick tour of the massive space. She had to see the *Mona Lisa*, the Winged Victory, and the Venus de Milo. Other magnificent pieces of art drew her attention, distracting her as time whittled away.

Three hours later, she headed to Sacré-Coeur. After pausing to take one last photo of the glass pyramid at the entrance of the Louvre, she vowed to come another time and discover more treasures. A quick glance at her watch showed it was past three o'clock. If she wanted to make it to Sacré-Coeur, check on the progress at the hotel, and call Alex on time, she needed to hustle.

From the Palais Royal—Musée du Louvre Metro station, she consulted a map as she boarded a train. Needing to change trains at Gare du Nord, she walked up four flights of stairs, following the signs around several twists and turns. Then she descended two flights, moving swiftly through the chaos. Just catching her train before the doors closed, she smiled in satisfaction. Riding the Metro was easy. Three minutes later, the train stopped at a station she didn't recognize, and her smug confidence vaporized. It should've been Anvers, her stop for Sacré-Coeur, but it wasn't. Before she could act, the doors shut, and she was on to another station.

She didn't have time to get lost, not today. At the next stop, she would get out, cross the platform, and take a train back to Garde du Nord. It wouldn't be a problem.

Determined to get back on schedule, she stepped out at the next station. The train pulled away, leaving her alone.

A lone sign dangled from the ceiling announcing arrivals and departures. The next train would not arrive for ten minutes. By the time it arrived, she could probably walk to Sacré-Coeur. She had to be close. There was no way she was going to wait in this dark station for ten minutes. If she went out to the street she could hail a cab.

Another sign, covered in grime announced she was in Pigalle. It sparked a memory she couldn't quite grasp. Following the signs for sortie, which she knew meant exit, she emerged from the subterranean cave and looked up at gray skies threatening rain. She hadn't thought to pack a jacket in the early warmth of summer.

Bringing her gaze down to street level, her mouth fell open in shock. A bright, neon pink penis rose and fell rhythmically in the window of the Sexodrome holding her vision hostage. She couldn't look, but she couldn't look away. Finally, she snapped a photo for Brigitte, who would love it.

Biting her lip, she murmured, "We're not in Kansas anymore, Toto."

Every direction she looked assaulted her senses with provocative images. This was Place Pigalle…Pig Ally. It was the most notorious epicenter for raunchy adult entertainment in all of Paris. People predominantly dressed in black with matching tattoos who sought adult entertainment milled in and out of shops as music blared. Rough looking men with hard expressions leaned up against scantily dressed, brightly made-up women in shop doorways.

Bumped from behind, she heard a metallic tinkle and look down toward the sound. A gold band lay next to her right foot. A tall, unshaven man picked it up and held it out to her with grimy fingertips.

"Yours," he said, trying to shove it into her hand.

"No," she said, holding up her hands in protest.

"Yours," he repeated, more insistently, his dark eyes narrowing in intimidation.

Turning away, she walked briskly on the cobblestone sidewalk trying to rid herself of the annoying man. He ran by her, bumping her shoulder hard and tossed the band at her feet again.

Blocking her, he reached out and grabbing her arm with his dingy fingers as he shouted, "Fifty euros."

Threatening tourists must bring in a good amount of money, but for Daisy, it only brought out her strong will and determination. With little conscious thought, she reacted with adrenaline-fueled anger. Hitting him as hard as she could with the bag of heavy souvenirs she accumulated on the day's adventures, she yelled, "Let go of me!"

Smiling, his teeth glittering with gold edged fillings, he tightened his grip. The feeling of being controlled by a stranger enraged her. She had flashbacks of her boss who'd gotten the wrath of the Strathmore stapler and it incited violence in her.

This horrible man, his scent—a mixture of cigarettes, sweat, and body fluids best left unmentioned—filled her nose in an unpleasant reality. He didn't have the right to touch her and was about to learn a hard lesson. Grabbing his forearms for balance, her well-aimed knee thrust forward and up, striking the intended target squarely in the crotch.

His smile faltered, his grip loosening, as he immediately bent forward to cradle his injured groin. Pushing free of him, she took off in a dead run. Neon signs flew by as her flight response kicked in. She ran down the cobblestone streets as the first drops of rain cooled her hot skin. His voice rang out behind her, a mixture of French and English profanity she thought it best to ignore.

Daisy kept running. The edge of the Moulin Rouge passed by, and she barely noticed. After a few minutes, she slowed to a jog, trying to catch her breath, and checking over her shoulder to make sure he hadn't followed. She took big gulps of air, nausea rising in her throat, heart throbbing painfully in her chest. She might have lost him for the moment, but she still didn't feel safe. Wanting to put more distance between them, she kept moving, pushing herself to keep up the pace. By now, she'd moved completely out of the neighborhood of sex shops and into more unfamiliar territory.

She would hail the first cab she saw, go back to the hotel, and order a very large cocktail from room service, which she'd enjoy after a hot shower to erase the memory of the stranger's hands on her body. Reaching into the back pocket of her jeans for what was left of the two hundred euros she'd packed for her afternoon of sightseeing, she found nothing. Thinking she had the wrong pocket, she reached into the other side of her jeans…empty. She'd been robbed. Her camera still bobbed around her neck, but she'd lost her money, her room keycard and even her new Chanel sunglasses. Tears threatened, but she fought them. There would be time for crying later. She had to find her way back to the hotel.

Thoroughly soaked, her legs threatening to drop her at any moment, Daisy stepped into the lobby of the Stark Intercontinental Hotel and walked stiffly to the front desk and waited for one of the desk staff to approach.

Almost immediately, a staff member she had gotten to know well over the past two weeks hurried to her. His name, she remembered, was Pierre. His handsome face turned wary as he took in her appearance. "Mademoiselle?"

"I've lost my key. I need another card for the corporate suite," she said, feeling guilty about the puddle of water forming on the new, plush carpet under her feet.

"That's a special key. It isn't one that we can reprogram," he explained.

"Of course not," she replied. "Could you just let me into the room?"

"Let me see what I can do. If I'm able, you'll need to replace the last two keys issued, yours and Monsieur Stark's, but it might be tomorrow." He explained that she would have to give Monsieur Stark the replacement key.

Her first corporate suite and now the whole thing had to be re-keyed because of her. She could think about it later.

"Do what you need to do," she replied.

"Are you sure you're all right, Mademoiselle?"

"I got lost and didn't have a jacket...then I got robbed," she offered, her voice trailing off as she reached for a box of tissues near Pierre.

Horrified, he pushed the box closer to her and asked, "Mademoiselle, were you hurt? Is there anything I can get you? Shall we call the police?"

"No Pierre, I'm fine, thank you. It was just a pickpocket. He got money and the card, not my ID."

Once on her floor, she was barely able to follow Pierre when he approached the suite door, inserted his master keycard, and stepped back. She thanked him, and then fighting the heavy door, she threw her weight into it, pushing it open as she heard an angry voice coming from inside. Had her pickpocket somehow found out which room she was in? It wasn't possible. The card didn't have a room number on it.

"Find her! I don't care what you have do to...just find her!"

Alex. He paced the length of the room, wrapped in a thick white towel, which hung precariously low on his hips. Bare-chested, he held the phone to his ear with one hand, while the other ran through his thick, dark hair in frustration. His chest muscles bulged as he literally pulled his hair out by the roots. A package of unopened cigarettes lay close by.

Standing on the marble foyer, the water silently dripping from her clothing onto the cool floor beneath her, she watched as Alex continued to yell into the phone. Alex was in her room. The comprehension that he wasn't just angry, but worried...about her...took several moments to register.

"She's been gone ten hours...."

At the sound of the door closing, he turned, the words fading on his lips.

"She's here," he said simply, his relief undeniable. Without another word, he tossed his cell phone toward the nearest chair missing it by a foot. In a few, barefoot strides, he was there, and she was in his arms. Her face brushed against his chest, resting against his warm, bare shoulder as strong arms engulfed her. Hugging him back, she breathed in his clean, masculine scent, enjoying his warmth.

"Are you all right? Are you hurt?" His voice was strange, the confidence gone as he rattled off the questions with machine gun precision.

Too shocked to speak, she shook her head as tears slid down her cheeks.

"Daisy, damn it!" he exclaimed, pulling back as he gently shook her by the shoulders. "Are you all right?"

"I'm fine," she announced, meeting the green eyes boring into her. "I'm not hurt, just cold…Why are you here?"

"We'll get to that later. Where have you been?" Softness now replaced with a hint of anger.

"Out. Familiarizing myself with the city," she replied, Luis's excuse coming back to her.

"The hell you were."

She was exhausted and freezing. His interrogation could wait. "Think what you want," she said, stepping past him heading for her bedroom as she muttered, "Hypocrite."

He followed her. "You scared the hell out of me. When I got here this morning, they said you were sightseeing, and you'd be back early this afternoon. It's almost ten o'clock…"

With her hand on the knob to her bathroom, she turned and said, "Fine, dock my pay. I really don't care. I got off at the wrong damn Metro Station trying to get to Sacré-Coeur. I ended up in Place Pigalle. There was this man…When I tried to walk around him, he grabbed me and I had to…well, I hurt him…" she said vaguely, "Then I started running and just kept going. I wanted to get as far away from him as I could. I got lost, really lost…I looked for a cab, Metro Station, any landmark I could find, but I was in the middle of nowhere. I checked my pockets and realized I'd been robbed. I found a phone booth and tried to call, but didn't have any money and the directions were, surprise, in French. I speak a little, but not enough obviously.

"By this time, it was raining, and I didn't have a jacket, so I was wet and freezing. I had to follow the setting sun to find my way back here and that is a little hard to do when it is raining. I've never been happier to see a familiar landmark in my life as I was to see this hotel. When I could see the marquis, I was still a mile away... By the way, all the lights should be replaced, they look old, but not vintage, tired old." Her voice cracked toward the end of her speech as he stepped close and pulled her to him.

"Daisy...I..."

"Oh, shut up."

He chuckled. After all she'd been through, he had the nerve to laugh. She tried to pull away from him, but he held her tighter, whispering, "Shhh...," his lips moving softly against her skin. "Let me hold you, you're absolutely freezing. I'll tell whatshisname to fix the bulbs on the marquee."

"Tell me something I don't know, genius. And his name is Luis."

He laughed harder and she twisted out of his grasp.

Hands on her hips, she asked, "Why are you in my bedroom? In fact, why the hell are you in Paris? Checking up on me?"

"I always stay in the corporate suite. Don't worry, I have my own bedroom. This hotel is important to me."

"Trust me, I'm not worried. I'm familiar with our employee/employer relationship you so pointedly outlined during my interview. You better not have smoked any of those cancer sticks," she said pointing at the unopened box of cigarettes.

"Daisy, please...get a shower, warm up before you say something you'll really regret. I didn't smoke any of the cigarettes, I just thought about it because I was worried about you."

She stepped toward the bathroom and stopped, muttering a swear word of her own. Teeth chattering, she managed, "I'm sorry about today. I shouldn't have taken the day off."

"You were entitled," he said. "Just don't scare me like that again. I've got enough people to worry about, you took about ten years off my life today."

Looking at him, trying to keep her eyes from traveling to his bare chest and the low hung towel, she realized these last few weeks they'd become friends. Yes, they started off on the wrong foot—now the whole thing almost seemed comical. He'd been through so much with his cousin the last thing she wanted was for him to be concerned about her.

She asked, "You were actually worried about me?"

"Don't sound so surprised."

"But…"

"I've had a lot of time to think in the last few days and I regret what happened back in Portland on the night we met. I almost gave credence to those nasty rumors you so enjoyed telling me at the interview," Alex said as his hands reached for her, only to stop short. "After my time in New York, I decided to fly over here and apologize for my behavior then and at the interview. I shouldn't have left you in the suite. I should have been nicer to you, more respectful. It isn't the way I was raised, and I forgot myself and for that, I'm very sorry."

"Possibly, we both have a few lapses of judgment to make amends for," she offered. "I shouldn't have drunk so much. And most of all, I shouldn't have been so eager to share that info I'd gathered on you. It was rather harsh. I just wanted to work hard for a company like this one—"

"Truce," he said, holding out his hand. Time passed, but Daisy finally grasped the offered hand, only to have both his hands enfold hers, warming them. "Would you consider a do over?"

"A 'do over'? What exactly did you have in mind?"

"We have a fireplace, and I can order some room service. We could try for a pleasant evening. Erase the bad of today."

"What about the employer/employee fraternization clause? I don't want to go back to wanting to call you, Mr. Stark. I can't do that. I care. I care too damn much."

"I've thought long and hard about it. I don't want to go back. I care too. I'm breaking the clause for us," he said. "That is if you are in agreement. If not, okay too. I don't want to make you feel uncomfortable. I just understand that life isn't forever, when happiness is in front of you, you should embrace it, forget the rules."

It was a bad idea all the way around and she wondered if his conclusions were based on grief, but for reasons Daisy chose to ignore, she heard herself say, "I want a hot shower and then I'd like to eat dinner, with you, by the fireplace."

"I'll call room service and you can get warmed up. Would you like me to bring you a cocktail?"

Thinking of how scared she'd been today, and what happened the last time she'd drank with Alex, she shook her head as Alex reached for the phone. "No, thank you. I'll be out in a jiffy."

"May I order for both of us?"

"Yes, that would be lovely."

Not trusting herself, she said nothing more before stepping into the bathroom and shutting the door.

With shaky fingers she adjusted the temperature in the shower and then stripped out of her wet clothes. She draped them over the edge of the enormous bathtub and stepped inside the glass and marble enclosure.

Alex had flown to Paris to see her. She needed to think about that for a while.

Ten minutes later, and after much contemplation, she was in her most comfy pajamas and one of the plush hotel bathrobes. She had quickly dried her hair, but it was still a little damp.

She wanted to take it slow and not make any mistakes. Nothing said slow like the milk bone dog biscuit flannel pajamas she had on.

All the lights were off in the suite except for the light of the burning fire from the fireplace. The night sky of Paris illuminated different areas of the suite as the city light fell through the windows.

Alex, who was also wearing one of the plush hotel robes, was busying himself with a bottle of champagne, fighting with the foil and then unscrewing the wire that held the cork in place.

Daisy took in the scene and tried to forget this was her boss. She remembered back to the café and the fun they'd had at Mother's Bistro and at the waterfront. And just like that, he was her Alex again and she was more than a little enamored.

Alex's hand paused on the cork when she entered the room. She smiled at him and said, "This is nice. I don't care why you came to Paris. I know you have work to do, but I'm glad you came."

"I came for you more than any other reason," he said, expertly pulling the cork and then filling two glasses. "I ordered us some champagne. I hope you like it."

"I like it, but I promise not to drink too much of it," Daisy said as she made her way to the couch and sat on one end of it.

He sat on the couch next to her and handed her a glass. "You're entitled and you've had a bad day. Are those dog biscuits on your pajamas?"

"Yes, they aren't the sexiest thing I have, but I'm still cold and they are warm, so I'm choosing comfort over sexiness. I thought you'd approve."

He put his glass of champagne on the coffee table and said, "Come here."

He didn't wait for her to follow his gentle order. Pulling her into his lap, he encircled her in his arms. She leaned back, her damp hair resting on his shoulder. They didn't speak, only sat by the fire until the doorbell rang and the person outside said something in French that Daisy couldn't understand.

Alex replied in French and gently pulled away from her. "Don't forget where I was because after dinner, we are resuming this position."

They ate Steak au Poive, with little, perfectly cooked vegetables and had chocolate crème brûlée for dessert.

Alex opened a second bottle of champagne and Daisy vowed not to make a fool out of herself, but mainly, she felt like melted butter. Every muscle in her body was relaxed. Alex held her on the couch and although they didn't speak, she thought it was the most intimate thing she'd ever done with a man.

"You finally warmed up," he whispered in her ear.

Snuggling against him, she replied, "You can take the credit for that."

"Are you tired?" he asked.

She could barely keep her eyes open, but she didn't want the night to end. Tomorrow, she was his employee again and she didn't want to go back. But it was not lost on her that he had yet to kiss her. Yes, he'd held her and snuggled against her, he'd even held her hand when they'd eaten dinner, but he hadn't kissed her.

"Come on, let's put you to bed," he said as he started to sit up.

She was glad she didn't have the pressure of making love with him, there were too many questions in her mind, but she would have liked to at least neck on the couch. She wanted to tell him that she didn't want the evening to end. Having him put her to bed like a baby, she didn't want that.

"May I ask you something?" he asked as they stood.

Here it comes, she thought. Maybe this was the big, this is why we could never be. I like you as a friend…

"Would I be crazy to suggest sharing your bed tonight? I won't try to seduce you, well, I might try, but really, I just want to hold you."

"You want to hold me as we sleep?"

"Yes."

"Will you kiss me?" she asked and knew she'd had too much champagne. Needy much?

His reply was to pull her close and kiss her like he had by the waterfront. Melting into the kiss, she couldn't believe they hadn't kissed until now. She was warm, she was fed, but she was hungry for this man.

He pulled back, his eyes sparkling in the firelight. "It is too soon, I know it, but when we kiss like that, I have a hard time not thinking of how it will be to be inside of you, feeling the heat of your skin on mine, tasting you—"

"You know what to say to a girl," she said.

"Come on," he said, leading her by the hand, "We both need sleep, so let's go pretend to sleep."

They went into her bedroom where she turned on a low light next to the bed, which they circled like tense cage fighters. She'd be damned if she'd make the first move.

"Pick your side," he said as he removed his robe and she discovered that he sported a pair of silk boxers with Snoopy dog heads on them and a white tee shirt. He looked all of seventeen, not the thirty-seven she knew him to be.

Daisy couldn't help it, she burst out laughing and then pointed.
"These were a gift from my niece last Christmas although I think her mother picked them out. What's your excuse, Miss Milk Bone?"

"They were also a Christmas gift. My mother gave them to me so I wouldn't get cold at night sleeping alone."

"Oh, what a waste. You're not going to be cold tonight."

"Something tells me I'm going to be uncomfortably hot."

"Count on it."

Daisy hadn't been spooned in a very long time, but having Alex hold her to him, his body protective against hers, was so much better than anything in her past.

She didn't need to worry about being kissed. Each time she moved or sighed or snuggled in the slightest way, Alex kissed her lips, her ear, her neck. And his hands roamed in unhurried fashion along every curve and dip of her body as if he were learning her.

She knew the moment he fell asleep, his weight feeling somehow heavier against her back.

Jerking awake much later, Daisy heard Alex whimper in her ear. They'd both been asleep so it had to be after midnight. He was dreaming, she knew, but the sound and the agony of his cries had her shaking him awake.

"Alex, Alex, wake up, you are all right," she said gently as she shook him.

He jerked awake, clutching Daisy to him as moisture leaked out of his eyes and gently fell onto her skin.

"You were dreaming," she said, and she held him to her.

"I was thinking about Adam," he admitted.

"Would you like to talk about it?" she asked as she turned so that they were facing each other in the dark.

"It is heartbreaking," he whispered.

"You can tell me. I'll keep it safe." And she meant it, nothing that happened between them would ever be discussed or shared with her coworkers.

"When he woke up, when Adam opened his eyes, I was the first one he saw. He knew. He knew about Melinda and A.J. He told me if they were okay, they'd have been the first people he saw, not me. What do you say to that?"

"I'm thankful you were there for him," she said as she pulled him to her. She held him close, much the way he'd held her earlier.

"I can't stop thinking about it," he said as he buried his face in the crook of Daisy's neck and let her hold him.

"Maybe you shouldn't try. Maybe you need to find the beauty in what they had. She was a lucky woman to be so loved. I don't know if anyone will ever love me like that. It is heartbreaking, but the love story is beautiful."

Alex kissed her then. A lazy, long kiss that spoke volumes to her. When he broke the contact, he whispered, "If you want the love story, you'll have it, Daisy. I know you will."

But as he spooned her again, he didn't say what she needed to hear, that they would have the love story.

The next morning, it was back to business. Daisy's plane trip back to Portland had been canceled. Alex said that he needed her in Paris for a few more days.

The torment of Luis started that morning. Although she liked Luis, she could understand why Alex was hard on him.

Alex questioned everything and rolled his eyes repeatedly as they went over every detail of the party again and again. They worked solidly through lunch and into the late afternoon, but no one noticed. Daisy had easier appointments at the dentist than watching Alex drill Luis. Finally, left with a list of questions, Luis held up his hand and asked for an early evening. Alex agreed.

"It's going to be fine," she said as they entered the suite in the early evening.

Alex said nothing, he just wrapped an arm around her waist and pulled her to him. He added a kiss that took her breath away.

"I've wanted to do that all day."

"I've wanted you too, as well."

"The question is, do you want to get out of this damn hotel for a few hours?"

She wanted to relive what they had when they went to Cinco de Mayo. "What did you have in mind?"

"Let me take you to my favorite arrondissement." He took her to an Italian restaurant in the heart of the Saint-Germain-des-Prés, where he spoke a mix of fluent French and Italian, ordering them something that included pasta, sun-dried tomatoes, and lots of cream, as well as the best margherita pizza she'd ever had. She watched as the pizza dough was tossed to the ceiling and then caught in the nick of time before it hit the floor.

They walked hand in hand along the lit streets near the Seine and looked at colorful macarons in pasty shop windows.

"Do you know what I could go for?" he asked.

She looked up at him and smiled, which earned her a kiss, then he said, "Ever had a freshly made crepe?"

She leaned into him as they stood by a street vendor and looked at the selection of crepes. She had Nutella, Alex had lemon. After they'd watched the artisan expertly make their crepes, they sat on a bench and pulled apart sections of their freshly made crepes from paper cones.

"Try this," Alex said, feeding her some of his lemon juice and powdered sugar crepe. It was delicious, but she loved her Nutella.

They made it back to their room by ten, the shank of the evening in Paris. Daisy felt warm and romantic, wanting more of Alex.

She thought of the new, sexy lingerie she'd purchased at one of the little shops near the hotel and wondered if tonight was the night she should break it out. The dog biscuit pajamas were going back in the luggage.

"I think I'll take a shower, wash away the streets of Paris," she said walking into her bedroom.

"Good idea," Alex said from the living room as she shut the door to the bathroom and tried to decide what she would do after the shower.

Pulling off her clothing, she stepped into the marble shower and let the warm water wash over her.

Just over the sound of the water, she heard a tapping at the door.

Sticking her head out of the shower, she asked, "Yes?"

"May I join you?" Alex asked.

This man, who'd haunted her for days, with the most perfectly sculpted body she'd ever seen, her boss, Garrison Alexander Stark wanted an invitation to join her inside the shower. Opportunities like this didn't come along very often. It was the logical next step in their, whatever this was.

"Only if you bring the champagne," she said, her body shivering a little under the assault of the warm water. Stupid girl, they didn't have any champagne in their mini fridge, why didn't she say water or soda? Something that wouldn't require a call to room service. She wanted Alex in her shower, in her bed, in her body, but sometimes stupidity got in the way. She should have thought before she spoke.

"Sounds good," Alex said, and Daisy heard the telltale pop of a cork from a bottle of champagne from the direction of the open bathroom door. She hadn't known that he'd apparently stocked the fridge.

A moment later, he was in the bathroom, a towel around his waist, a bottle in one hand, glasses in the other as she peered through a small opening of the shower door from the safety of the marble shower.

Alex's towel hit the floor with a soft thud as he opened the shower door and stepped inside to join her.

Daisy leaned her hands against the marble, shut her eyes and waited. His warm hand ran gently along her skin parting the stream of water flowing down her back. She moaned happily at the onslaught of sensation.

After several moments of this sweet torture, she opened her eyes and turned her face to meet the emerald eyes gazing back at her. Somehow, they appeared more luminescent in the subtle light. He paused to bend and pick something up. She accepted one of the long-stemmed champagne glasses he offered. Taking it from him, she drank the refreshingly cool liquid in one swallow and felt the tickle all the way to her stomach. He followed suit, then took her glass and placed both empty flutes outside of the shower.

Turning her back on him, she faced the water and let the heat sluice over her body. Despite its warmth, she trembled which she associated more to the man than to air temperature.

"Cold?" he asked.

"I think it is more from anticipation than temperature. I want your hands on me."

Strong hands gently touched her shoulders then moved down the length of her arms. The hair on his chest tickled her back as he brushed up against her. His hands moved lower, sliding along her rib cage and finally up to cup the undersides of her breasts. Soft, warm lips again worked their magic dancing along her neck and up to her jaw line.

"Like this?" he asked.

"That's a good start," she said.

Need and lust for this man bubbled inside of her. She'd spent hours thinking of how his hands would feel on her body, choreographing every touch in her mind. Last night had been a tease, but this was so much more. He wasn't going to wear his snoopy boxers and she wasn't going to wear her milk bone pajamas.

Her imagination failed to adequately capture the reality that was looming ahead. She wanted to rub against him, feel the full impact of his body against hers, but what she needed was to have him inside of her, filling the emptiness she was all too aware of.

He turned her just enough to touch his lips to hers, but this time it was different, more intense. Warm lips tasted of tickling champagne and long denied passion.

His hands roamed over her back and reached down to cup her bottom, then he tasted her, gently moving his tongue between her lips as he lifted her, pulling her close against his hard length. She gasped at the first intimate touch of his body to hers. She ran her fingertips over the hard contours of his chest and then rubbed against him, his coarse chest hair teasing her nipples.

"Come here," he coaxed, stepping back, and extending his hand in offering. He led her to a marble ledge at the back of the shower and sat. Hands on her hips he pulled her close, his mouth level with her breasts. When his lips covered one rosy tip, she moaned. Smiling up at her, he drew circles with his tongue. She watched his mouth suckle her, felt the heat all the way to her toes. Without warning, her knees buckled and gave way.

Catching her before she fell, he pulled her onto his lap and cradled her protectively. Her hands explored him, slowly moving lower, brushing against him with feather light caresses, marveling at his size and velvety texture of his erection made slick in the water.

"Easy, beautiful," he warned. "I'm getting a little too excited."

"I don't think that is a bad problem to have," she said with a small smile.

With infinite patience, he stood, guiding her to the warm water streaming from the showerhead. Putting a generous amount of the hotel's complementary bergamot scented Hermès Eau D'Orange Verte shampoo in his hand, he massaged her scalp with powerful fingers that unwound her by degrees. An exotic mixture of citrus and spice perfumed the air as he worked his magic. Forever after, when Daisy thought of Paris, it was that woodsy, exotic scent that would bring about her most sensual of memories.

After she'd been thoroughly lathered and rinsed, he grabbed a washcloth and a bottle of shower gel in the same scent as the shampoo. He rubbed the soft, foam filled cotton over her skin paying particular attention to her breasts. Shutting her eyes, she felt his breath; warm on her cheek, as his cotton sheathed hand slipped between her legs and touched her where she most wanted him.

She leaned into his hand, hearing the washcloth drop as he explored her with his gentle fingers. He lingered, his fingertips expertly touching her. Spreading her legs, she leaned against his chest to give him better access. He touched her softly at first and then began to get serious about his discovery. She let out a small scream of pleasure, encouraging his touch as a torrent of passion awakened and soared within her. Turning her head, she puckered her lips, wanting more connection. Bending, he fastened his lips to hers, their teeth bumping as their tongues tantalized one another.

Alex pushed Daisy flush against the cool marble wall and leaned into her, kissing her, his lips and tongue making love to her mouth as his hands pinned her gently against the hard shower wall. She lifted her legs and wrapped them around his waist, needing to get closer. He slipped inside her in one easy thrust, and she sighed contentedly. This, this is what she wanted, this is what she needed.

Groaning, he pulled back, helped her feet back to the marble floor and slowly slipped out of her, leaving her to feel bereft for the loss. It wasn't enough, she needed him.

"The first time we make love isn't going to be in a shower, Daisy, especially when we have a nice big bed in the other room."

"Is that what we're going to do?" she asked with a tremor in her voice.

Cupping her breasts with his hands, his words came out in a tortured growl, "As soon as we get out of this damned shower…"

"I'm in no rush," she lied as she grabbed the shower gel from where he'd dropped it and started her sweet assault on his skin. Moments later, he was leaning against the marble and saying, "Daisy, you are killing me."

"Good," she replied, just as the doorbell interrupted them. Alex responding with a soft, "Merde."

Alex rinsed away the richly scented lather and stepped out of the shower, quickly toweling off and grabbing his robe on the way to the front door.

Daisy turned off the water. Happy for a moment to herself, she toweled off slowly. She wasn't going to think about tomorrow or next week. She wouldn't deny herself the pleasure of his body, not one more day, not one more minute. She wasn't her mother and history was not repeating itself. She'd met Alex before he'd become her boss. They were both single, healthy adults in the most romantic city in the world. She'd worry about tomorrow…tomorrow.

Luis was on the other side of the door with some last-minute reports. Alex took the papers and shut the door in his face without a word. The reports were bogus, Luis was checking up on them and they both knew it. Luis could crawl back into the hole from which he'd emerged.

Daisy would be the first employee he'd ever slept with, well, since he was seventeen and the Swedish parlor maid at their hotel in Oslo offered him a massage. It wasn't like she was his employee…

No, the maid had been his *father's* employee. He'd been an innocent boy...

Having heard the shower turn off moments after he left Daisy, Alex moved around the suite and turned out all the lights, the fireplace and city providing all the light he wanted, and then he called to Daisy. She appeared, wearing the hotel robe, her hair wrapped in a towel. Her eyes looked larger in the firelight. She moved shyly toward him, coming off the adrenaline rush of their shower. When she was an arm's length away, he opened his robe and welcomed her.

Despite the warm shower, her skin was cool against his. His erection nestled at the juncture of her legs. Helping it along, he swayed a little, enjoying the texture of her skin.

Without another word, he picked her up, her legs going around his waist once more as their robes and towels dropped, and he carried her back to her bedroom. The lamps on the nightstands were turned to their lowest settings, soft and seductive. Pulling away the covers in one quick motion, he gently eased her back against the pillows then stretched out beside her, his hand settling on her breast.

Her skin was the color of peach kissed with shadows of blush and blonde. Where she was fair and light, he was dark and tan. They kissed and touched, exploring the contours of each other's bodies until he thought he might explode. She responded to each touch, her body a finely tuned instrument he intended to play.

Extracting himself, he said, "I'll be right back."

Daisy sat up, caution in her voice. "Where are you going?"

"I'm trying to be responsible."

A minute later, he tossed a new box of condoms onto the nightstand, slid between the sheets, gathered her into his arms, and kissed her as his hand slipped between her legs picking up where he'd left off.

"Forgiven?" he asked, as he made slow, gentle circles in her heat.

"You were never in trouble," she said softly. Within seconds, her hips rose off the bed in rhythm to his touch. Through practices he'd mastered over the years, he brought her quickly to her first orgasm. When she cried out, her fingers dug into his back as she bucked against his ministrations. He kissed a trail from a tight nipple to the column of her throat. She clung to him, running her fingers through his damp hair.

"You're driving me crazy," he murmured, reaching for the small box on the nightstand. Ripping the package open, he freed the condom and sheathed himself.

"I want you inside me, now," she ordered.

Settling between her legs, he noticed that she trembled with even the smallest touch. Her sensuality beat within her. He savored the moment, growing still and locking his eyes to hers. Slowly, he leaned into her, bringing their lips together as he nudged himself inside her heat. With great care, he began his onslaught, determined to make each second last a minute. He teased her a bit, he knew he shouldn't, but he wanted this to last.

Daisy wanted to scream, scream with frustration and pleasure. He was teasing her with the ultimate joystick, rubbing himself in her warmth but refusing to push inside her. He'd brought her to orgasm quickly, but it wasn't enough. If he kept this up much longer, she wouldn't be opposed to begging.

Lifting her hips, she pushed against him, hoping he'd slip inside. Employing a little purposefully seductive talk, she said, "I've wanted you since the café. Wanted you deep inside me, making me scream…"

"That makes two of us," he said, but only allowing the tip of his shaft to enter her. One glorious inch, inside and then out, rubbing, teasing her flesh…

"Please, Alex…what are you waiting for?"

"Tell me what you want."

"Alex, damn it," she said, punching his shoulder, "Make love to me!"

"Like this?" he asked as he pushed into her with one long stroke.

When she didn't respond he got worried.

He stilled, his hand reaching up to cup her face. "Are you all right?"

"Don't you dare stop or I swear, I'll kill you…"

Smiling down at her, he moved, slowly pulling out and pushing back in. Her breath came out in quick, hard jerks with each of his intimate caresses.

"Easy," he said, his hand resting on her cheek.

Her body relaxed by degrees but held him tightly within her. Wrapping her legs around him, she pulled him deeper, noticing that his emerald eyes glinted with feral intent.

It all felt so wonderful, but she needed more and didn't hesitate to ask for it. "Harder, please...Alex...please?"

"Does this feel good?" he asked.

"Yes...yessss..."

Their coupling turned to frenzy as he rode her climax to the final shudder and then succumbed to his own.

They lay quietly for several moments, looking into each other's eyes until the intensity made Daisy look away.

"Hey," Alex said, his thumb running along her jaw line, concern in his voice. "Where did you go?"

"I'm right here."

"Are you okay?" he asked, but now the concern held a deeper emotion and Daisy sensed vulnerability in the powerful man.

"Yes, I'm fine."

"Did you like that?" he asked, his smile carnal.

She nodded and said, "It was okay."

"Okay?" he said with incredulity.

"Nice, I guess?"

"Hmm...some nice instruction, then 'okay' and 'nice'?" he asked, rolling onto on his back and looking up at the ceiling.

Running her finger along his cheek, she said, "Well, yes."

"'Okay' and 'nice'?" he asked in a tone so skeptical, so concerned that she could no longer control herself and started laughing.

"You're a little faker! It was fantastic and dirty and just fantastic," he said, repeating himself as he pulled her close. He kissed her as she laughed. He kissed her until she could barely breathe for her laughter. He kissed her until she found her breath and started kissing him back. When kisses weren't enough, he slid inside her and this time he didn't make her beg.

An hour later, she lay in the crook of his arm, her warm body snuggling against his. She had to admit, their second round was better than the first.

"When are we flying home?" she asked.

"Of all the things I thought you might say, that wasn't one of them," he said as his hand made small circles on her skin.

"It's just that the date has been moved several times, so I want to see what I should expect."

"I don't want this adventure to end," he said, honestly.

"I don't either," she said, wondering what next week, next month might look like. She didn't want to think about it. She was sleeping with her boss, despite anything they'd said to each other, there it was.

"Why don't we check on the other Stark International Hotels? I think I want you to visit the other hotels involved with the anniversary party. It should give you some perspective into Stark International Hotels and you'll get a chance to see what everyone else is planning." It sounded like an idea he'd come up with on the fly, while they were laying there in bed, but he hadn't. The idea had come to Alex sometime on the flight to Paris. With the rate he was changing his schedule and the schedules of everyone around him, sooner or later, there would be talk and the rumors would start. He felt the first twinges of regret.

He couldn't help himself though. After seeing Adam, Alex needed something—not something, someone…Daisy. They'd not finished what they'd yet to start. He felt short changed that first night at Cinco de Mayo, he wanted more time with her but knew that wasn't the smartest thing to do. He was a traveling bachelor—and who would ever want to hook up with someone who's never around—which was why he kept his relationships at one and done. Well, until he'd become the CEO and before he met Daisy.

Then if fate couldn't have done it better, there was Daisy a.k.a. Deirdre. He knew then and there, Stark International Hotels needed her; and from a personal standpoint, he certainly wasn't going to let her get away. Things couldn't have worked out better.

"If we hadn't made love, I'd be sent on the next plane home?"

Treading carefully, he said, "No, your plane ticket still would've been changed."

"When did you decide on this plan?" she asked, looking at him suspiciously.

Did anything get by her?

"I thought of it a couple of days ago. It's a good idea, besides, you'll be able to see more of Europe."

"Will you be joining me?" she asked, her hand smoothing out a wrinkle in the sheet with nervous precision.

"Of course, I'm the boss. I can do things like that. Besides, I'm not about to leave you alone in three of the most romantic cities in the world. I'll be right by your side."

She abandoned the sheet to kiss him, placing her hands on either side of his face. He broke away from the kiss first.

"Stop looking at me like that," he ordered softly, her blush having more effect on him than he wanted to admit.

"Like what?"

"Like a kitten enjoying a bowl of cream," he said as he rolled over, pining her body to the mattress. "Or a lioness who just ate some small woodland creature."

"And don't you just love it?" she asked.

He did, but his feelings for her scared him a little.

CHAPTER NINE

Daisy awoke slowly, sprawled in the middle of the bed as late-morning sunlight filled the room. Swimming in the twisted linen, she noticed that a now familiar solid body of warmth was gone. Alone, she stretched tight, resisting muscles, and sat up too quickly, her head spinning. Sinking back into the soft mattress, she contemplated going back to sleep, but her curiosity as to where Alex had gone made her throw back the covers. Standing on wobbly legs, she walked to the bathroom and stepped into the shower.

The warm water lapped her body, easing her fatigued muscles and the telltale soreness between her legs. She deserved every little discomfort. Despite her protests to the contrary, it would appear she was much more like her mother than she wanted to ever admit. Like mother, like daughter, she was making love with her boss. But Alex was different. This had to be different.

She pictured her father, Blaine Maxwell. She'd never called him 'Dad' because she had never really known him and never would. He'd died ten years ago. Blaine was her mother's boss and they'd had an affair although Blaine was married to someone else and had children. Somewhere in the world, she had two sisters she'd never know and who probably would never want to make her acquaintance.

She'd only seen Blaine four times in her life. He didn't embrace the idea of being a father to a bastard child. She was a complication at the end of a mistake that he didn't want to be reminded of.

In truth, her mother never regretted her relationship with Blaine, and she regretted getting pregnant. She regretted Daisy. Daisy put the wake in her mother's clandestine life of smooth sailing.

During her childhood years, whenever things got tight, her mother would find a way to get extra cash. It was strange to think of your own mother as a mistress to a man who happened to be your father. On good days, she liked to think they loved each other. But on most days, she figured they just liked to have sex with each other.

Forty minutes after waking up alone, Daisy emerged from the bedroom, wearing a pale peach silk suit.

The lavish suite was hauntingly quiet. The previous week she'd lived in it alone and never noticed the absence of noise. Now it was Alex's absence, which permeated the space, changing not only the very air she breathed, but also the suite itself. Grabbing her new replacement keycard, which had been delivered yesterday, she decided it was time to see just what was left of her career at Stark International Hotels.

Walking through the lobby, she was alert, but uneasy. Why hadn't Alex left a note or awakened her when he left? They had both come down at the same time yesterday, but they hadn't had a night of hot sex the night before either. No breakfast and diminishing confidence placed a solid rock in her tender gut.

Had they been a one-night stand? When had he left the suite? Was he so used to leaving women in his bed that he hadn't given her a second thought?

The doubts were growing legs when Alex appeared from around a corner with Luis. They stopped talking when they saw her, and it was Luis who spoke first.

"Daisy, oh my goodness, yesterday was so busy, I didn't get a chance to tell you how worried we were when we heard you got robbed. Pierre alluded to it, but Alex just filled me in about the details of the incident in Pigalle." Closing the distance between them in a few quick steps, he grabbed her in a tight bear hug. Over Luis's shoulder, she regarded Alex for the first in the morning's bright light. His slow, appraising smile took her breath away, unhinging her from the inside out. She was, at the very least, still employed.

"I'm sorry," she said, feeling guilty. "I knew we had other things to discuss yesterday."

Luis filled the silence. "I feel responsible. I had promised Alex that I would keep you safe. I let him down. I wish you had called. It must have been terrifying. You said nothing about it yesterday, I thought you'd just gotten lost in the adventure."

"I didn't want to mention it. It is a little embarrassing. I wasn't robbed at gunpoint or knifepoint or anything like that. It wasn't scary. He just bumped me and grabbed my arm."

"It is an extortion technique used on tourists," Luis said.

"But he could have bumped you with a knife," Alex said, his voice a sharp edge inserted into the conversation as he stepped toward her, angling his body strategically to prevent Luis from hugging her again.

"Mon Dieu!" Luis exclaimed.

"I am fine. I didn't mention it yesterday because it wasn't still in my mind. It was over. I'm very sorry I worried you…both. It is just a memory. It was day before yesterday, it is over."

"I should've taken you myself," Luis said.

"No need, I'm here. I'll have to keep a close eye on you, Daisy," Alex offered, giving Luis a predatory look that was edged with cool indifference toward the lesser man. Wasn't he worried that Luis would guess the nature of their relationship?

They ate an early lunch at a nearby café, Luis further explaining his updated vision of his party to Alex, and Daisy noticed the tension she'd witnessed yesterday was no longer as strong. Daisy watched the men go over the budget and the details, heard the warning in Alex's voice as he told the other man he expected him to open the hotel on time. Luis looked nervously to her for reassurance, although they'd gone over the timeline and numbers endlessly yesterday to assure they were correct.

"We've come a long way in a very short time," she offered. "I think Luis made us good promises yesterday and today that can be achieved, we just need to give him the time and space to make it happen."

"Looks better than it did a month ago, but I'm still concerned," Alex stated flatly, his lips tight, his expression formidable.

"With Daisy's help over the last several weeks, we've nailed down many of the details. I'm glad to know she'll be staying a little longer."

"What?" she asked, not understanding.

Alex's eyes bore into the other man. "I had a feeling she would be helpful to you, but she is needed elsewhere. She will be accompanying me as I go to the next hotel."

"How much longer do we have her?"

She didn't like being talked about as if she were a piece of furniture.

"We'll be leaving on Saturday. I'm in need of her assistance starting this afternoon." Alex announced, staring pointedly at the other man.

Daisy rolled her eyes; she couldn't help it. A bone between two angry dogs playing tug of war had more dignity. Both men ignored her nonverbal protest, but then she caught Alex raising a single eyebrow in her direction. Heat licked up her skin and she used the menu as a fan.

After lunch, they bid goodbye to Luis and stepped into the elevator, Daisy silently taking in the navy suit that wrapped Alex's large frame perfectly and the emerald patterned tie, which exactly matched his eyes. He was wearing Cordovan Gucci loafers and some exotic cologne that called to her more primal of senses.

Staring back at her, he asked, "Yes?"

"Nothing," she replied as the doors shut.

"Let's try that again," he said, wrapping his arms around her and pulling her to him. When they were nose to nose, he kissed her.

"That's definitely something," he replied, briefly breaking contact with her lips to grin at her just as the elevator doors slid open.

Still not answering, she walked ahead of him to the suite. Once the door shut behind her, she unbuttoned her jacket slowly and turned toward him. His eyes followed her fingers and focused on her breasts stretching against the creamy lacy camisole she wore underneath.

She asked, "May we define how exactly you are in need of me? I wouldn't want Luis to get the wrong idea."

"I could give a shit what Luis thinks. He's too handsy with you."

"We're friends."

"If you snapped your fingers, Luis would push me out of the way to get to you."

"I don't want Luis, I want you," she said not missing the satisfaction glowing in Alex's eyes. "What did you have in mind for our afternoon?"

He smiled and said, "I need you to accompany me on a little sightseeing. I thought I'd take you to Sacré-Coeur, the Musée d'Orsay, and maybe do a little shopping on the Champs-Élysées."

"Really?"

"Yes," he said, closing in on her, but not making any moves to touch her.

"All in one afternoon?"

"What we don't get to today, we'll do tomorrow. And if you don't stop looking at me like that we aren't getting out of this room."

"Would that be so bad?"

"No, but I want you to see the sights. I can make love to you all night long, but you can only get into the Musée d'Orsay during visiting hours."

"Is that a promise?"

Alex picked up a brochure and then dropped it again. "The Musée is only open during the day."

"That's not what I meant," she said, playfully pulling at the knot of his tie.

"I know what you meant, you little sex-crazed seductress," he said, stepping away from her. "That's why I let you sleep in this morning. I want you...well rested. Now change into something touristy, so we can burn a little daylight and get back here."

An hour later, they were at the Musée d'Orsay. Taking her hand as they walked from place to place, he showed her everything from Degas's *Ballerinas* to *Whistler's Mother*. They ended the day at Sacré-Coeur. Dining later at a little café in the Saint-Germain-des-Prés again, they laughed over a bottle of wine.

"You really like this area of Paris," she said, more of a statement than a question.

"It is my favorite. I hope you like it."

"I do," she said.

Two days earlier she'd been wandering the streets of Paris alone, thinking she might never find her way back to the safety of the hotel or ever see this man again. Now, she sat next to him, and they were dressed in casual clothes much as they had been the first day they met. Had it not been for the business that brought them to Paris, they resembled any other couple strolling along the boulevard.

Kissing her palm, then nuzzling her neck, he said, "Just wait until you see Rome."

"Is that our next stop?"

"Yes, then London."

"I can't wait."

"Once you see how the Stark International Hotel Villa Roma is doing with their celebration, you'll want to fire Luis yourself."

"I like Luis, he is a very sweet man," she said, adding, "So, you're really taking me with you?"

"That was the general idea," he grinned, showing a single, sexy dimple.

"Staying with me?"

"That was the general idea unless you require your own room and a good night's sleep…"

"No special requirements for me," she said, but it was with effort that she stayed to light topics. "I seem to sleep better when wrapped in your arms."

"I like the feel of your naked little body next to mine," he said.

"Sounds like we both need each other," she said.

Wiping his brow in mock fear, he elicited another smile from her. "How about walking back to the hotel? It's only six blocks."

Looking at the setting summer sun, striping the sky with pink and lavender, she replied, "That sounds absolutely perfect."

This was what love felt like, she thought and wondered if someday she would tell their children that this was the night she knew she was in love with their father.

CHAPTER TEN

As planned, Alex and Daisy left for Rome the next day. As they rode to the airport, a sense of unease fell over Alex. He probably should have told Maria he was bringing Daisy. Maria was not only very territorial about their relationship, but when you added her hot-blooded Italian heritage, you were playing with dynamite. He asked a lot of Maria, but after everything she'd dropped in his lap—the rules, the secrecy—he wasn't feeling especially sensitive to her feelings. But Daisy was now a part of his life. And it wasn't as if his relationship with Daisy had anything to do with his relationship with Maria. They were two, completely separate entities and he intended to keep them that way. He only hoped the women wouldn't kill each other.

Making sure all the women in his life were happy was turning into a full-time occupation.

Alex raised the interior glass between them and the driver of the limo.

"I think Luis is going to miss you a little more than he should."

"I tried to help where I could. I hope I did some good," Daisy said, feeling a strong sense of accomplishment.

"I think you did some great," he confirmed and with a raise of an eyebrow, added, "Too great, but that isn't what I'm talking about."

Turning toward him, she asked, "What do you mean by that?"

"He likes you and can't stand me," he announced without malice.

"Maybe you bully the poor man."

"Maybe he's an idiot," Alex replied.

"Maybe he doesn't approve of us. Maybe he thinks I'm sleeping my way to the top. We haven't exactly been discreet. Maybe that is a discussion we should have at some point."

Sometime, over the last couple of days, worry had settled in, getting under her skin. If Alex thought it would undermine his authority to be sleeping with her, he might reassign her or even ask her to leave the company.

"How can we be discreet when we stare at each other like we'd rather be alone and making love?"

"What?" she asked.

Running his gaze along her body, he added, "You look sexier by the moment, if that's possible. You look like you've had good sex and want more. It isn't a bad thing, but I see it and I like it."

"I don't look sexier. I look tired. Are you bothered that the staff knows? Or maybe they've learned to look the other way..."

"Daisy, please," he said, choosing to ignore her small jab. "You're a member of the staff and besides, Luis is French. I'm pretty sure he's had a lover in the past or has one now. I'm also pretty sure if I hadn't shown up a few days ago, he would have been glad to take my place in your bed."

"That wouldn't have happened. Luis is my friend. He'd never make a move on me."

"Yes, he would have," he said, with a certain confidence that made it hard to argue the point. "And then I'd have had to kill him."

"Oh, stop with the posturing, it doesn't matter because I don't feel that way about him. Not the way I feel about you."

Looking at her with his blazing green eyes, he unhooked her seat belt and pulled her onto his lap. Slipping his hand under her skirt and up her silk covered leg until he found the juncture of her thighs, he stroked her through her silk panties. The rush of heat had her squirming to get closer to him.

"I told you," he whispered as he continued to draw circles over the dampening fabric, "You're irresistible."

"You're messing with me."

"And you like it."

"I do," she said, as she reached down to cup him through his suit trousers.

By the time the limo stopped, and the door opened, Alex and Daisy were sitting away from each other, prim and proper.

They boarded the most luxurious plane Daisy had ever seen. The interior was done in cream leather with bird's eye maple trim. Sitting across from Alex in one of the oversized chairs in the main cabin, she tried not to think about what had almost happened in the limo. It was like being thirsty and not having anything to drink.

Once airborne, he warned, "Don't get too comfortable."

"Why?" As a fair-weather flyer, she was already feeling the first twinges of panic.

"We're going to finish what we started in the limo." He unbuckled his seatbelt, stood, and held out his hand. She caught it, swaying with the turbulence as they walked toward the rear of the cabin.

He opened a small door, which led to a compact bedroom. The bed was done in the same cream color, matching the main cabin, only the linens were silk with a quilted fabric headboard and bird's eye maple trim.

Pulling her close, he shut the door behind them and locked it. Then he reached into the pocket of his blazer and pulled out a condom as Daisy forgot all about the turbulence and started unbuttoning her blouse.

Much later, he ran his fingers softly through her tousled hair and whispered, "Welcome to the mile-high club, Daisy."

They managed to dress and be somewhat presentable by the time the pilot stepped through the cabin an hour later to open the cabin door for them. Alex thanked him for the smooth flight, but a speechless Daisy could only blush and avoid eye contact.

Inside the waiting limo, she giggled as she leaned back into her seat.

"What's so funny?" he asked, reaching for her hand.

"I've always heard of people doing things like that. I just never believed they actually did."

"Of course, they do. All the time. Today, it was us," he offered nonchalantly.

As his words sunk in, she felt the all too familiar rock in her gut. Just how often had he bedded another woman in his flying bedroom?

"What's the matter?" he asked, squeezing her hand.

When she didn't answer, he asked, "Have I ever told you how much I value the way you say what's on your mind?"

"You've never said that to me."

"Talk to me. Don't push me away, beautiful."

"Would it be rude to ask how many other women have been on your plane?" she asked.

"Hmm…I really couldn't say. It's the family plane."

"That's not what I meant, and you know it. How many do you remember taking into that bedroom?"

"Are you trying to ask me how many women I've slept with?" he laughed, deflecting her by not answering the question. "Not this again. Daisy. You must live in the present, not in my past. I've told you that those stories were exaggerated. I'm not one-tenth the womanizer you want to make me out to be."

"One-tenth would still be a lot," she pointed out.

"And now you're part of the one-tenth," he retorted, hitting a nerve.

Grimacing, she let go of his hand.

They rode in silence for several minutes then his voice, low and contrite, offered, "Daisy, I'm sorry."

"Not as sorry as I am."

"Daisy, please, had I known you'd react this way, I'd have suggested we watch a movie instead of what we did on the plane…are you at least having a good time?"

"I was until about ten minutes ago."

"So, the majority of the time you've spent with me since I came to Paris has been enjoyable?"

"Yes, but—"

"Then be happy, Daisy and enjoy the moment."

They drove the rest of the way in silence as his hand found its way back to hers. She'd said her piece, but the rock remained firmly lodged in her stomach.

The limo pulled up in front of the Hotel Villa Roma where a tall, dark-haired woman in a tight red business suit and four-inch red snakeskin heels waited, impatiently tapping her foot. She was beautiful, dark, and exotic. Her makeup accentuated her sculpted Sicilian features expertly.

Daisy would have known the woman anywhere. She'd only stared at her photo in *Vanity Fair* about a hundred times. This woman was Alex's Italian lover in the flesh.

In that perfect moment of recognition, Daisy could not have felt more stupid or used. Why had she agreed to go to Rome? Well, she had to admit, her eyes were wide open now.

The woman greeted Alex warmly, kissing each of his cheeks leaving a red lip print before giving him a tight, full body hug. Turning to introduce Daisy, he stepped back and placed his hand on the small of her back.

"Maria, I want to you to meet our new Associate Marketing Director for European Operations, Daisy Miller. She will be helping to oversee the anniversary parties, especially in Paris, where Luis seems to need a little extra help."

"Buon pomeriggio, Daisy," she greeted, offering a weak handshake. "How lucky you are to be working with Alex. He's so wonderful."

"Thank you," Daisy replied, watching as the other woman regarded her coolly with icy green eyes.

Trying to maintain her composure, Daisy stepped inside the elegant hotel and stared at the completely white lobby accented with red as she followed Alex and Maria to the front desk. The website hadn't done the space justice. It looked nothing like the hotels in Portland or Paris. Modern and eclectic, it was sexy to the point of hard-core porn, if a hotel could be called sex on a stick. Maria Medici, Alex's ex- or current or whatever lover, now the hotel manager, fit right in. She was like Barbie doll with a figure that defied normal female proportions. And how she walked on those heels, Daisy couldn't begin to understand.

At the front desk, speaking in rapid Italian, Maria discussed the accommodations with her staff and handed Daisy and Alex keycards. Alex said something to Maria in Italian, and she gave Daisy a curious look. Snatching the keycard out of Daisy's hand, Maria spoke again to the clerk.

A moment later, she handed Daisy a different card, explaining, "I didn't know you were sharing the suite with Alex."

Daisy looked at Alex, who had conveniently started a conversation with the desk clerk ignoring the interaction between the two women.

"Yes, we are," she said.

Without missing a beat, Maria smirked and said in a bored tone, "For now, July."

"July?" Daisy asked.

"How do you say in America? You're the flavor of the month. You're Miss July."

Daisy laughed despite the alarm bells sounding in her head and said with a surprising amount of self-control, "That was almost funny coming from, let me guess, a bitter Miss December?"

Alex returned before Maria could respond, but she had the nerve to look insulted. Narrowing her eyes, she seethed as Daisy smiled.

"Well, I don't know about you ladies, but I'd love to get settled and then have a look at the anniversary plans over dinner. Would you please make the usual reservations, Maria?"

"I already have, but only for the two of us. I didn't know you'd be bringing along a trainee," Maria snipped.

Without his usual smooth cadence, he quietly reprimanded the other woman. "Daisy isn't a trainee. Change the reservation. We will see you at eight." Then he grabbed for Daisy's hand, leaving Maria to stare after them.

Once in the elevator, Daisy asked, "Do you have surveillance cameras in here?"

"Sure."

Daisy grabbed Alex by the lapels of his suit jacket and pulled him to her for a kiss. He responded, pushing her into the wall and kissing her as his leg pushed between hers and lifted her off the ground.

"You constantly surprise me," he whispered.

"Get used to it," she said, sucking on his bottom lip.

"Try to wait until we make it to the suite. I like being the CEO and I don't want scandal in the form of video."

Once inside the modern space, decorated in black and white, they threw their clothing to the floor as they kissed and headed for the nearest flat surface.

Pushing Alex back on the bed, Daisy straddled him and searched his pockets until she found the one containing his stash of condoms.

"You're killing me," he said, with a moan as she ripped the wrapper with her teeth.

"Are you dying happy?" she asked, taking him inside of her.

"Yes," he managed through half closed eyes.

Later, Daisy sat up from the tangle of sheets. She could just make out the Colosseum in the distance.

"My god."

"What?" Alex asked sleepily, kissing her shoulder.

"The Colosseum."

"That's nothing," he said, getting out of bed and returning a moment later in a plush hotel robe. In his arms he held a second robe. Holding it open, he said, "Put this on and I'll really show you something."

Standing in front of one of the tall, modern windows, he pointed, "See that?" Wrapping his arm around her shoulder, he announced, "That's the Vatican. The Spanish Steps are just to the west. And do you see that round dome?"

"Yes."

"The Pantheon."

"Wow," she marveled.

"Tomorrow afternoon we're taking a tour of all of them."

"I can't wait."

Nuzzling her neck, he replied, "This is wonderful."

"Um-hum," she murmured, closing her eyes.

"What was that in the elevator, Daisy? I thought you were going to have your way with me."

Eyes jerking open, she replied, "No, nothing like that in an elevator."

"Does this have something to do with Maria?"

"The green-eyed viper?" she asked.

Alex tensed and she knew she'd crossed the line. "Daisy...that viper runs this hotel. She's consistently in the top three most profitable properties in the entire company. Despite her cool exterior, she is very good at what she does. I like her."

"How exactly does she do that?"

"Daisy," he scolded, "Watch her, you might learn something."

"She hates me, and the feeling is kind of mutual."

"You don't know that. You just met her. Give her a day or two to get used to you."

"Doesn't matter. It's a chick thing and a territory thing. We're both claiming you," she said. "I win."

"That's absolutely ridiculous. Maria and I are old friends. She is protective of me, nothing more or less. Don't worry about her."

"I think I will worry about her." Running on pure female instinct, she said the words with certainty.

"You have nothing to worry about." Touching his lips to hers, he asked, "What did she say to you while I was talking to the desk clerk?"

"I think it is best you don't know." She focused on the Vatican in the distance. She didn't trust her emotions and wasn't sure she could trust Alex either.

"Daisy, she is harmless, but if she is being overtly mean, I'll deal with her."

"No one, who looks like that, is harmless."

"Would you like me to have a word with her?" he asked as he absently ran his hand along her spine in a move meant to reassure, but only annoyed her further. "I have no problem talking to her."

"No, that would only make it worse. Let it go."

"Then I guess you'll just have to trust me that you have nothing to worry about."

"Never said I didn't like a challenge."

At precisely eight o'clock, they met Maria in the lobby and got into a waiting limo. Dinner was at an elegantly dark hole-in-the-wall restaurant with large prosciuttos hanging from the ceiling. Over what was one of the longest dinners of her life, Daisy listened to Alex discuss every element of the party with Maria. Every now and then Maria would speak in Italian. Alex would ask her politely to speak in English and she would shoot Daisy a nasty glare.

By the second of their five-course meal, Daisy grew tired of staring at Maria's cleavage squeezed into a tight black dress. It came close to ruining the best cappellacci di zucca she'd ever eaten.

"We have all the masks and the costumes. It'll be beautiful," Maria exclaimed, using her hands as she bent toward Alex exposing a generous amount of her olive skin.

Daisy looked down at her own front. The simple black sheath dress she wore was about as different from Maria's as it could get. She felt dowdy and unattractive across from the flamboyant woman. Alex must think she looked like a nun.

"You've almost doubled your budget since the last time we talked. I hope the expense will be worth it," Alex complained.

"Alex, I don't know why you scold me. You know in the end you'll give me whatever I want," she said, with a sexy half-smile.

Daisy bit her lip to keep from hissing.

"Damn it, Maria. You're spending too much money."

Maria pouted and pursed her lips as she whined, "What would you have me do? Carnevale is sexy and mysterious. A person becomes someone else. They live out their fantasies. I can't do it halfway."

"All I'm asking is that you keep your budget in mind."

"It'll be spectacular," Maria said simply.

Alex sighed in frustration and turned to Daisy. "You might not know about this, but once a year in Venice…"

Daisy held up her hand to silence him. "The theme of her party is Carnevale Di Venezia only you're doing it in Rome… Roma? Right?"

"Sorry," he replied, placing his hand on her thigh under the table. "I didn't mean to sound condescending."

Maria smirked, but Daisy ignored her and placed her hand on top of Alex's.

"Tomorrow, I want to make sure Daisy gets a complete tour of the hotel and meets the management team."

Maria scrutinized her then. "She speaks no Italian. What is the point? It will frustrate everyone."

"The point is to get her familiar with the hotel and the staff. You'll also give her a sample of your marketing materials and a copy of your current marketing plan." His tone made it clear that it wasn't a request but an order. It pleased Daisy to see him speaking up on her behalf, but she also realized she might have to be alone with the other woman.

Then Alex said the sweetest words she'd ever heard. "You know, I haven't given the hotel a thorough inspection in over a year. Don't worry about the language barrier. I'll go on the tour as well and am more than happy to translate for Daisy when she meets the staff."

After the grueling three-hour dinner, the only redeeming quality being the food, Daisy was more than ready to leave. She'd had more than she could take of Maria and was ready to explode. It was an iron test of her will to keep quiet and maintain her cool. She had a lot of questions for Alex, and he wasn't going to like any of them one bit and she didn't care.

He paid the check as the waiting limo pulled up and then held his hand out to Daisy eliciting an eye roll from Maria.

They drove back to the hotel in silence, but when they arrived outside the modern entryway, Alex put his hand on Daisy's knee to stop her from leaving. He turned to Maria, "Buona sera Maria, we'll see you tomorrow."

"You aren't coming in?" Maria asked, looking at Daisy.

"No, I want to show Daisy something."

Smugly, Daisy settled back in her seat as the car drove away, leaving Maria at the curb like trash.

"Where are you taking me?"

"Someplace that can only be appreciated at night. Here," he said, handing her three coins from his pocket.

"Are you taking me to the Trevi Fountain?"

"Shh…you'll ruin the surprise," he replied, bending to kiss her cheek.

"You're enjoying this touristy sightseeing stuff, aren't you?"

"Yes, it's fun watching you see it for the first time. Almost like seeing it for the first time myself."

She'd planned on laying into him, demanding answers about Maria, but his tone and the way he was looking at her, made her hesitate. Quite simply, she didn't want to ruin the mood.

When the limo stopped, Alex popped open the door not waiting for the driver and held out his hand.

"Beautiful," she murmured, looking at the bottle-green water reflecting off the white marble structure with the Pantheon in the background.

"Come on, we'll get closer." He pulled her to an open space away from other tourists.

Standing next to the fountain, she studied the carvings and listened to the rushing water.

"Don't forget your coins."

"Is there something I should say?" she asked.

"No. Just think about your wishes and toss them in."

"Are you going to toss anything in?"

"Maybe one," he answered.

"Hmm…what should I wish for?"

"If you say it out loud it won't come true," he warned.

"That's an old wives' tale."

"Humor me," he replied, flinging his coin high into the air. She watched as it fell into the water with a loud splash.

She made her wishes, which had much to do with the man standing next to her and tossed the coins separately. The third one made an especially large splash, which was appropriate, for it was the most important.

"That one is coming true for sure," Alex proclaimed, kissing her cheek.

"That would make me quite happy," she said with a gleeful chuckle.

"What did you wish for?"

"Hey, old wives' tale, I can't tell you…"

He laughed, "Well, if you're not going to tell me, I'll have to introduce you to my old friend, limoncello."

"Lemon cello, a yellow musical instrument?"

"No, silly, you like lemons right?" he asked, walking her toward a little sidewalk café in front of the Pantheon.

"I love lemons. I have to admit, I liked your lemon crepe in Paris."

"Then you'll love this."

They sat at a small café table watching the tourists walk by, looking at the Pantheon in the warm summer evening. The waiter appeared and Alex ordered in Italian. That was another thing she didn't know about him. Not only did he speak French, he also spoke Italian.

"Just how many languages do you speak?" she asked.

"English, French, enough Italian to get by and I should learn Arabic, but it is a hard language."

"Impressive," she said. Daisy had purchased the Babbel French Language course and was struggling to answer the questions that would tailor the experience for her.

He shrugged, "Necessary part of doing business."

Within a couple of minutes, the waiter returned with a bottle of vibrant yellow liquid which he stuck in a bucket of ice, and a plate of amaretto cookies.

Alex poured each of them a small glass, dipped a cookie into the liquid and held it out for her to taste.

"Oh, that's good," she said, savoring the tart fresh lemon against the sweet almond cookie.

Alex touched his glass to hers and then drained his limoncello in one swallow. After a small grimace, he gestured toward her glass and encouraged her to do the same. Daisy did, feeling the sweet alcohol all the way to her toes.

Two hours later, Alex pushed her against the wall of the elevator as it lumbered to their suite. Lifting her body against the highly polished wood, he pinned her in place with his thighs. Her legs wrapped around his waist, straining the fabric of her straight skirt as she kissed him. Tongues met playfully, passionately as he reached under the hem of her dress and hooked his finger around the lacy edge of her panties. Within seconds, the offending scrap of lace was ripped away.

Struggling with his fly and zipper, he shoved what was left of her panties into pocket of his dinner jacket.

Daisy wanted him, would have let him make love to her in the small public place if he hadn't regained control in the nick of time.

"Hold on," he said more to himself than to her. When the elevator stopped and the doors opened, he pulled away from the wall with her arms and legs wrapped around his middle. Carrying her, he stepped into the hall, barely managing to open the door to their suite.

Once inside they ripped at each other's clothing, struggling to break free from anything that acted as a barrier between them. And then, for Daisy, the world spun and not just from the sweet-tart lemon liquor.

Peals of church bells signaling Sunday Mass were painful gongs beating in Daisy's head. She struggled to open her eyes against the bright morning light and automatically reached for Alex. He was on his stomach, facing her, his palm resting on her breast. Stirring, his hand moved in small circles, caressing her gently. She snuggled against him, whispering a throaty, "Good morning."

"Good morning, beautiful."

"Please stop yelling."

Smiling, he fought to open one eye, "Limoncello."

"Shh…" she whispered, giggling.

He kissed her ear and asked, "We didn't make love in the elevator, did we?"

"We made it to the bed."

"Good, because it's the last thing I remember. That's not the kind of corporate video the board members need to see."

"I'd get fired," she said, moving her hand up stroke his hair.

"We'd be fired," he corrected.

"Oh god, I feel sick."

Alex picked up a trash bin from his side of the bed and handed it to her.

"Very funny," she said, tapping him lightly on the arm.

He chuckled and leaned back into the pillows.

"Don't ever let me drink limoncello again," she announced.

"That's a promise I cannot make."

"Enabler," she said as she sat up, the world spinning as nausea threatened to overtake her.

"Stay in bed, try to sleep it off," he said, groping for her hand blindly, his eyes closed once again.

"I have to brush my teeth."

Standing, she slowly meandered to the bathroom, going through her normal morning routine much more slowly. In the shower, she slumped against the cool tiled wall and moaned.

A few minutes later, she heard Alex at the sink performing the same ritual. He stepped in the shower beside her, his hands running over her smooth wet skin. Sighing in pleasure, she leaned against him for support.

"I need to wash my hair, but my arms are too heavy to lift over my head," she complained, her face smashed against his hard chest.

"Allow me."

"Thank you, just be gentle, because it hurts."

"Your hair hurts?" Alex laughed, his whole body moving.

"Stop it. You're making me seasick."

When his laughter grew louder, she pulled away from him to lean once again against the cool marble.

"I'm sorry sweetheart, but you're cute all hung over," he said, kissing her until she all but forgot about her hangover.

CHAPTER ELEVEN

After three whirlwind days in Rome, they left for London, none too soon for Daisy. For reasons she couldn't understand, Alex defended Maria in everything she said or did. Daisy wondered how long ago they'd been lovers. However long it had been, Maria was still licking her wounds. And she really, really didn't like Daisy.

Would she end up feeling like Maria some day? Maybe they would one day bond and end up discussing Alex as a past experience. She didn't think they'd ever be friends, but anything was possible.

Hard as it was to admit, she'd learned a different perspective of the hotel business while in the other woman's company.

It was raining when they boarded the corporate jet bound for London. As soon as they were airborne, Alex pulled Daisy into the small plane's bedroom. Sinking onto the bed intent on a repeat performance of their last flight, they were interrupted mid-kiss by the insistent wail of Alex's cell phone. Glancing at the caller ID, he apologized and went back out into the main cabin.

Daisy was left to browse through a stack of movie magazines as Alex settled into a deep conversation. She listened, trying not to eavesdrop, but unable to escape his voice. The conversation focused on the company's new hotel in Dubai. She'd tried to find out everything she could about the jewel in the Stark International Hotels crown, but while listening to Alex, she garnered more information in a few short minutes than she had in a several hours of searching on the internet. The project was over budget and there were issues with the contractors. Occasionally, she'd glance up from her magazine to find him watching her. Despite the harsh tone he used with the person on the other end of the line, there was no anger in his expression when he looked at her.

He was still hashing out the problems when they landed in London an hour and a half later.

"I'm sorry about that," he said as soon as he hung up. "There are so many issues and delays, I don't know where to begin."

"Sounded like you had a handle on it," she replied and quickly added, "I'm sorry, I wasn't trying to eavesdrop."

"I didn't say anything that's secret," he said, taking her hand as they strode across the tarmac to the waiting stretch limo.

Thirty minutes later, they arrived at the majestic Stark International Hotel London, which was reminiscent of the elegant Portland property. They were greeted by an older, stout-looking man, the hotel manager, Benjamin Renwick. Daisy immediately made the correct assumption that he was a snobby stuffed shirt and didn't like him on sight. She had a hunch the feeling was mutual.

"Alex, good to see you again," he said, completely ignoring Daisy. He ignored her in much the same way Maria Medici had, but without the added glint of jealousy. Daisy took in the formal lobby as the men exchanged small talk. When she heard her name, her head snapped to attention.

"Benjamin, I want you to meet our new Associate Marketing Director for European Operations, Daisy Miller. She's my personal consultant on the anniversary party. Her thoughts and opinions are very important to me."

It was the first time he'd ever introduced her as if she belonged to him. She wasn't sure how she felt about that but had a strange feeling he was trying to be protective. The other man's jowls shook a little as he extended his hand to her, but he kept his eyes on Alex as he said, "We have everything under control."

"I'm sure you do, but I want to sit down and hear your plans for myself," he said as Daisy sensed the palpable tension between the two men.

A bellboy awkwardly handed each of them a key and disappeared.

"It's too bad you wasted your time coming all this way. I could have emailed the plans to you."

"I wanted to visit and show Daisy your operation. Are you available for dinner?" Alex asked.

Jowls shaking, he asked, "Seven? In the main dining room?"

"Fine. Please bring Vivian. I haven't seen her in a long time," Alex replied, glancing at Daisy.

"Well Alex, since you're bringing your mistress, do you mind if I bring mine instead of my wife?" the other man asked with smug satisfaction.

The verbal slap hit Daisy across the cheek. She froze, her face turning bright red. Obviously, word of their affair had traveled throughout the organization. Alex stiffened, his posture rigid, as he took a threatening step toward the other man, "Excuse me. I'm fairly certain I didn't hear you correctly."

Renwick smirked, not at all chagrined. "Is that what they're calling this kind of arrangement these days?"

Alex's face became an expressionless mask. Turning to Daisy, he said, "Please go and get settled in the suite. I need to have a discussion with the staff. I'll be up shortly."

Unable to respond, feeling every bit her mother's daughter, she nodded and quietly stepped away from the mounting fury.

Alex stopped a passing bellboy, "Take Ms. Miller to the corporate suite and get her anything she wants. Understand?"

The young boy was wide eyed, "Yes, sir, Mr. Stark. Right away."

Daisy spent the next half hour walking around the well-appointed royal blue and carnelian suite trying to calm down. Was this the way her mother had felt, the mistress of a powerful businessman? She thought of the chatter and rumors, the hurtful comments she'd overheard as a child. She'd made a promise to herself to never repeat her mother's mistakes. In less than a month at her new job, she'd followed her mother's career path almost completely. All she wanted was to do her job well. But the passion she felt for Alex had a life of its own.

Was that how her mother felt in the beginning? Much more importantly, how would it end?

She walked to the window and stared at the Parliament buildings and Big Ben. She wasn't sure how long she stood there waiting, but she jumped at the sound of the door even though she'd been anticipating it. Turning, she regarded Alex, saying nothing, wanting him to speak first. He sat on the nearest couch and rubbed his brow with his hand.

"I'm sorry about that, Daisy. It was totally out of line. And it will never, ever happen again."

"Word travels fast," she said flatly.

"It's not that. He's been bitter since I took over two years ago. He wanted to be the CEO and lobbied for it. Now, he looks for anything he can use as leverage to get me removed from my position."

Turning to stare once again at Big Ben, she murmured, "This thing...whatever it is between us...could cost you your job. Could cost me my job."

"No," he said, incredulously.

"You made it sound pretty bad. I'm the leverage," she replied, looking at him over her shoulder.

"Daisy, my family has the majority of the stock. Of the family, I'm the largest shareholder. All Renwick is trying to do is force my hand or slap it. I either have to fire him or help the woman in my life develop a thicker skin."

She turned all the way around, looking at where he sat slumped on the couch. "Is that what I am? Am I the woman in your life? Or am I the flavor of the month?"

"Damn it!" Alex shouted as loosened his tie. Nothing since he'd stepped into that café in Portland had gone according to plan.

"Why didn't you tell me who you were when I met you? You lied about your job, where you lived. Are you going to keep lying? Lie about this thing between us?"

"I'm as surprised by this thing between us as you are," he said, feeling like an idiot.

"I'm sorry I'm so inconvenient."

"What's wrong with you today?" he asked as he stood, walked to the bar, and pouring himself a drink. Thinking better of it, he fixed her a glass too.

"Answer one of my questions. Any one of them will do."

"You're very complicated," he demurred, walking toward her holding out a crystal glass with two fingers of bourbon. "I wish you could just enjoy what we have."

When she didn't reply or take the glass from his extended hand, he asked, "Would you please join me for a drink?"

Through clenched teeth, she ordered, "Make the answer simple."

"Fine," he said, grimacing as he tasted the amber liquid. "When I met you…I wasn't sure what we were going to be. I didn't know if I'd know you for a day, a night, or hell…forever. I was taking a day off when I stepped into a café that first time, and I couldn't stop myself, I had to keep going back. Nothing has been the same since the moment I got up the nerve to ask you if I could join you at your table."

"Do you regret it?"

"No, not in the least," he said, shaking his head.

"But you're keeping your options open," she concluded, her lips tightening with anger.

This was no good. He needed to calm the situation down. The last thing he needed was a spurned lover who was an employee. Besides, he didn't think he could let her go, not now, not ever. "Daisy, I spent two hundred and fifty nights away from home last year."

"So what? Is that a declaration or an excuse to move from woman to woman?"

There hadn't been anyone since he'd taken over the running of Stark International Hotels. Hell, he'd been celibate for two years before Daisy. There hadn't been time and he'd found that the excitement of a quick affair had lost its appeal. He didn't want that anymore. No, something had changed along the way. Daisy was the first woman that made him think he could be with one woman for the rest of his life. Adam had been right—when you know, you know.

"What I'm trying to say is that I'm not a man who settles in one place for very long."

"Or with one woman?"

"Those are your words, not mine. This isn't just about me. I don't know what is going on with you, but I sense you have trust issues. Until you tell me what is going on in your head, we don't have a chance. You've got to learn to trust me," he said. It was a low blow, but he was on some level disappointed in her. She thought the worst of him. Did she think the worst of all men?

"That's a convenient thing to say when you're the one scared of commitment."

He hadn't seen her this angry since her interview.

Pulling his tie free, he tossed it to the side. "I'm scared of the wrong kind of commitment. I don't want to be with someone who always suspects the worst of me, like you do. For example, if I tell you that you don't need to worry, you don't need to worry."

When she didn't reply but looked at him with hurt in those big blue eyes, he marched into the bathroom and slammed the door behind him. He didn't want to say anything he might regret more than what he'd already said. He needed a moment and a very cold shower to cool off.

Fighting back tears, Daisy got ready in a different area of the suite. She put on the new black dress she'd bought in Rome. It was off the shoulder, sexy, but not too revealing. She'd looked forward to having Alex see it, but now she didn't know why she bothered.

Looking in the mirror, she added her fake pearls to her ears and throat, swept her hair up into an elegant twist and added perfume to her pulse points. Occasionally, she dabbed at a wayward tear with a tissue, which was exactly what she was doing when Alex saw her. She could see his face in the reflection as he leaned against the doorframe and stared. Without a word, he walked up behind her, placing his hands on her waist. He leaned down to her ear and whispered, "I'm sorry."

Shutting her eyes, she let out a long breath. She didn't want to repeat her mother's mistakes, nor did she want to be a fool, but she wanted to enjoy each minute she had with him. The question was, what made a man as powerful as Alex marry a lover? Her father never married her mother, would Alex ever want to commit to Daisy or were they destined to be in this same spot five, ten, fifteen years from now? Would he fall as deeply in love with her as she was with him?

"I'm sorry, too," she said, turning so that she was facing him. Kissing him lightly on the lips, she asked, "How much time do we have before dinner?"

"Twenty minutes, but I don't mind making them wait," he said. "No one talks to you like that and gets away with it, not even me."

"I won't be my mother," she said, leaning back into his arms.

"What does your mother have to do with us?"

She knew he didn't understand, so she took a deep breath and began.

"My mother and father were somewhat like us, but I hope nothing like us," she said, wiping away a stray tear. "My father, who I never knew shy of a couple of awkward meetings, was my mother's married boss. They had an affair that lasted for years, most of my childhood actually. I was the unwanted result that no one talked about. I was the mistake. A physical reminder of something that should never have happened. I promised myself that I'd never do anything as stupid. Yet, here I am, the hypocritical daughter. And I'm loving every minute of it."

Alex wiped another tear from her cheek, his expression softening. "I'm not your father; you're not your mother. Besides, neither one of us is married. Let's savor this and take it one day at a time. I love what we have. I love the passion and the need I have for you. I can't have a life without you in it, Daisy. Give me a little time to figure out what that means. Be gentle with me."

"So, I'm not fired?" she asked, smiling as she looked into his sparkling emerald eyes.

"Not even up for consideration and not part of this conversation. This is about us," he said, bending to kiss her. Then, he added, "We are both in uncharted territory, let's enjoy the sweet moments. And every moment I've had with you has been sweet with the exception of the last couple of hours, for which I'm sorry."

"Thank you," she said and took a step closer. He pulled her to him, his arms wrapping her securely in an embrace.

"I'll take that as a yes. Now, how do you like this room in comparison to the others you've seen on your tour through Paris and Rome?" he said, as he ran his hands along her sides, caressing her curves.

"It's cozy, the smallest of the three," she mused as she looked at the fireplace.

"Would you like a fire later?" he asked, kissing her temple.

"Yes, because it is cold here for July."

He chuckled, cupping her bottom with his hands, "I'll enjoy making love with you in the firelight."

"We have to make it through dinner first. I really can't stand that ass who is your manager."

"Don't ever stop that," he said, guiding her toward the front door of the suite.

"What?"

"The feistiness. I like it too much. You're a hard shell with a soft center. It's lovely, smart, and very sexy. You are my truth barometer on all things."

Daisy felt the blush heat her cheeks. Just when she wanted to cut him off at the knees and suspect him of the worst, he surprised her.

"Was he kidding about his mistress?"

"He wasn't kidding. They have an arrangement."

"And his wife knows about it? And puts up with it?" she asked, thinking of the ugly man she'd met. No woman in her right mind would want to be with that man.

"I really don't know or care. It's his business. Our London operation is one of the more profitable in the family."

"But not as profitable as Maria's," she offered.

"No, are you starting to warm to Maria?" he asked tentatively.

"No, and I'm pretty sure I loathe Benjamin, too," she said, picking up her small black handbag.

Daisy liked Mrs. Renwick and couldn't understand why she was with her husband. Unlike him, she was the height of dignity and class, welcoming Daisy warmly.

"How do you like working for Stark International Hotels?" the silver-haired woman asked, with an elegant English accent.

"I've had a wonderful time in Paris working with Luis Gardot." Noticing Mr. Renwick's scrutiny, she added, "His party should be very interesting and different. Hopefully, it will go off without a hitch."

Benjamin Renwick himself spent most of his time trying to talk civilly to Alex. Daisy could feel the tension between the two men but listened with interest as Alex discussed the new hotel in Dubai. "I'm flying over there in a few days to check on things. The construction is difficult. A lot of American contractors are trying to become rich on the cheap labor and we're starting to see the effects. Then I need to fly to New York to attend the services for Adam's family."

"I can't believe that happened to such a beautiful family," Mrs. Renwick said and then asked, "How is Adam?"

"Devastated," Alex replied. Each day he called to check on Adam, either calling Adam directly or members of their immediate family. Each time Alex got off the phone, he would hug her, holding her a bit more tightly than he had in the past. Daisy would hold him back, tighter, and longer than he held her because he needed the connection and the comfort.

She wouldn't be going to Dubai or New York. Alex told her in Rome that she would be going back to Portland and beginning the promotions for the Intercontinental as soon as possible.

Adam was home from the hospital now, the funeral was in a few days, and Alex wanted to be there, of course, but selfishly, Daisy wondered what would happen when he returned to Portland.

Mr. Renwick had turned remarkably pleasant. She wondered what Alex had said to him and realized she probably didn't want to know.

"Don't you like the scallops?" Mrs. Renwick asked her halfway through dinner.

Daisy looked down at her plate. Cold, semi-raw scallops on a bed of pureed broccoli and leeks lay unappetizingly before her. Distracted with thoughts of Alex leaving and their earlier fight, she'd paid little attention to her food until this moment. The thought of eating anything turned her stomach. "I had a large lunch."

"You didn't eat lunch," Alex interrupted. "Daisy, get something you like. It's fine to send it back."

"I don't know if I could eat anything else. I'm sorry, but I'm really not feeling very well," she said, picking up her glass of ice water and drinking it down. In the time it took to explain, she'd grown warm and uncomfortable, breaking out in a sweat. She would not vomit. She would not do any such thing in front of Alex or the Renwicks.

"Are you all right, my dear?" Mrs. Renwick asked.

"I think I might need to go back to the room. I'm so sorry for having to leave," she said as she stood, as did Alex and Mr. Renwick.

"Call the front desk if you need anything," Alex said, adding, "I'll be up soon to check on you."

"Thank you," she said, shaking hands with the Renwicks and then added, "Take your time. I'll be fine."

Back in the room, she lay on the bed with a cool cloth on her head. The nausea passed within minutes. Her stomach growled, but nothing sounded particularly appealing. Raiding the mini fridge, she ate some cheese and crackers, changed into her new Parisian nightgown, which she had yet to wear in Alex's presence, and crawled into bed.

An hour later, Alex quietly entered the suite and undressed in the bath. Having stripped down to his silk boxers, this time Clifford the big red dog, he slipped under the covers.

"It's okay, I'm awake. How was the rest of the evening?"

"Horrible because I can't stand Renwick. How're you feeling?"

"Better, but food doesn't sound appealing," she said, as she stripped off her nightgown.

"You must be feeling better," he said, helping to free her from the gauzy pink garment.

"You'll be gone for over a week. I need to make the most of my opportunities while we have them."

He stripped off his boxers and pulled her into his arms. "I agree, but I won't be gone forever, and I have a very nice suite in Portland. You'll love it."

"I can't wait to see the ceiling in the bedroom," she said, and leaned in to kiss him.

The need to erase the memories of the earlier fight fueled their passion. When he slipped inside her, she whispered, "Careful."

He stopped moving, his voice tender. "What's wrong?"

"You forgot something."

"Damn, I'm sorry. I got caught up."

"It's okay," she replied, savoring the feel of him. "Can you stay awhile?"

"A minute or two shouldn't hurt."

Eventually, he eased out of her and returned with a condom in hand. As he sheathed himself, he said, "That reminds me of something I've wanted to talk to you about."

"Now?" she asked, feeling bereft for the loss of the intimacy.

"Yes, it's timely. The thing is, I like being inside of you with nothing between us," he explained between kisses. "Would you be open to making that happen?"

What he said sounded a little like commitment. Odd, but that is the first thought that entered her mind.

"Like the pill?"

"Sure, or whatever," he said, rubbing his hands along her thighs.

"It would mean we were exclusive," she said, as he spread her knees and settled between them.

"You're right," he whispered, slipping inside of her with soft groan. And when he made love with her that night, something felt different, good, but different.

CHAPTER TWELVE

Daisy finished packing and tried to keep her emotions in check. Despite the rocky start, they'd had a good time in London, spending four nights mixing business with pleasure. She'd spent very little time with Benjamin Renwick, concentrating on the rest of the hotel staff. An idea for an expanded European promotion was forming in her mind. Alex liked the idea when she suggested it and asked her to start mapping it out as soon as she returned to Portland. Today, her fifth and final day in London, she would catch a plane home in the early evening and Alex would take the family jet to Dubai. He would join her for late lunch as soon as his final meeting was over and then they'd head to separate corners of the world. Dabbing a tissue to her eyes, she felt stupid. It wasn't like she wouldn't see him again, he just had to sort out the mess in Dubai and attend probably the saddest funeral in the history of funerals.

He would be back in Portland in a week or two, but what happened then? Would he call her and ask her out? Would it be assumed that she would be in his bed? Oh, the drama of it all! She had to let it unfold, which she wasn't good at. She was driven in all things—unfortunately these things extended beyond her career. This was one area where she had to be cool, act cool, let him come to her. Yeah, right.

The phone rang in the bedroom just as Daisy finished zipping her suitcase. Perfect timing. Thinking it was Alex calling her from the lobby, she hurried to the phone.

"Hello?"

"Well, hello," the familiar voice said. "I'm looking for Alex. Do I have the right room?"

It was a voice Daisy instantly recognized and hoped she'd never hear again. *Satan.*

"You do, but he isn't here right now, may I take a message?" she said, hoping he wouldn't recognize her voice. She had to tell herself to calm down. She would not lose it, not now.

"Sure sweetie, just tell him Peter called and I want to find out if I can stay in the corporate suite or in his loft when I come for the funeral in New York. I know I can't get a ride on the plane 'cause Alex will be coming from Dubai with his chicky, Maria, but I thought I'd check on my accommodations."

Peter Crawley, her former boss, the man who she'd hit with the stapler. Her enemy like no other. She should not have settled. It still made her angry. He'd gotten off easily, too easily. She hoped the stapler left a scar.

"You're going to the funerals in New York?" she replied, hoping she sounded stupid.

"Of course, Adam, Alex and I were the three musketeers at Wharton. I'm shattered for Adam. We are all best friends."

"Are you traveling alone?" she asked. What about Claire?

"Yeah, my wife is pregnant again so she's staying behind."

Daisy tried to swallow down the bile that was rising in her throat. Alex was best friends with Peter?

"Yes, I see. I'll give Alex the message."

"Thanks sweetheart. You're the secretary, right?"

"Yes," Daisy said. "Goodbye Mr. Crawley."

Daisy dropped the phone back into its cradle, disconnecting the call. She was in shock, everything coming to pass. Alex and Peter were friends? They went to Wharton together. She ran to the bathroom and threw up her breakfast. After she cleaned up, she looked at the phone as if it were a snake as she thought about what to do next.

"Please, please, please…" she murmured as she grabbed her briefcase, searched for, and found a brochure for the Hotel Villa Roma.

The third time she dialed the number she got it right. A moment later a voice answered, "Prego."

She asked for Maria and waited. The man on the other end of the line spoke in a string of Italian she couldn't begin to decipher.

A moment later, she had another earful of Italian and repeated her earlier question in English.

"This is Signorina Medici's office," a woman replied.

"May I speak to Signorina Medici, please?

"And you are?"

"This is Daisy Miller with Stark International Hotels. I'm just confirming Mr. Alexander Stark's meeting agenda in Dubai. When will Signorina Medici be arriving?"

There was a long pause, the sound of shuffling papers and then, "Signorina Medici will be joining Signore Garrison Stark at Leonardo da Vinci Roma airport at five o'clock departing for Dubai International Airport on Stark One Star…Is there a confusion?"

Daisy terminated the call. Alex was picking Maria up in Rome with the family plane.

Her next conscious thought was of being on a British Airways flight headed home. Somehow, she'd picked up her luggage, taken an elevator to the lobby, walked out the front door of the hotel and grabbed a waiting taxi. When the driver asked her where she wanted to go, she didn't hesitate, "Heathrow."

Half an hour later, they were able to get her on an earlier flight and she was gone. Gone from the suite where Peter had shattered her happiness. Gone from London. Gone from Alex.

She sat dazed in the first-class section, staring straight ahead. The stewardess went by several times, asking her again if she were all right. Finally, accepting a ginger ale to calm her troubled stomach, she held the glass in a death grip and let her mind wander.

She'd dismissed every bad rumor she'd read in article after article about Alex's womanizing ways after spending time with him. How long had they been together? Was it just twelve days? He'd changed her world in a dozen days. And she'd believed him. Falling for him.

She couldn't believe she'd been so completely stupid to ignore every sign. He'd been playing her from the start. For all she knew, he arranged for Peter to call their suite. Maybe it was his way of ending the affair and not having to say or do anything.

And of all the luck! How could Alex and Peter be friends? Could Alex know anything about her and Peter, that he was her boss? That couldn't be, could it? She was just getting herself all the more upset with each thought. What upset her the most was Alex's omittance of telling her Maria was joining him in Dubai.

Twelve hours later, she stepped inside her apartment, hauling luggage behind her. Her cell came to life, ringing. One glance at the caller ID showed it was an international call. Ignoring it, she went into her bedroom, stripped out of her clothing, and took a shower. While drying her hair, the cell rang again. When she declined the call, the caller disconnected, not leaving a message. A quick scan of the caller ID log showed the international caller had called ten times in the past few hours, her cell just now catching up after being on airplane mode.

Powering off her cell, she put it in her handbag and felt the pain all the way to her gut.

Sinking into her own empty, cold bed, she felt the tidal wave of emotions roll over her. Alex was best friends with Peter Crawley, her worst enemy. Could she be more stupid?

Her mind went to all the dark places she'd tried to avoid while flying home. When he'd arrived back at the suite and found her gone would he have been happy? Was this part of their game? Did Maria like to get jealous and then take it out on him when they next met? He had more than enough stamina to make love several times a day. Had he made love to Maria on the family plane? Was he making love to Maria right now?

Unable to sleep, she got out of bed and meandered to the kitchen for a glass of cool water and drank it too fast. A minute later, the cold liquid hit her stomach and she was instantly nauseated. She barely made it to the bathroom in time to wretch everything from her stomach.

The next morning, she heard her alarm clock and rolled over, reaching for Alex before remembering that she was home and alone.

After a cold shower, she slipped into one of her more comfortable suits and drove to her office. She had work to do. For not having been at Stark for very long, she was surprised by the amount of email and voicemail waiting for her attention.

The last voicemail on her office phone was from him. "Call me, Daisy. As soon as you get this."

Why should she? He would have some excuse or lie ready, but she knew the truth, had heard it for herself, he was part of Peter's pack, what else did she need to know? She consulted her watch. It would be early evening in Dubai. Hopefully, she'd disturb him and Maria.

Punching the number to his cell, she steeled herself, wishing she hadn't eaten toast that morning. "Daisy?" he answered on the first ring. "What the hell happened to you? Are you okay? Where are you?"

"I left," she replied quietly.

"What? What are you talking about? Why did you leave like that? Do you know how worried I was about you?" His anger was real, but it was the sentiment behind it that she questioned.

"You'll get over it."

"What is wrong with you? What happened?"

"I just realized what I meant to you," she said. "Anyway, your friend Peter called. You should call him back."

"Okay, fine, but what do you think you mean to me? I just don't understand any of this," he said.

"I don't mean a damn thing to you," she said and slammed the phone into the receiver.

The next two weeks were pure torture. She sat in her office and put together a detailed campaign for the Stark International Hotel Paris and established relationships with the other hotel managers in Europe. Luis Gardot called her every day to run ideas by her, getting more nervous with each day. When she wasn't in the office, she was at home, walking aimlessly from room to room, wondering what Alex was doing. His trip had been extended without explanation. The nights were the worst. Her body craved him. She reached for him in the dark and when she realized he wasn't there, the tears would come. If she wasn't crying, she was fighting the ever-present nausea. She started wondering if she'd picked up a stomach bug on her trip.

"I'm worried about you, kid," Brigitte said when she called her after returning to Portland.

"I think I have an ulcer," Daisy complained.

"That would be the lesser of several evils. Take some Tums, but promise me if it doesn't get better, you'll see someone."

"He is best friends with Peter," Daisy said.

"That sucks so bad," Brigitte said. "Does Alex know you sued Peter?"

"He's got to know, they had to have talked."

"Good riddance, Daisy. You got rid of Peter once, don't let him back into your life."

"Do you think they set me up?" Daisy asked.

"That would take planning I don't think they are capable of. Not these men—women maybe, but not men. Did Peter know it was you?"

"I don't know, I don't think so—but I won't put up with this," Daisy said. Only, Alex was a lot harder to walk away from than Peter had ever been.

Early one morning, she sat behind her desk and stared at a page of headlines. The lines blurred a second before a fat wet tear smeared the ink on the paper. She missed him and hated herself for it. He'd lied to her from the start, and she'd fallen for it, hook, line, and sinker. She wiped away her tears and looked out her window. At least she was getting used to the windows. Not that she'd have a chance to enjoy them. When Alex returned, he'd no doubt fire her, but maybe she'd quit first. How long would it take her to find her next job? How far away would she have to move? And how long would she feel dirty inside?

On the fifteenth day, her back was turned to her door, and although she heard someone enter her office, she didn't think it was him. But when the door slammed shut, she knew he was standing on the other side of her desk. Gripped with a mixture of sadness and disappointment, she turned to face him. Before he uttered a word, she could see his anger bubbling from every pore. He had no right to feel angry. If there was anyone who should be angry, it was her.

The last fourteen days had been hell. Daisy refused to take his calls unless they were business related and then she would only respond by email. Dubai was awful and then he'd been there for Adam. And all the while, he'd been racking his brain wondering what the hell had happened with Daisy.

During the hours he'd spent reflecting on every minute of his time with Daisy, he had come to two conclusions. One, he had hurt her or offended her in some way, and it had been so devastating an insult that she was holding the largest grudge he had ever seen. Or two, and this was the option that scared him, something was very wrong with her. If it was the latter and not the former, he needed to accept the fact she was a mess and walk away.

Stepping into her small office, he slammed the door behind him scaring Daisy out of her skin.

Her back was turned, but he'd seen her jump and when she finally faced him, none of the warmth he'd come to recognize in her eyes at the sight of him remained.

"Welcome home, sir. Did you have a nice flight?"

Enough of the bullshit, he was going to get answers. Tersely, he asked, "What the hell happened?"

"You lied about Maria, and I caught you. Game over." She decided not to address Peter; if Alex brought it up, fine, but she decided she didn't even want to go there.

"After our first day together, I never lied to you about anything." He had omitted some things, but nothing that had anything to do with them or their relationship.

Standing defiant, hands on hips, she let the unfamiliar fury she had for him seep from each and every pore. "The more interesting question is: Do you ever stop?"

"What happened, Daisy? You're the one who left. I think I deserve an explanation."

"No sir, I returned. Leaving would have meant I quit. I've decided I like my job, so we will have to find a way to get along. Or fuck it, I will quit. I haven't decided yet."

"What happened in London?" he asked, trying to soften his voice. "What happened between the time I left you in our bed and the time I came back to an empty suite?"

"I think the more appropriate question would be: What happened after I left? What did you do next? Did you and Maria enjoy your flight to Dubai?"

She was talking in riddles, intent on him figuring out something he couldn't begin to understand. "All I know is that I thought we were going to have lunch together, I returned to an empty room with no explanation. I felt like an idiot and looked like a fool. The CEO of the company sick with worry over you *again*, who simply decided to leave without a word. I'm a laughingstock."

"I know what you did," she stated, shooting daggers at him with her eyes.

"Tell me. Tell me so that I'll understand."

"Please Alex, just leave me alone. I don't want to do this anymore. Just let me do my job and let's forget what happened between us and if it can't be forgotten, I'll go," she said, her face showing the pain she felt. He wanted to circle around the desk and pull her into his arms. But behind the vulnerability, he could see her anger.

This was all wrong, but he was smart enough to know he wouldn't get any further with her today. But it wasn't over between them. It was only the beginning. Nodding in agreement, he walked numbly to the door, paused on the way out to offer a parting remark, "I'll respect your wishes, Ms. Miller."

"Hope you had fun with your friends," she replied.

"What?" he asked, pausing by her door. What the hell was she talking about?

"You'll figure it out," she said and went back to her work.

For the next two weeks, they barely spoke. He sent her emails but didn't set foot in her office. If she wanted to play this game, he'd show her how it was done.

Maybe if she went away, far enough away to still be close to home, like Seattle, Daisy mused, maybe they hadn't heard of how she liked to be pulled into sexual situations with her bosses. She shook her head and fought tears. She was her mother's daughter. What was it about Miller women that they couldn't resist their bosses? Why couldn't they meet decent men who wanted to marry them and share their lives with them? Well, she had resisted Peter, but that was easy. She didn't care about him, didn't want him, not like she wanted Alex. She had been a willing participant. She'd wanted Alex and it had paved the path to where she was right now—in a mess.

Deciding to take a walk on her lunch hour to clear her head, she left her small office. In the hall, a little girl in a bright summer dress flew past her in a blur of pink and pigtails.

"Freeze!" Alex shouted fiercely, from the proximity of his office door a few steps behind her.

Both Daisy and the little girl froze. She turned to find Alex smiling at the little girl standing ten feet away. Slowly, he bent down, opened his arms, and shouted, "Unfreeze!"

The little girl laughed as she ran, jumping into his waiting arms, shouting, "Uncle Alex! I missed you!"

A tall, raven-haired woman in a pretty white suit nodded to Daisy and kept walking until she stood next to Alex, now holding the little girl in his arms.

"She insisted on seeing you today. Thank you for making time." The woman kissed his cheek and looked back at Daisy.

"No problem," he replied.

Daisy turned and continued down the hall.

"Oh, Daisy," he called after her.

"Yes, Mr. Stark?" she answered politely. It was the first time he'd spoken to her in sixteen days, not that she was counting, but she was…

"I'd like you to meet my sister and my niece."

Approaching cautiously, she felt thoroughly inspected by all of them. Alex motioned to the raven beauty, "This is my sister, Rebecca Wilder."

Rebecca was tall like her brother, but her green eyes were slightly less brilliant than Alex's. All the good, strong family features that made the Stark men handsome and the women beautiful, the striking, chiseled features, the deep-set eyes and seductive smiles graced both of their faces. Something about Rebecca was familiar to Daisy, but it would be several weeks before she realized what it was.

"Hello," Daisy offered, trying hard to smile as she extended her hand.

"Ah, so this is the Daisy I've heard so much about," the woman said, knowingly, "Very nice to meet you."

They shook hands as Alex looked down at the little girl of four or five and said, "And this tree monkey is her daughter, Emily."

"I'm not a tree monkey," the little girl protested, looking at Daisy shyly.

"Of course, you're not," Daisy agreed. "I like the butterflies on your dress."

"Thank you," Emily said politely.

Daisy made her excuses and turned away. He'd been talking to his niece on the phone, not a lover. If she'd been wrong about the phone call, what else was she wrong about?

She called Brigitte that evening.

"How are you holding up?" Brigitte asked.

"How long does it take to fall out of love?" Daisy asked.

"I'll have to get back to you on that," Brigitte said.

"Why did I do this?"

"You went for it, I think that is incredibly brave," Brigitte said.

"Or incredibly stupid."

"Stop beating yourself up. Do you want to grab some nosh, and chat?"

"No," Daisy said, "I feel kind nauseous from all the stress."

"Okay, but if you aren't better in a couple of days, see a doctor. You might have picked something up eating all that raw shit in France."

Daisy pictured the large plates of tartare that Luis had eaten in France, with gelatinous raw eggs resting on top of the mangled, seasoned filet and knew she was going to be sick. "I've got to go," she said and hung up on Brigitte, barely making it to the bathroom in time.

A week after meeting Alex's sister and niece, Daisy stood stiffly in front of thirty-five of her coworkers and Alex at the weekly staff meeting. She had seven minutes to present her marketing plan for the Hotel Intercontinental Paris. If they liked it and Alex approved it, they would test it as soon as the hotel reopened. If the campaign was successful after implementation, they would launch it with nine other hotels in Europe. Based on the results from a European launch, it could go company wide.

Her nerves were getting the best of her as she prepared to rollout her plan to Alex and the rest of the staff. Aware of his gaze drilling into her, she held her head high and spoke with authority. By the end of her allotted time, she could see heads nodding in encouragement. She fielded questions for another couple of minutes until she felt her breakfast of dry toast start to curdle in her stomach. Why had she been stupid enough to eat anything? Her bug was still wreaking havoc with her, sadly she still hadn't felt a hundred percent since she returned to Portland. Maybe Brigitte was right, she had some stomach thing from France raging in her tummy, creating chaos.

Holding steady, she finished answering the last question and to her surprise, everyone clapped, including Alex. She made it back to her chair next to Don. He leaned toward her and whispered, "You made me proud."

"You're just saying that."

"Definitely not. You brought a fresh perspective we've needed for a long time. Since you're my hire, you're making me look good. Nice job, Daisy."

Alex walked to the front of the room, his mere presence quieting the group, "Good job, Ms. Miller. Now, I want to discuss the European anniversary party…"

Bile rose in her throat, racing for escape. Pushing her chair back, Daisy stood and ran for the ladies' room.

Barely making it the bathroom, she kneeled on the cool tile floor inside one of the stalls and wretched into the toilet. Leaning up against the stall wall, she began to cry. What was wrong with her? Did she have an ulcer? Was she seriously ill? Sure, she'd been nervous, but the presentation had gone well. She had to call her doctor and find out what was going on. First, she would have to face Alex and apologize for interrupting the meeting. He'd stopped speaking the moment she stood. No doubt, he'd want to talk to her about the disruption.

The ladies' room door opened and closed softly. If she were discovered sitting on the floor, they might do something crazy like call for an ambulance. Before she could stand, there was a knock on her stall door. Gazing down, she noticed a pair of polished Cordovan Gucci loafers and beige trouser legs. Squeezing her eyes shut, she murmured several curse words in rapid succession.

"Daisy?" Alex asked, his voice sounding hesitant. "Are you okay?"

"I'll be fine. It must have been something I ate."

"Open up and let me see for myself."

Pulling herself up, she leaned on the wall for support and slowly opened the lock with shaking fingers, as she said, "I'm sorry, I didn't mean to interrupt the meeting."

"Don't worry about it. Just open the door."

She did as he asked, looking at the floor, not wanting to face him.

"You don't look fine."

"I was sick," she said, not wanting to look up at him. "It made my mascara run. You shouldn't be in the ladies' room."

"It's my building, my ladies' room," he said, his expression flat as he stared down at her. "This wasn't a case of nerves was it?"

"I've never been sick during a presentation. Nervous yes, but never sick."

He looked away from her, shaking his head.

"Was the meeting still going on when you left?" she asked.

"Yes."

"Does everyone know you're in here?" she asked, sitting down on the small bench next to the sinks.

"I couldn't care less what they think," he replied, walking to the sink, and running several paper towels under the cold water. He wrung them out and handed the cool cloth to her.

"Thank you," she replied and started to stand. He held out his hand and she grabbed it for support. He pulled her up easily, breaking the contact as soon as she was steady. She glanced in the mirror. As she had feared, her makeup was a mess.

"When you get done in here, come to my office. I think we need to talk."

"I…"

"Daisy, please." After a moment's hesitation, he placed his hand on her arm and gave it a small squeeze.

Ten minutes later, after she'd fixed her makeup and rinsed with mouthwash, she walked along the hall knowing she was about to get fired. He would fire her for the way she was behaving, not to mention running out of an important meeting. Everyone she passed asked her if she was all right. She admitted something hadn't agreed with her stomach and kept walking, feeling self-conscious.

She knocked on the double doors outside Alex's office and waited. He opened them and invited her inside. She headed for the chairs in front of his desk, doing a mental inventory of what she would need to pack from her office.

"Why don't we sit over here?" he asked, indicating the couch.

Hesitatingly, she moved to the far end and sat on the espresso brown leather. He sat next to her, crowding her space.

"How're you feeling?" he asked softly, "You look pale."

"I'm nervous," she replied and looked hopefully at her proposal from the meeting, which had been placed on the coffee table in front of them.

"You're worried about the proposal? Daisy, it's good. I think you should launch it for a couple of other hotels to give it a fair test. I'm sure AMEX will enjoy the opportunity to work with us on that level."

She had approached American Express, and they had agreed to participate in the campaign, sharing ad dollars. "They said they'd love to work with us on a larger scale."

"Good, I'm approving it with expansion," he said, and held out his hand. "Congratulations on your first major proposal."

She shook it and waited.

He looked at her, smiled sadly and said, "I think it was the limoncello."

"What?" she asked, confused. The very thought of limoncello had her stomach roiling.

"I don't think I wore a condom the night we drank limoncello. I'm sorry. I was pretty drunk and pretty turned on," he admitted, looking at her with a mix of pity and concern.

"What does it matter now?"

"Daisy, you're pregnant."

Gaping at him, she shook her head. "No way." But in the back of her mind, she started counting the days. With the new job and the travel, she was late. Very, very late. She couldn't be pregnant. It wasn't supposed to be this way for her. She wasn't her mother. She didn't have a baby without a loving husband.

"Well," he asked, "Is it possible?"

Instead of replying, she looked down, noticed the subtle pattern on the beige carpet blur as tears filled her eyes. It was not only possible; it was probable.

"It's okay, don't worry," he said, wrapping his arm loosely around her shoulders in support.

"Don't *you* worry—" she said, pushing away from him. "I'm capable and will handle this on my own. Let me know if you want me to give notice, I'll understand. I'll take care of it, but I'm having the baby." She did everything her mother told her not to do and now she'd fallen into her footsteps, having a baby with her boss. She was a woman who thought a dog was too much responsibility—how was she going to do this? She was almost assuredly pregnant with Alex's baby.

"Daisy, stop it," he said, placing his hand under her chin and forcing her to meet his gaze. "I told you before, I won't let anything happen to you. We'll get married as soon as possible. Everything will be fine."

"What?" she asked, her head spinning. "Marry you? No way."

"If you're pregnant, we're getting married."

"You must be kidding. You don't love me."

"I like you more than you know," he said, adding, "I really like making love with you. I like you when you're not calling me a womanizing lothario or whatever antiquated term you like to use to describe me."

"That's just it. You're not a man who stays with any woman for very long. Eventually, you will leave me. No thank you. I don't want the pain of being left for someone else. I want the man in my life to love me completely, unendingly." She was standing but couldn't remember getting up from the couch.

He stood, his voice stern. "You've never trusted me, fine. Maybe you never will. Believe me when I tell you I haven't been with anyone else since the day I met you."

She shook her head. "Tell that to Maria. She called me the flavor of the month. That hurt, a lot. And then Peter—"

"Peter?" he asked, shaking his head. "You mean when he called and left me a message in London? What does he have to do with anything? This is the second time you've mentioned him, and I just don't understand."

"Does it matter?" she asked, "I know all about Maria and Peter and New York."

"You know nothing. And you trust me when I tell you this," he said, his voice angry, angrier than she'd ever seen him. "No child of mine is going to be raised wondering why their father didn't marry their mother. I don't care if we divorce the day after you have the baby…we're getting married. I won't have what happened to you or my little sister happen to our child. I'll make the arrangements. All you have to do is pick out a dress, show up, and say 'I do.' And try to remember one more thing, remember the way we felt about each other when we made this baby."

Without saying a word, she turned on her heels and ran out of his office.

Chapter Thirteen

For the next two days Daisy was in a thick fog, barely sleeping, and just going through the motions of her life. Alex hounded her with emails and phone calls. *When was she seeing her doctor? Was the pregnancy confirmed? When was the official due date? When was her first ultrasound, he needed to know so he could book it on his calendar.? How was she feeling? Had she told her family yet? What kind of engagement ring would she like to have? Where would she like to get married?* He had incredible nerve!

Daisy ignored every communication from him that wasn't business related and did a slow burn at the idea of marrying him. Five minutes before she left for her doctor's appointment to confirm what she feared was true, she emailed him a simple acknowledgment: *Doctor 4pm today.*

He met her at the elevator.

"No," she sneered, baring her teeth.

"I'm going with you," he replied flatly.

"Forget it."

"You really want to be a martyr, don't you?" he asked, his voice raising. "You don't want to think about anyone but yourself."

She cocked her head, appearing to think on it for a minute.

"Yes," she whispered, "the thought of someone marrying me, who doesn't love me, has that effect on me."

"Think of our child. Think of how we felt in Rome."

"I would, if I could get past that you're only doing this to ease your own guilt. Then, I'm reminded of all the publicity this will generate for your parties. *Playboy Gets Snared. Hotel Baron Marries His Pregnant Employee.* It should be quite the tabloid fodder."

"Well, at least your work isn't suffering," he struck back. "Glad to know you're thinking of the marketing angles."

Ignoring the jab, Daisy stepped inside the elevator and said, "Go away."

"Lady, I'm not going anywhere," he replied as the doors slid shut, giving him the last word.

Two hours later, she was back at her apartment with a big bottle of prenatal vitamins and a handful of pamphlets on the different stages of pregnancy. She changed into her bathrobe, stretched out on her couch to listen to her favorite Diana Krall album on her iPod as she contemplated her completely messed up life. She'd never felt so alone. Alex had surprised her when he'd said "our" child. It made her heart skip a beat, but then the altercation had escalated. Could she really marry him knowing he didn't love her but just wanted to legitimize their child? She knew what it was like to grow up without any acknowledgment from a father. She wouldn't let it happen to her child.

A knock at her front door woke her from a fitful sleep. She wavered as she stood not sure how long she'd been dozing. Maybe if she ignored the knock whoever it was would go away. The knock got louder, and she only hoped it wasn't her mother. She didn't know what she'd say to her. She had a feeling this might be the final nail in their relationship coffin.

A glance out the peephole made her realize it was worse. Alex waited in the narrow little hall. How did he even know where she lived? Damn the HR file! Begrudgingly, she opened the door.

Still dressed in a suit without his tie, he stepped inside carrying two large bags of take out from Marrakesh. The day they'd met, she'd told him about Marrakesh. The Moroccan restaurant was her favorite for takeout. He'd remembered, damn him!

"I'm sorry, I didn't know you were resting," he said by way of greeting.

"It's fine," she said and added, "Besides, you brought food and I've been throwing up all day, so now I'm hungry."

He followed her to the kitchen and placed the bags on the counter as he checked out her small apartment and offered, "I didn't think you'd call, but I thought you might be hungry. Then I worried the smell might bother your stomach."

Opening one of the bags and inhaling, she said, "Let's hope I never lose my appetite for Marrakesh."

"That would be a tragedy," he said, looking around her space. "How long have you lived here?"

"Four years, since college," she replied, grabbing two plates from the cupboard. "It's no penthouse or New York loft for that matter, but it's my home."

"I've loved this old house for years. Never thought I'd know someone who lived here," he said, graciously ignoring the dig. Then he picked up the bottle of vitamins and asked, "So, I was right?"

"Congratulations," she said sourly, busying herself opening containers and adding spoons. "I'm going to have a baby."

"We are having a baby."

"You're the sperm donor and I expect nothing more."

"Daisy, damn it, you're not alone. We, the two of us are having a baby. I'm in your life, get used to it. You're having my baby, our baby."

"Sure," she said, shooting daggers at him with her eyes.

"It's going to be okay."

"Just so we are clear, you're not trying to persuade me to get an abortion or put the baby up for adoption because I won't do it. It is so early I could still lose it," she said, her voice cracking as she lost her cool control.

"I hope you don't lose the baby. This baby, our baby, is meant to be here, to be ours," he said, stepping toward her and pulling her into his arms. "I wouldn't ask you to do the other. I wouldn't want you to."

Having him close was exactly what she needed and what she feared. She didn't want his pity. She wanted his love. For a moment, she enjoyed the feel of his arms around her, so familiar, so perfect.

"Well, that's something we agree on," she said, coolly.

"Once we are married—"

"No, I don't want to talk about the marriage of legitimacy. Not today. I'm a modern woman, I don't need to be married to have a baby."

"Okay, we won't talk about it today, but tomorrow we will."

Eventually she pulled away and returned to dishing up their dinner. They sat down at the little table in her kitchen, not speaking for a long time, but acting politely civilized. Finally, she asked, "You mentioned your sister a few days ago and what happened to her. What did happen to her? I thought she was married."

Taking his time, he replied, "My older sister, the one you met, is married. I told you about my younger sister."

"And?"

He shrugged, "She's my father's love child."

"Your father had an affair?" How could they have this in common?

He took his time before speaking, unfolding his napkin, and smoothing it in his lap. "My parents were happily married for almost forty years; at least I always thought they were. My father died two and a half years ago in a motorcycle accident while my parents were vacationing in Greece. My mother was devastated. She was a complete mess for the first few months. I stepped in and started running the company.

"A few months later, I was going through my father's papers and discovered all this information about this little girl," he paused to take a sip of his water and took a deep breath before continuing.

"I hired an investigator, who looked back into my father's travels. Turns out my father had a year-long affair. The woman got pregnant. It appears my father had people help her and set up a trust in the hopes she'd go away. It wasn't the most gentlemanly thing he could do, but I think he did the best he could. He loved my mother, and she didn't find out, not then anyway. She was splitting her time between Portland and New York, raising my sister and me."

Daisy groaned and pushed her plate away. She didn't like the direction this conversation was headed.

"My father's lover died in childbirth. My sister ended up with an adoptive family. She has memories of a tall, dark-haired man who resembled me, visiting her when she was a child. She tells me

I have a very strong resemblance to my father at the same age," he explained.

"So, you've met her?" she asked.

Smiling a little, he said, "Yes."

"You didn't date her, did you?"

Alex chuckled. "Leave it to you to think the worst. Even in my most vile of womanizing days, I wouldn't date my own sister. I can honestly tell you I've never been attracted to her although I like to think she is rather pretty. I'm very protective of her."

"I am sorry, I probably shouldn't have said that."

"Probably not, but I don't mind."

"Do your mother and sister know about her?"

"My mother had a feeling, which I confirmed. I think it broke her heart. Then I had to tell my sister, Rebecca."

Daisy shuddered, wondering if her father's family knew of her existence. Somehow, she doubted it.

"The Stark women are a loyal tribe, and my younger sister isn't going to be invited to join, which makes me really sad. She was convicted and sentenced before she could even defend herself. Kind of like your story."

"Do you think they'll ever want to meet her?"

"No, but I've made sure they don't know too much about her. I've had a hard time getting to know her myself, but we've started to connect."

"Where does she live?"

Hesitating, he offered, "She's very private about her life. I'd have to ask her permission before I tell you anything about her. I've said enough that she'd be angry."

"I'm the mother of your unborn child," Daisy protested.

He chuckled, "I like the way your mind looks for opportunities. Look, you're one of four people, five if I count the detective, who even know about her. I want to respect her privacy. Once we are married and the time is right, I'll tell you all about her. Maybe you could even meet her someday…I'd like her to be a part of our child's life."

"Our fathers sound like they were cut from the same cloth," she observed, ignoring the child comment.

"I just wish my father was alive so I could talk to him about her. Try to understand how he could do this to my mother. How he could do this to my little sister."

"It's probably for the best you can't talk to him. Try to remember what you loved about him."

"I do. He was a wonderful father to Rebecca and me. Now, maybe you can understand why I want to get married. I want our child to know he or she is loved, no matter what happens. I want the child to have my name. I want to be there for him or her and you."

"I thought we had agreed not to talk about the sham marriage tonight."

"I can't help myself," he said as his hand covered hers.

Pulling away, she said, "You shouldn't feel you have to marry me, Alex. I know you have other irons in the fire."

"Oh, I forgot, you know me. Have you ever thought I want to marry you?"

"No," she said, shaking her head. "I think you feel obligated."

"I don't. Are you trying to tell me you won't marry me?"

"I haven't decided yet."

"I see."

"You will regret me and then the baby," she said. "It's only a matter of time."

"You've already predicted the bleakest future possible. You know, Daisy, I make my own decisions and I've decided I want to marry you. Once I make a decision, I give my all to it." Pausing, he added, "We can get married any time or place you want, but I'd like to make plans and get it done before the anniversary party."

"Gee, that soon? How romantic…"

"The press would have a field day if they found out you were pregnant. I don't want the Paris Affair to be the focus of the anniversary parties. I'd much prefer it be billed as our honeymoon. I guess I'm a hopeless romantic that way."

Then it all came together for her. It was just another business deal to him, a merger needing to happen. As far as he was concerned, they were in the middle of the negotiations. She hadn't known this side of him. She'd seen glimpses, even liked his powerful side.

It would be so different if he loved her. If he said the three magic words she'd have married him at City Hall tomorrow. How easy it would have been for her to say, *I love you*...but if she said it to him, they'd be wasted words. Yes, after all this Daisy still loved this man.

"You've thought it all out, haven't you?" she asked.

"Yes. If you turn me down, I'll keep changing tactics until you change your mind." His eyes were cold, no longer twinkling, but menacing in their intent.

Shutting her eyes, she came to a kind of peace. At least if she married him, she would get to see him, to be with him.

"Fine," she said with no enthusiasm. "I'll marry you."

"Good, I'm glad that's settled...so easily."

"By the way, I think I hate you," she whispered.

He smiled sadly. "You're entitled. I got you pregnant, now I'm demanding you marry me before a large company function so I can show you off to the world..."

"Hate you." The irony was that she was pretty sure if she told him she was falling in love with him, he probably wouldn't marry her.

"When can we do this?"

"Oh, you mean the wedding?" she replied sarcastically. "I thought maybe you wanted us to have mutual tetanus boosters or flu shots."

"I do like your sense of humor. Do you want a big or small wedding? Obviously, we don't have a lot of time, but I've got the resources to make it a very nice event. We can take over the Columbia Ballroom in the hotel and invite whomever we want. But we don't need to stay in Portland. If you'd like, we can fly to Paris or even New York. It doesn't matter to me."

She had always hoped it would matter a great deal to her groom where they got married. Feeling worse than she had all day, she offered, "We could get married at the rose garden in the park blocks and then have dinner someplace downtown just the two of us."

"Daisy," he said, tentatively placing his hand over hers, "Money isn't an issue. You can have whatever you want."

I just want you. I want you to give up every other woman but me. I want you to love me. I want Maria Medici out of your life. I want your best friend to be anyone but Peter Crawley.

Daisy was still reeling over the coincidence. How in the world could they even be friends? At some point she supposed she'd have to tell him Peter was her boss and that he had harassed her—oh God, would he think this was something planned, that she'd set up Alex to marry her? *Ok you really need to calm down and focus,* Daisy tried to tell herself.

"I really don't want to involve a lot of people. I'd prefer to elope," she said.

"What about your family?"

"I'm an only child. My father died years ago. I call my mother about once a month. We are very different people, and she would only add to my stress. Better she finds out later. I don't need her drama now. How important is it to you to involve your family? Because I'll marry you as soon as you can arrange a minister."

"We can keep it small," he said, picking up her hand and kissing it softly in an uncharacteristically sentimental gesture. "I think I should go and let you get your beauty sleep. Unless you'd let me stay?"

"You should leave."

Seeing him to the door, she stifled the urge to touch him, initiate intimacy. She needed to be held and comforted, but she wouldn't ask for his affection. If he didn't offer it freely, she wouldn't beg.

"Oh, and one more thing," she said. "If Maria Medici or Peter Crawley are at our wedding, I won't be."

Before he had a chance to reply, she slammed the door in his face.

The next morning, Alex sat at his desk, staring at nothing in particular. He and Daisy were having a baby. Once the shock had worn off, he found he liked the idea of waking up next to Daisy every morning. When had he fallen for her? He'd like to think it was because she was making herself out to be quite a challenge, but in truth, the moment she'd looked up at him with her big blue eyes, he'd been captivated.

She was setting herself up to hate him. Fine, he'd turn it around. It couldn't be any harder than what? His transaction in Dubai?

Dealing with Maria? There were a host of much more difficult things in this world. Only one thing still bothered him. He understood why she didn't like Maria, but what had Peter done to her? He'd asked Peter more than once about the conversation in London, but Peter said he just left a message to call him. He hadn't said anything that would cause such upset in Daisy.

Yet, she knew something about Peter that she didn't like, and the thought was very concerning.

Needing a distraction, he typed an email and smiled broadly before he hit the send button.

Daisy closed her eyes trying to shut out the world as her head pounded. The ping on her computer alerted her to an incoming email from Alex, subject line: RINGS.

Please be available at noon today to look at rings.

Groaning, she picked up her phone and dialed his office. When he answered on the other side of the wall next to her own, she said, "Is this really necessary? You don't need to buy me a fucking ring."

"I don't need to buy you a fucking ring. I want to buy you a fucking ring. A fabulous fucking ring I might add. There is a difference. See you at noon, my future wife."

"You are an asshole."

"Yeah, but I'm about to be your asshole. I'll even get a ring, too. See you at noon."

"Wait!" she exclaimed, before he could hang up. "We need to talk. I've been thinking and I've got some questions…"

"I'm listening…" he said, matching her tone.

"Do you want me to stay in my apartment after we're married? Will I still have my job? I think I can work from home, just come in for staff meetings. I should keep my name, don't you think? Is there a prenup you want me to sign? And what about child support? If we get that settled up front, I'd feel better."

"Let's take one thing at a time. After we're married, I want you to move into my suite here in the hotel. As for your job, I need you.

If you want to stay home once the baby arrives, you can. I'll hire someone else for your position, but I won't like doing it. Maybe you can be a consultant. We will work it out. You won't be signing a prenup unless you have one for me to sign so we won't be discussing child support. I'd like you to take my name. I guess that makes me a bit old fashioned, but I like a family to have the same name."

Daisy Stark. Mrs. Alexander Stark. A shiver lapped along her skin.

When she was silent too long, he asked, "Will you at least take a look at the suite?"

"It would be helpful when the baby comes if I were living with you, so you can help with diaper changes," she answered, wishing she could see his face during this conversation. "What about your loft in New York?"

"I'm keeping it, but with the headquarters in Portland, the commute is impossible. And I like being close to my family. With you and the baby, I've decided it's a good idea to make Portland my home base at least until the baby comes and you can both travel."

"I'm telling you now, I don't know if I can be a stay-at-home mother."

"Darling, whatever you decide, I've decided to make your office larger. I'm going to knock out the south wall and create space for a nursery."

"You're kidding me," she said, looking at the wall in question.

"Nothing is too good for our marriage or our child. I've got a conference call coming in. I'll see you at noon."

Three hours later, Daisy stared numbly at a large tray of sparkling diamond rings, her heart beating loudly in her chest. Alex hadn't been happy until the jeweler brought out the rings with the "large stones."

That same jeweler, who couldn't stop smiling, was making himself busy at the other end of the store to give them some privacy. She studied Alex, who was picking up ring after ring and judging the quality of the diamonds.

"This is crazy," she whispered.

"What?" he asked, turning his attention away from a large diamond solitaire.

"We aren't in love." She wanted to say: if you loved me, this might be fun, but I know you don't. Why go through the motions?

He put the ring down and wrapped an arm around her waist, his hand splaying her hip. "Does this mean you can't decide and want me to pick one for you?"

Barely able to think with his body touching hers, she whispered, "You're being a little too sweet today. It's hard to remember I hate you."

He smiled and dipped his head to kiss her. Not a peck or quick kiss, a long, languid connection she felt all the way to her knees. His lips moved to her cheek and finally her ear where he whispered, "I have three favorites. Why don't I show them to you? You can pick the one you like best."

Catching her breath, she muttered, "Damn you."

He chuckled and began selecting his favorites.

One of the three he picked was her favorite, a beautiful, round, 3.0 carat, white diamond on a band of baguettes.

"This is your favorite."

"It's obscene." And gorgeous.

"It's still your favorite."

"How do you know that?" she asked, more curious than she was willing to let on.

"I know you better than you think." Slipping it on her finger, he said, "See? Perfect."

When he asked the jeweler for a selection of matching wedding bands for both of them, she just stared at him.

"What do you think?" he asked trying to decide between two different styles of platinum that would complement her ring.

"That one," she said pointing to the slightly larger band. If he wanted to wear a band, she wanted to make sure it could be seen.

"I'd like our wedding rings to be out of the same chunk of platinum. How fast could you make a couple of bands?" Alex asked.

The jeweler explained an expedited timeline and added cost that Alex apparently could live with.

Daisy grabbed the case for support when Alex handed over an unusual-looking credit card to cover the immense cost without hesitation.

"Would you like to wear yours Ms. Miller?" the jeweler asked.

"Yes, she would," Alex answered, taking the newly sized ring, and slipping it on her finger. He kissed her hand and then her lips.

She'd missed kissing him. It had been over a month and now that he'd broken the dry spell, she didn't want it to stop. "Thank you, Alex. It's absolutely beautiful." It was the most beautiful piece of jewelry she'd ever seen. He kissed her again and this time, she kissed him back.

"I missed this," he said.

"What?" she managed.

"Kissing you," he said, and kissed her again.

She was weak and very, very hormonal. If he suggested seeing one of the rooms in his hotel, she'd have made love with him. What was wrong with her? Instead, he suggested lunch at the Heathman Hotel. Little did he know how close he'd come to being mauled.

"You're not serious?" she asked.

"Your stomach's been growling for the last hour. You need food."

"But they're our competitor."

"I like doing research on them. Besides, they have this mango, crab, and avocado salad I really like," he said, taking her arm as they waited at the crosswalk.

"I've had the salad," she replied, looking down at her ring in the sunlight. "Our restaurant should do something similar, without the watercress."

"My thoughts exactly."

"My former employer thought of the Heathman as competition as well. We copied at least five of their dishes, that salad included," she said, knowing she was babbling as she stole glances at her ring. She wasn't thinking and it was about to get her in a lot of trouble. "We stacked it in a round tower and called it the South Sea Dungeness Salad."

Alex stopped walking and turned to her. "That was my favorite salad at my friend's restaurant. Oh my god, you worked there."

Daisy stuttered, "Well, I—"

"Did you work for Davis and Crawley? Are they the hole I sensed on your resume?"

"I worked with Brigitte as a consultant. She'd worked for Davis and Crawley first. Then, I got a job there. I loved it until I started reporting directly to Peter. So, yes," she said. "I worked for Peter until I couldn't, until he forced me to leave. Brigitte had left by then, so I started consulting with her. It paid the rent." Well, this had to come to fruition sooner or later, might as well be now, Daisy thought.

"You're the one who threw the stapler at Peter and almost ruined his marriage. He had to get thirteen stitches." From Alex's tone, she couldn't tell if he thought that was terrible or not—he just said it like *matter of fact*.

Daisy remembered the blood breaking out on his forehead, the call to 911, and then how everyone turned on her, everyone but Brigitte.

"He deserved it, but why should I think you would believe what really happened?" she asked as they stood in front of the Heathman, the sun making it hard to see and uncomfortably warm, but the conversation had become so dramatic that neither of them moved.

"Try me," Alex said, his eyes narrowing in possibly anger?

"He made me an offer I could refuse and tried, but he wouldn't take no for an answer. Then, he tried to force the issue, so I defended myself. The stapler injury didn't need to happen, but he came toward me, I felt scared, so I picked up the nearest thing."

"He has a very nice wife. We were good friends in school. I introduced them," Alex replied, then asked, "Did you have an affair with Peter?"

"No, I didn't. I know Claire, and I like her despite who she is married to. She is also pregnant by the way," Daisy whispered as she pulled the ring off her finger, handed it to Alex, raised her head high, meeting his gaze. "I should have known you were too good to be true. I told you this wouldn't work. Anyone who is friends with that monster would never be anyone I'd consider marrying."

Peter called London, Daisy left, now it was starting to make sense. *Peter had lied.* It had almost cost him Daisy.

She turned and strode away, leaving him standing on the sidewalk and staring after her.

He caught up with her a block later as she walked along Broadway Street crying.

"Daisy," he murmured, as he walked beside her. "I'm not Peter. You have to understand I heard a very different story from him. I don't want anyone in my life who scares you."

"Let me guess, he told you he turned me down?" she asked. "I got psycho and threw a stapler at him? Maybe he said we had an affair, that he broke off. It never got that far. I'd have never let Peter touch me."

"I'm sorry, you caught me off guard."

Raising his arm to place it around her, to comfort her, she stopped him mid-motion. "Don't you even think of touching me. Just tell me the story he told you."

"Daisy, please," He tried to move closer as she straightened her stance backing another step away. "Ok—Peter mentioned the blonde when the lawsuit was going on, but I didn't know it was you. I didn't know you. Why didn't you tell me when we first got together? Why did you leave it off your resume?"

"Sure, like I wanted to ever bring that up, especially with my new boss who I *wanted* to have seduce me? Come on! I couldn't risk anyone asking me about that horrible experience and especially you—it was the exact opposite with Peter. He tried to force me to have sex with him in order to keep my job. I had to defend myself when he didn't like my answer. I had to fight him off," she said, spitting out the last words as if they burned. "No one should have to go through what I went through. What really upsets me, he'll do it again to some other unaware employee. How can you be friends with him? How can you be friends with that animal?"

"I can't. You and the baby are my main concern."

Looking down at the sidewalk, her black suede high-heel shoes toyed with a crack in the pavement. Shutting her eyes, she shook her head and through clenched teeth said, "I really, really hate you for being friends with him."

"You have your reasons," he said with a nod then continued, "but that doesn't mean our child should suffer. A week from Saturday, I'm going to be in the rose garden with a minister and a couple of witnesses, not Peter, and not Maria." Maria wouldn't care, Peter was a different story altogether. He needed to have a word with his soon to be *ex* best friend.

She responded, "I need some time to think about this. And if you were his friend, what does that say about you?"

"Not a lot, but you can be assured that you never have to see Peter again."

"Prove it." She turned and left him on the sidewalk to stare after her.

He looked down at the large diamond now on his pinky finger. Daisy was unlike any woman he'd ever known. Usually, he was able to get that kind of thrill from a business deal or a hard negotiation. But never with the women he dated. They were demure and pleasing, rarely contradicted, or stood up to him. Daisy was the exact opposite of every woman who had come before her.

He wanted to chase after her, get the ring back on her finger, but there was another pressing matter that needed to be taken care of.

Back in his office, Alex picked up his cell and found the number in the memory and waited.

"I'm glad you called, how is Adam?" Peter asked. "After the funeral I've been trying to stay in touch with him, but he's been aloof, totally expected I'm sure."

"He's a mess. Listen, I have to go to the bank across the street from your office. Thought I could stop by. I've got something to tell you."

"Sounds good," Peter said, completely misreading Alex's end of the conversation.

Alex usually invited Peter to his office because Peter liked Alex's office, but that was before Daisy. Peter would never set foot in Stark International Hotels again. Later this afternoon, their friendship would be officially over. Alex was certain after he shared the story with Adam that he'd feel the same way.

Funny how you could know someone for a significant portion of your life but not really know them? It wasn't foreign to Adam and Alex that Peter often had mistresses, or willing girlfriends on the side, in fact they were fairly certain Claire was aware, or at least that is what Peter told them. A mistress was one thing, however; they are aware of the situation and elected to be with you. It was a whole other ballgame when you were forcing someone for sex. That was demented and beyond his purview. And totally unacceptable. The fact Peter had tried to seduce his Daisy now made it Alex's business. This would get ugly, at least Alex hoped it would.

He took his time walking toward Peter's office. It was less than a mile, but he needed time to think. His father liked to say that in life, every relationship you ever have has a beginning, middle, and an end. You are lucky if you get any choice as to any of the stages.

When he arrived, Peter's secretary, a blonde, blue-eyed, young twenty-something in a tight suit told him that Peter was expecting him.

"Hey bud, come on in and shut the door," Peter said, getting up and coming around the side of his desk to shake Alex's hand. They'd met in college, been the best of friends ever since. But Adam had always had issues with Peter, thought he was a jerk, and now Alex knew why.

In fact, Alex once believed the only positive thing about his father's death was that he'd have the option to move to Portland permanently to run the company and that would allow him to be closer to not only to Rebecca and Mitch, but Peter and Claire.

Alex sat across from Peter and thought of what he wanted to say. "I'm getting married," Alex announced.

"Holy shit," Peter said and buzzed his blonde receptionist. "Hey sweetie, would you bring us two of the 25-year-old Macallan's neat?"

"Yes, Mr. Crawley."

A minute later, the woman in the tight suit arrived with a bottle and two glasses. She shimmied a little which did not escape Alex's attention.

"You and the Italian chick, can't say I blame you, she's fucking hot. Cheers!" Peter said raising his glass to Alex.

"You're wrong," Alex said, taking a sip of the Macallan.

"What? Not the hot Italian chick?" Peter asked, not understanding.

"It is the woman you talked to in London," Alex said.

"But she's just your secretary."

"No, she does work for Stark International Hotels, but she isn't a secretary."

"When did this happen?" Peter asked.

"In the last few months. I hired her, and realized like Adam once said, when you know, you know. I know. Hit me like a ton of bricks."

"How did Maria take it?" Peter asked.

"How are any of my hotel managers taking it? Why should they care?" Alex responded.

"But you and Maria—"

"We're nothing, never have been, never will be."

"You're passing up on the spicy Italian for a lowly secretary?" Peter asked.

Alex shook his head. "As I said before, she isn't my secretary. She is my marketing associate for European operations."

"Well shit, I'll call Claire, we'll have you over for dinner, meet the woman who finally took Alex off the market. She must be pretty special."

"Thanks, she is very special, but I'm not sure I'll be able to convince Daisy to spend an evening with you, despite how lovely Claire is," Alex said, and took a deep hit of the Macallan. Shit was about to go down.

"Daisy? Daisy fucking what? What is her fucking last name?" Peter asked. Alex thought he could see sweat form above his friend's upper lip.

"You know, which is why I'm here. Daisy Miller is who I'm marrying, she worked here. She sued your ass for sexual harassment."

"You are marrying that little blonde cock tease?" Peter asked. "What the fuck is wrong with you?"

"Did you not take no for an answer?" Alex asked. "Did you try to force yourself on my girl?"

"Alex, who are you going to believe, me or that little cock tease? Has she pulled you into her honeytrap, maybe sucked out a few of your brain cells?" Although Peter was trying to lighten up the conversation there was nothing humorous about it in the least, and he was soon to find out.

"Let's be clear, I believe her. I don't believe you. Now, why don't you do what you're good at, acting inappropriately..."

Alex stood and started walking toward Peter, let him see how it was to be attacked by someone who was bigger and stronger. Peter wasn't a small guy by any means, but Alex had a good five inches and twenty pounds on him, and his now ex-friend was going to feel a world of pain. And Alex hated to admit it, but he would enjoy every second of the altercation defending Daisy's honor.

The next morning, Alex stepped into Daisy's office and sat in a chair across from her. She was typing and ignored him until she finished her email. She'd had a sleepless night and was mad at herself. Her life was a complete mess, had been in a downward spiral ever since she met Garrison Alexander Stark.

Pulling her attention from her computer screen, she glanced at Alex and said, "Yes?"

Alex lifted his hand. The garishly large and expensive ring he'd bought her the day before dangled on the knuckle of his ring finger on his right hand. Glancing at it, she noticed the skin beneath the ring was purple. In fact, all the knuckles on his hand were bruised. With closer examination, she saw a few nasty cuts that needed bandages.

"What happened to your hand?" she asked.

"I've defended your honor. Now, the least you can do is wear the ring I bought you."

Oh, goodness. "Peter?"

"Yes, we had a little talk. It didn't end well for him."

"What happened?" she asked. Happy Alex believed her, valued her and their baby more than his friend—hopefully, ex-friend.

"I beat the crap out of him for what he did to you and the lies he told. I also hit him a couple of times for his lovely, long-suffering wife, Claire, who I like very much."

Placing her hands flat on the desk, she pictured the scene between the two men, couldn't quite believe it. "Did you really punch him?"

"Several times, more than two, less than six," he said and then pointed to a small purple bruise on his chin. "He threw the first punch. I threw the rest. I admit, I baited him, but he did throw the first punch. He wanted to celebrate our engagement by hosting a little get-together at his house, but once I told him your name and that you wouldn't go, it went downhill from there."

"How do I know this really happened?"

"I suspected you wouldn't believe me," Alex said, pulling a cell phone from the breast pocket of his charcoal suit coat, then retrieving something on his phone with a few presses and swipes of his finger, holding it up for her to see. It was a picture of Peter Crawley holding up his hand to block the camera, but she could see his bloodied nose. His right eye was swollen shut and no doubt well on its way to being black.

"You did that?" she asked. "You gave him a bloody nose and a black eye?"

"Yes, I don't usually go for that kind of thing, I like to fight with my brain, but I wasn't getting through to him and I thought the situation called for it. He used his physicality to intimidate women, and I simply let him know how it felt to be on the receiving end. I defended your honor. No one abuses my future wife."

"Wow," she said, her heart beating faster at the thought that he'd defended her. "What did he say?"

"He admitted to calling you in London and insinuating that Maria was my girlfriend."

"He called her your chicky," she corrected, holding up her hand. "I don't think I want to hear anymore."

"Fine, then we start fresh. I don't want any more time or energy wasted on Peter or what he has said or done. I handled it and he will never bother you or I again, agreed?"

It wasn't a negotiation, but an edict.

"He lied and no one believed me," she said, not willing to forget so easily.

"I believe you," he said. "It cost you a job and hurt your reputation. I lost a friend, a best friend, who wasn't the man I thought he was. In the end, we've both lost a great deal."

"I'm sorry for both of us."

"You can make me feel better right now," he said, with a wiggle of an eyebrow indicating the ring gleaming on his battered finger.

It was so beautiful that she would feel guilty wearing it. It should be on the hand of a bride whose future husband loved her, but he'd taken care of the man who bullied her. That meant something.

Leaning forward, Alex picked up her left hand and placed the ring on the third finger. Admiring it, he said, "It looks good there."

"It looks beautiful," she managed, feeling her throat tighten with emotion. *Damn hormones.*

"Yes, now that we have that settled, can I count on you to be at the rose garden a week from tomorrow?"

He was still on track to marry her. Unsure of what to say, she nodded and waited.

"Good," he answered. "I'm leaving for Europe tonight. I'm in negotiation for a hotel I've had my eye on the Amalfi Coast in the town of Positano. Don't worry, I'll be back in time for the wedding."

"You're leaving?" Daisy already felt his absence, which was crazy since they were just finding their way back to one another.

"I've wanted the hotel for two years." Reaching into his pocket, he pulled out a keycard, which he handed to her. It was different from the rest of the room keys she'd seen. It was heavier, more permanent. "This is your key to our penthouse. I'll email you the movers' contact info. They are waiting for your call. And if you can't break your lease and incur a fee, just contact Janice in accounting. She will cut you a check from my personal account to cover the cost. She will also take care of the movers' bill. Let them pack everything. I don't want you lifting anything heavy.

"Start thinking about how you want to decorate. My things arrived from New York last week. I want you to do anything you want to the place. I just ask one thing...I like to live in calm, peaceful surroundings. If you want to paint the walls red, leave me one room of beige. Deal?"

"Okay," she said, looking down at the keycard.

"That also opens my office and about every door in this building."

"You trust me that much?"

"If I don't trust the mother of my child, who can I trust?" he asked, as he stood and walked around the desk until he was on the same side as she. Leaning down, he kissed her softly on the lips. He pulled back, smiled, and kissed her again. Her hands found his shoulders then encircled his neck and before long just their lips didn't seem to be enough.

He pulled her out of the chair and into his arms, and she leaned into him to let the last few weeks fade away.

He stopped first, his lips slowing then departing and leaving her feeling bereft. His child grew inside her. She wanted him to love her. When he pulled back, she felt tears spring to her eyes.

"Darling, what is it?" he asked, cupping her chin.

Shaking her head, she held the words she wanted to speak. *You don't love me, but I'm completely in love with you.* "I'm sorry you lost a friend, but I'm really happy you told him about us."

"I gained you," he said, and she couldn't speak. "Don't worry about anything. Move in. Enjoy yourself. And when I get back, the real adventure begins."

She leaned against him again, felt his lips brush her temple.

"I've got a plane to catch, but if I didn't," he whispered, and she nodded knowing exactly what he meant.

"We've wasted a lot of time, for that, I'm sorry."

"We can make up for it when I get back," he said as he walked toward the doorway.

A moment later, he paused and said, "See you a week from Saturday."

CHAPTER FOURTEEN

On Saturday, exactly one week before her wedding, Daisy tried on one white frothy concoction after another at Trudel's Wedding Boutique. It wasn't every day you tried on wedding dresses while the owner of the bridal shop had a coronary over the idea that she had a bride that was getting married in a week.

"We only have a handful of dresses to sell you. The rest take too long to get here. I just really don't like being in this position," Trudel complained.

"Okay, let's make the best of this," Daisy said, "Let's see what you've got."

"Well, I'm not even sure I have something in your size."

"I understand. Try your best," Daisy said and noticed that Brigitte was just shaking her head.

"What?" she asked her friend Brigitte who was witnessing the exchange from a padded pink chaise. Brigitte was on her second glass of champagne…

"I guess I'm in shock. It isn't every day that your best friend calls you and says, 'Hey, what are you doing? I'm getting married in a week and I need a dress.' I mean, like a few weeks earlier, you were sure it was over. He didn't care and he didn't love you. Now, you're getting married and have a ring on your left hand that looks heavy enough to wind you up in physical therapy."

"It is complicated," Daisy said.

"It's actually quite simple, you love him and you're pregnant."

"I do and I am," she said, looking at her friend. "But I'm not sure the love part is mutual."

"Don't give up, the main course hasn't been served yet. Just go with it."

"Am I making a huge mistake?" Daisy asked. "Am I ruining my life?"

"Ironically, I've never seen you so happy. Seriously, Dazs, you're glowing. And can I remind you that you are in love?"

"I do love him," Daisy whispered as she looked at her ring and smiled.

Despite all the warnings from the wedding shop owner, the available dresses kept piling up, so the concern of having no inventory in her size didn't appear to be as problematic as predicted. However, nothing was right. Everything was too complicated. She wanted simple. In the end, she asked for the most unadorned dress they had. When Trudel returned five minutes later, Daisy knew she'd found the one. Off the shoulder, three-quarter-length satin dress nipped in at the waist with flowing skirt, but still hiding her baby bump. It wasn't pure white. It had the faintest hint of color she decided to call blush.

"Oh my," Daisy said when she saw it.

"I really shouldn't be selling it yet, but it just fit the bill and a little birdy told me you were having a baby," Trudel said, looking conspiratorially at Brigitte. "I respect that you are doing the right thing by way of the child."

"You do good work, Ms. Trudel. That's the one," Brigitte agreed.

"You just like the color," Daisy said..

"It is gorgeous and brings out your peaches and cream skin."

"It will work."

"He'll be beside himself with you in that dress, you look good enough to eat," Brigitte said with a wink, and then clamped her jaws together, making a biting sound.

"He never, ever leaves marks," Daisy chided.

"Too bad, but just one look at you in that dress, he will want to leave his mark."

Daisy hoped so. She wanted him to love the way she looked. She wanted him to want her as badly as she wanted him.

The best part was the dress fit and didn't need to be altered. Ms. Trudel wanted to do a little of this and a bit of that, but Daisy refused. It worked. She left the salon carrying it in a large white garment bag.

On her way back to her car, she passed by Mario's, the most exclusive men's store in town.

"Is it weird that I want to buy him a little something?" Daisy asked, as she paused at the entrance to Mario's.

"I think that you should after he dropped what, like fifty grand on that ring?"

"Closer to one hundred."

"Holy shit, girl."

Daisy picked out an expensive silk tie with matching pocket square the exact color of her dress. It was ridiculous to think Alex might wear it, but it didn't stop her from buying it or having it gift wrapped.

On Friday morning, six days later, Daisy stood inside her apartment and looked at the accumulated stacks of boxes. At nine o'clock, just as Alex had told her in one of the businesslike daily emails she received from Italy, the movers knocked on her door. She watched them pack up the life she'd had for the last twenty-six years in a matter of minutes. Once they left, only the empty shell remained.

Ten minutes later, the cleaners arrived to give the apartment a final once-over so Daisy wouldn't have to. Alex had thought of everything.

It was real now. She was moving into the penthouse of the Stark International Hotel Portland, marrying the head of the company, and having his baby in a little under seven months. Not knowing whether she should laugh or cry, she picked up her keys and left her apartment for the last time.

Twenty minutes later, she arrived at her new home and watched as movers unpacked her things. The twelve-foot-high ceilings and large windows of the penthouse looked out at the city, and made the space seem huge. A couple of the rooms were filled with nondescript hotel furniture and Alex's furniture, just the bare minimum to make the space livable. Boxes of Alex's belongings lined one of the walls in the large dining room. The living room and master bedroom had atrium style windows curving skyward, which gave the illusion of open airiness, but didn't trigger her vertigo. It was a good place to watch the stars at night. She wondered if Alex ever did. She wondered if they ever would.

After much deliberation, she placed her suits, jeans, and casual clothes next to Alex's in the master bedroom closet. The kitchen looked warmer with all her Italian ceramic canisters lined along the cool granite. The movers set up one of the bonus rooms to be an exact replica of her old living room. Even the pictures were hung as they had been in her apartment. The guest bedroom resembled her old bedroom. Having her familiar things around her made her feel better, but by lunchtime, the movers had left, and she was alone and exhausted.

Instead of laying on Alex's bed, Daisy stretched out on her own bed and stared up at the ceiling. She tried to calm her mind. In less than twenty-four hours, she would be married to Alex. She would be Mrs. Garrison Alexander Stark. However, the groom had to arrive home and still want to marry her for that to happen. It was a lovely dream or a complete nightmare; she didn't know how it would come out yet.

The hotel landline phone next to the bed rang. She ignored it. She hadn't given the penthouse number to anyone. Last night she had broken down, called her mother and told her that she was dating Alex. An hour and a half later, after she'd heard every bad outcome that would come from dating her boss, she admitted they were moving in together. Her mother blew a cog and vowed not to speak to her daughter for at least a week until she 'calmed down over Daisy's poor decision.' Surprise! How would she react when she found out they were really married? If her mother had reacted differently, she might have told her. Did Alex's family know? How about his sister, Rebecca? Had he told her?

Therefore, the ringing phone would be for Alex. The last thing she needed right now was to pick up the phone and end up talking to one of his girlfriends or Peter or his sister. Her cell phone rang next. She glanced at the caller ID. An international call from Alex. It had been for her all along.

"Hello," she answered dryly.

"Daisy?"

"Yes, Alex?"

"Did everything go all right?"

"Fine. How about you?"

"Are you okay? You sound tired."

"I am tired."

"Are you taking care of yourself?"

"Yes."

"What did you have for lunch?" he asked.

She waited too long to answer.

"I thought so. Room service will be bringing you a grilled cheese sandwich and tomato soup and because I wasn't sure what you liked, they are also bringing you a club sandwich and French fries."

"Alex!"

"Darling, if you aren't going to take care of yourself, I will."

How could she argue with kindness? "Thank you," she said and meant it.

"Okay, listen, I've had a change of plans."

Of course, here it comes, she thought. "I'm not getting back until tomorrow, I just wanted you to know. I'll see you at the rose garden."

"What?" she asked, sitting up. "You're not even coming back to the suite?"

"No, my plane gets in early tomorrow afternoon. I had a feeling this might happen, so I have my suit waiting in another room at the hotel with everything I need. I'll shower and change there."

"Why not just come back to the penthouse?"

"Daisy, that's bad luck," he chided. "I can't see you on the day of the wedding, before the wedding."

"Please Alex, if you're running late or need to reschedule, just let me know. I don't want to be stood up at the rose garden. I don't know what I'd do. It would really upset me."

"I'm going to be there. You worry too much."

"Well, I have something for you. It's no big deal, and you don't have to wear it."

"What?" he asked, sounding curious.

"I just saw it and thought of you because it kind of matches my dress."

"The bellman will be there in about five minutes. You can give it to him, and he'll put it in the room with my suit."

"Really, you don't have to wear it."

"Daisy, have you ever thought that I might want to because it is from you?"

She didn't know what to say to that, so she asked, "How did it go in Amalfi?"

"I don't know yet. Maria is working on the family for me."

Hackles rising, she saw red. She was having his baby, but couldn't he give up his Maria for at least the duration of her pregnancy?

"I couldn't have done this without her. She's been fabulous. The family loved her. She paved the way for us." His gushing had her seething.

When she didn't respond, he continued, "Did you get settled in? Tell me, is everything okay? Does it look okay?"

"Fine, everything is fine," she answered. "But I think I'm going to be sick, so I have to get off the phone."

"Morning sickness still? Have you talked to your doctor—"

"I have to go." She hung up and punched her pillow. *Maria.* He'd spent the week with Maria. What the hell was she doing marrying a man who was still close to another woman whom she was sure had once been his lover? Something was going on with them, she just needed to get to the bottom of it. Marriage was about two people—three was a crowd, and Maria needed to know that as soon as Alex and Daisy were married, Maria was part of the past.

CHAPTER FIFTEEN

Sleeping was a futile effort for the woman who wondered if her groom would make it to the wedding or choose to stay in Italy with a woman who resembled Sophia Lauren. Daisy tossed and turned, then canceled her wakeup call and breakfast. If she could eek out any sleep, regardless of the time, she'd consider herself lucky.

Waking in her bed at noon, she meandered to the enormous granite and stainless-steel kitchen and tried a buttered English muffin and some fruit. It all tasted like sawdust, perfectly matching her mood. Years from now, today would either be one of the happiest days of her life, or bar none, one of the worst.

She didn't have a crystal ball; she had no idea what she was doing.

At least she wouldn't be alone, Brigitte would be there for her. She had several other close girlfriends who would be mortified to know she was getting married without them. But she had avoided calling them, there was too much to explain. When they found out she'd eloped with the owner of the Stark International Hotels and was pregnant with his love child, there would be hell to pay, but Brigitte was excited, caught up in the romance, fine let her be…

Still in her bathrobe, she curled up on her couch and watched one of her favorite chick flicks. She should be packing for Europe. They would be leaving on Monday to finish the details before the big round of parties, but the thought of packing made her nervous. Besides, she'd need something to do tomorrow.

At three, she showered and washed her hair. By five, she was dressed and walking nervously from room to room, her strappy silk high heels clicking musically on the hardwood floors, matching the beat of her heart. She wanted Alex to be there, not because of his promise to marry her, not because of the baby, but because he wanted to be there for her. She wanted to see truth in his eyes when he spoke his vows. And when they came back to the suite, she wanted him to treat her like a wanton bride on her wedding night.

"Stop dreaming, Cinderella," she chided, as she heard a light knock. A young bellman, who she recognized from the day before, waited in the hall holding two large boxes with chicly sloppy pink silk bows.

"Ms. Miller? These are for you," he said, smiling appreciatively at her as he placed them on the dining room table and left.

As she carefully tugged at one of the bows, finding it hard to mar the perfection of the elegantly wrapped box, whiffs of green floral hints assaulted her senses. The larger of the two boxes held her bridal bouquet protected under frothy sheets of white tissue paper. Creamy peach roses, white dendrobium orchids, and delicate strands of ivy created a stunning arrangement. Recognizing the roses as Blushing Ladies, her stomach fluttered and tightened reflexively. Alex had remembered the rose from Mother's Bistro, their first date. Shutting her eyes, she inhaled their sweet smell.

Fighting back a stray, sentimental tear, she opened the second box and found an assortment of small, individual roses, which were wired and taped with florist ribbon for her hair. A black velvet box tied with a peach ribbon lay casually among the delicate buds.

Reaching for the box, she saw a simple card:

If these don't work with your dress, you don't have to wear them. —A

How had he known the color of her dress? Had he had someone open the box and show him the tie? Probably. The box held a pearl necklace and matching earrings the exact hue of her dress. They were large, freshwater pearls closer to the size of quarters than peas. Twenty minutes later, she smiled at her reflection. The pearls looked like they were made exactly for her and her dress. Her first strand of real pearls. Next to her ring, they were the most beautiful thing she owned. She was suddenly very happy that she'd thought to get Alex a matching tie.

At 5:40, she passed through the lobby, heads turning in her wake as people regarded the unescorted bride. Ignoring the attention, her thoughts drifted to her mother. If they had a better relationship, if she hadn't been so similar as to make the same exact mistakes, they would be sharing this day. She promised herself, if she and Alex were still married in two years, she would ask him for another wedding and invite their families and friends. If they made it. She wouldn't consider the possibility, especially when she knew with no uncertainty that the groom wasn't in love with the bride. No matter what happened, they would always be a part each other's lives. Their child would forever connect them. If that was all of him she could have, she would find a way to handle it.

The black limo waited for her as Alex promised. The ride to the park was hindered by summer traffic slowly meandering through the city. Staring down at the bouquet of flowers clasped tightly in her hands, the roses blurred before her eyes. What would she do if he wasn't there? Alex wasn't cruel.

She would let Brigitte take care of her if things went sideways. Brigitte would be there. And in that moment, she was happy she'd shared the news with her friend.

The limo stopped and the door opened, the late afternoon sun momentarily blinding her. She wished she'd thought to bring sunglasses. Then all she could see was Alex leaning toward her. Handsome in his black suit with the tie she'd given him, he smiled almost hesitantly and extended his hand.

"You look beautiful," he offered, his voice tight.

"Are you all right?" she asked. She could see his tension. Was he finally having second thoughts?

"You're eleven minutes late. I was getting nervous."

She smiled then, her face lighting up at the thought of him worried that she might stand him up. Just then she heard a click and knew a photographer had snapped a picture of her looking at her groom with happy adoration.

Alex wrapped his arm around her waist and walked her to a large, trellised area covered with roses where a minister waited. The photographer and the minister's wife, not to mention the crowd of rose garden visitors who'd gathered at the sight of the dressed-up couple, acted as witnesses. Brigitte ran to her and kissed her on the cheek and then kissed Alex.

"Treat her well or I'll hunt you down and kill you," she said, just loud enough for Daisy to hear.

"I understand and I promise to take good care of her," he said, giving Brigitte a kiss on the cheek. "I'm glad you could be here today."

"Thank you," Brigitte said, and added, "You're right, he is handsome."

Daisy looked away, but Alex smiled as Brigitte took her place behind Daisy. And Don, one of her favorite people from Stark International Hotels, the man who had once been slated to be her boss, slipped in behind Alex to act as best man. He winked at Daisy and told her she looked beautiful.

Daisy's breath caught in her throat as Alex said his vows. The tenor and intensity of his words went straight to her heart. She smiled at him and promised to love him forever, meaning each and every word. When he slipped the wedding band on her left hand, the light caught the sparkling band from a hundred different angles. It was a platinum eternity band covered in diamonds, which fit perfectly against her engagement ring. She met Alex's emerald eyes, now twinkling with mischief.

"What is this...why?"

"The plain one next to your ring didn't look right," he replied. "I wanted something that matched you...something with a little sparkle."

She reached up, looped her arm around his neck and pulled him down for a kiss. She was vaguely aware of people whistling and clapping in the distance as Alex prolonged the moment by dipping her in his arms.

The minister cleared his throat as Alex straightened slowly, setting her vertical once more. "Sorry about that," he apologized sheepishly.

As she slipped the plain platinum band on his finger, she hoped he would never have cause to remove it.

When the minister declared they were husband and wife, the crowd applauded. Alex pulled Daisy into his arms, dipped her, and kissed her again. Gently he stood, pulling her with him, trailing soft kisses over her cheeks. He unfolded a tissue from his pocket and wiped away tears she didn't know she'd shed.

One look to Brigitte, and Daisy could see that even she wasn't immune to tears. They invited her and Don to dine with them, but they both declined, Don looking sheepishly at Brigitte and she smiled coyly.

"Really?" Daisy observed.

"Just drinks and dinner," Brigitte admitted as she walked away with Don.

"Be nice to each other," Daisy said.

"Call me tomorrow, Mrs. Stark. You lovebirds have a good night."

"Don isn't married," she said to Alex.

"Widower," he replied. "And I didn't like the way he used to look at you either."

She laughed and he kissed her again.

Alex and Daisy dined at Fenouil, a beautiful French restaurant in the Pearl District, not far from their wedding venue. They stepped through a blonde sunstone tile entry which glowed in the late afternoon sunlight as twelve-foot-high French doors opened wide to welcome the warm summer breeze. Thin curtains moved seductively, dancing over the pale stone floor. Fenouil was not usually in Daisy's budget. In fact, she had forbidden herself from going to any restaurant in the Pearl District until she'd built up her savings. An issue she no longer had.

They dined on a menu pre-selected by Alex. Forgoing champagne, they drank French sparkling cider. Feeling overly sentimental, nervous, and not at all hungry, Daisy picked at her food, occasionally glancing at her bejeweled hand. She had a husband. The excitement mixed with a healthy dose of disbelief left her wordless.

"Mrs. Stark looks a little shell-shocked. Are you all right?"

It took her a moment to understand he was talking to her.

"I am," she admitted, shyly looking up to meet his eyes. "Just a little shocked."

"Why?"

"You really married me," she said, placing a hand to her chest as her throat tightened.

"Of course," he replied matter-of-factly, his eyes narrowing with concern. "Daisy, really, are you okay? You're flushed. I'm worried you might faint."

"I'm fine. It is just the last two weeks...I think I was more stressed than I thought," she admitted, dabbing at her eyes with her napkin. "Today, I convinced myself you'd stand me up or tell me why you couldn't marry me."

He sat back, looking hurt, as he said, "You think that little of me?"

"No, that's not what I meant. Three months ago, I was unemployed, thinking my life was spiraling downward. Then I got the call from Stark International Hotels for the interview and I met you in a café."

"And during the interview you accused me of a bunch of bad things," he reminded her.

"See what I mean? How can you be happy about marrying me?"

He paused, took a sip of his water, and looked at her with narrowed, serious eyes. "You're the only woman I've ever asked to marry me."

"Alex, I need to say something to you and then I don't want to have to say it ever again. I want a clean slate."

"Okay."

She held up her hand. "I don't want to know about the other women in your life up until this exact moment. Not yesterday, not last year. The past is over. I have the expectation that while you're with me, you'll be with me. From this day forward if I find out that you've got a girlfriend on the side or have had a fling with someone while you're traveling, I'll leave you. I won't tolerate the behavior of either of our fathers."

He filled the silence that followed by folding his napkin carefully, his expression never changing. Then he leaned close, and she prepared for the worst. "Okay, I'm starting to feel the jet lag, do you mind if we get a doggie bag and head home?"

"Doggie bag? You don't have anything to say about what I just said? What I need in this marriage to stay?" Not that she wanted to fight, but she'd said a lot.

"Well, I didn't get any sleep on the plane and your expectations seem reasonable, so I agree with them, but I do have a question."

"Okay," she said, nervously.

"Are you sure you don't feel deprived not having a big wedding?"

"No. Please, let's stop talking about this. I told my mother we were dating and that we were moving in together. She almost burst a gasket. I thought she might explode so I didn't tell her anything else. She told me she didn't want to talk to me for a while, which is how she gets when she is angry. I'll call her in a week or two, maybe. How about you?"

"My mother and older sister's family are spending a month on Martha's Vineyard. I told my sister we're seriously dating. I'll tell her we had a spur of the moment wedding when they get back. With any luck, she'll break it to my mother."

"They'll think I'm sleeping my way to the top."

"They would never think that. My sister said nice things about you after meeting you. She is very mellow, unlike my other sister who was born to fight."

"Did I deprive you of a big wedding?"

"No, not at all. I preferred something discreet, but after all those people today with their cell phones taking photos of our quiet little ceremony."

"Why didn't you sleep on your plane?" she asked

"I wasn't on the family plane. My mother and sister used it for Martha's Vineyard. That's something you should know, my mother and sister trump us for the jet. It can be annoying. I had to fly commercial to get home to you. Coach. Middle seat. Next to a screaming baby. It was a twelve-hour flight, and I was awake for every moment of it. In fact, I've been awake for almost twenty-seven hours, which is why I'm kind of boring and not as enthusiastic as I feel," he said, consulting his watch.

"You really wanted to marry me," she said, more to herself than to him.

"Of course," he replied, signaling the waiter for their check. "Daisy, we are having a child."

But what if they weren't? Would he have ever married her? What if she lost the baby tomorrow or next week?

Twenty minutes later, they walked through the lobby of the Stark International Hotel aware of people turning to watch the handsome newlyweds.

"I think our secret is out, Mrs. Stark," Alex whispered, as they waited for their private elevator.

Outside their suite, Alex paused, smiling down at her. She returned the smile wearily and waited. When he didn't open the door, realization kicked in.

"Alex, no!" As if she had any control of the situation.

"I told you, I'm superstitious," he said, easily lifting her into his arms. He carried her inside and kicked the door closed behind them. Walking directly to the master bedroom, he gently dropped her in the center of a large four-poster bed. They sank into the large mattress together. The sheets had been turned down invitingly and sprinkled with red rose petals. Stretching out alongside her, he wrapped his arms around her, pulling her close.

She met him halfway when he leaned in to kiss her. The soft touch of his lips reminded her of that first time, that first day by the waterfront. With each kiss he placed on her skin, her body became more pliant, ignoring all the warning her brain tried to volley at her cynical heart.

She let her hands roam over his broad shoulders and down his back, feeling the taut fabric of his suit coat under her fingertips. He'd worn the tie she picked out for him and now she felt the cool fabric tickling her collarbone.

"You smell like roses," he whispered in her ear, as he gently fingered one of the delicate blossoms in her hair.

"I know you're tired."

"Not too tired."

"Then maybe later you could deflower me? You know, take all the flowers out of my hair?"

He sat back from her, his lips curved into a sly smile as he ran his hands over the smooth blush satin, tracing the seams of her bodice with his fingertips.

"Why is it that we've never talked of your past, yet mine has been examined and dissected?" he asked. "Who came before me? Whom should I hate with the heat of a thousand suns for deflowering you the first time?"

Smiling, she said, "There was no one that mattered. I've only had a couple of boyfriends. One in college, one after, and then came you. I think you'd like them both. They are both still on my Christmas card list."

"I hate them both," he said, taking her face in his hands as he whispered, "This Christmas we are going to send out a joint card and let them know you are off the market, Mrs. Stark."

Daisy wanted to accuse him of being a hypocrite but a card announcing her status would also be announcing his. She decided not to point this out as she wanted to enjoy her wedding night and not spend each moment fighting. If there was any chance at happiness, it started with them, and this night, their first of hopefully many to come.

"I'm not only off the market. I'm pregnant with your child," she added, as his hand immediately rubbed that part of her body where his child grew inside her.

"It's been a very long six and a half weeks since we last shared a bed..."

"I've missed you," she admitted, rubbing her hand along the buttons on the front of his shirt, "I've missed having you touch me..."

"That's the nicest thing you've ever said to me." Hands gently covering her breasts, he moved softly over the contours of her skin. "I've missed you, too."

"You wore the tie," she said, reaching out to touch the blush-colored silk.

"It matched your dress perfectly."

"So did the pearls. They're beautiful..." She stumbled over her words, feeling shy and awkward. He kissed her then, a deeper kiss that resonated with the gathering butterflies in her stomach, sending shivers along her skin.

"It's time to begin the deflowering," he said, moving back so that she could sit up. "Come here."

With great patience, he removed every rosebud and pin holding her blonde mass of curls in place. As soon as the roses were dispatched, he ran his fingers through her hair eliciting a sound of pure pleasure from her lips. Pulling her into his lap, he went to work on the dozens of tiny buttons running down her back.

"How did you ever get these buttoned?"

"Tenaciously, but your limo driver helped me with the three that I missed."

He paused, his hand stilling in mid-motion. "You should've had someone here for you. Why didn't you? Why didn't you ask Brigitte?"

She didn't want to explain that her friends would have been shocked and thought she'd lost her mind for marrying her boss after two months of knowing him. Clearly, her mother had not been an option. Brigitte had offered, but she wanted to be alone. "When it came down to it, I only wanted you."

The fabric slid down over her arms as he kissed an exposed shoulder. When she was wearing only her pale blue bra and panties, he asked, "What did you borrow?"

"Hmm?" she asked, distracted by the sight of him removing his jacket, then the tie, followed by the unbuttoning of his shirt with slow, unhurried deliberation.

"I recognize the gold bracelet you're wearing, so that is the 'old'. The 'new' is your dress and necklace. The 'blue' is the silky lace covering your lush body. What did you 'borrow'? I think this proves I'm not the only superstitious one."

Bending down, she removed her blush-colored silk sling-back and pulled a penny from where it rested just inside the lining. "You really are superstitious, but it has rubbed off on me. Here you are. Thank you for the loan."

He looked down at the penny in his outstretched hand as if it were a prized treasure.

"I took it from that pile of change on top of your dresser," she said, gesturing toward the large walk-in closet in the corner of the room.

"Thank you. I'm sure I would've missed it," he said with a small smile as he pocketed the penny. Then he reached for the clasp on her bra.

By the time they were naked, she was impatient to have him inside her, but he had other ideas.

They'd only been together a short time in Europe, but they'd learned a variety of ways to please each other in those twelve days. Still, Daisy didn't know what to think when he abandoned her on the bed and disappeared into another room. He returned a moment later with candles, which he lit and set around the bedroom.

"I meant to do this before the deflowering," he said as he made a beeline for his luggage, which had been delivered while they'd been off getting married.

He returned to the bed with a little box.

"What's that?" she asked, sitting up on her elbows.

"I bought it in Positano. Luckily my Italian is just good enough to get me in trouble. It is very high-end massage oil, heck I think it is food grade," Alex said as he opened the box and extracted a small, sealed bottle. After he took off the wax and extracted the cork, he smelled the contents and smiled.

Pouring some of the liquid from the bottle into his hands, he rubbed them slowly together and smiled at her in the candlelight.

The scent of vanilla filled the air and then she was drowning in sensation as his hands slid over her skin spreading the warm oil liberally. She watched his fingers move over her, focusing on the platinum ring he wore on his left hand that announced to the world that he belonged to her.

Daisy heard erratic breathing and understood it was her body's response to his touch. When she thought she couldn't take another minute of his sweet torture, he settled at the end of the bed and gently nudged her knees apart.

Heat radiated off her body in waves as she thought of what he was about to do to her. She wanted to yell at him to hurry, but with one wicked smile, he dipped his head and feasted on her tender, engorged flesh.

The moment his tongue touched her skin, she bucked and screamed in release. He didn't stop sucking and licking her until she'd stopped quaking beneath him. Then, showing infinite patience, he slipped inside her and stroked her until she thought she'd die from pleasure of it.

Alex watched Daisy sleep in the pink light of the early morning. Her chest gently rose and fell in perfect rhythm as she clutched a pillow and slept peacefully.

He shook his head in sad realization. She thought he wouldn't show up to marry her. She thought he was only marrying her because she was pregnant.

He didn't know if he was more hurt or disappointed. He would have to tread lightly, convince her that she could not only trust him, but that she could love him as much as he loved her.

It seemed so incongruent to him that his feelings were so different from hers. For the first time since his father died, hell, maybe his whole life, he was happy. Since the moment he'd met her, he hadn't had a moment's peace. He'd never known such passion, such fear, such, well…love. He was in love for the first time in his life. What a roller coaster ride the last few weeks had been. If someone would have told him that he would have lost one best friend and found another, he wouldn't have believed it.

She was scared. From a young age her mother had made her feel like a mistake. It would take time and patience for her to understand that she was his greatest gift, the gift he'd always wanted and never knew if he'd get. If for no other reason that his life was to show this one woman what it was like to be loved, his life had purpose.

Daisy stirred; her face scrunching up as it fought an encroaching sunbeam. Her arms stretched out, searching for him. He dropped his towel, got back into bed, and reached for her. Content once more, she snuggled against him, and he felt hope surge in his heart. They would have a great life. They would be very happy.

He moved his hands along her skin, waking her gently. His mouth replaced his hands, his hair, still wet from his shower, tickled her. She murmured happily putting her hands in his hair.

"Good morning, Mrs. Stark," he whispered, as he lavished attention on one of her nipples with his warm tongue.

Her eyes fluttered, then opened, "What time is it?"

"Early," he said, kissing a path along her neck. "Too early for anything but sleep or making love."

"I need a shower," she said.

"It can wait," he said, reaching for a soft mound. "Your breasts are getting larger."

"No, they're not, I'm only six or seven weeks along," she argued, as her hands ran over his skin.

"I know every inch of you. They're bigger and they're vanilla flavored," he argued, cupping her breast before moving to her other nipple.

"Ohhhhh," she moaned. "You win, they're bigger."

"And a lot more sensitive."

Moving his hand down, he eased it between the cleft of her thighs and said, "You're already wet for me."

"Only you," she said, relaxing her legs to give him better access. When she was panting, he rolled onto his back and lifted her, so she was astride him and gently lowering onto his erection.

Her blue eyes sparkled as she looked down at him as she said, "It is a good morning, Mr. Stark."

Kissing him quickly, she teased him with her breasts, swinging them just out of reach above his lips. He grabbed a passing nipple and sucked softly on it, giving it a playful tug with his teeth.

"You don't play fair, Mrs. Stark."

She was beautiful, a woman who fully embraced her passion. Placing his hands on her hips, he guided her on his body, moving her in lazy circles as she gently squeezed him in her velvet vise. As her body pulled harder on his, he matched her, pushing up into to her until her breath came out in short rapid gasps.

Minutes later, they lay panting, their bodies still connected, their room flooded with sun and the scent of vanilla and sex.

"Are you bringing that stuff with us to Europe?" she asked, her words labored.

"I will, but it isn't like we need it," he said.

"But I haven't gotten a chance to play with it yet. Spill it all over you and rub it in."

"Hell," he replied. "When we're in Italy I'll buy us a gallon."

Later, after they had taken a long, playful shower, Daisy sat on a bar stool and watched Alex make her breakfast. She'd had no idea he could cook. Watching him expertly chop vegetables, she could tell he was no novice.

He caught her watching and put down the knife to pour her a glass of orange juice he delivered with a kiss to her forehead. "Drink it. It's loaded with vitamins. Good for you and the baby."

"What are you making?"

"Frittata. Unless that doesn't sound good to you."

"It sounds good."

"What would you like to do today?" he asked, as he put the creation in the oven.

"Well, since we leave for Europe tomorrow, I'm thinking probably pack," she replied, as little tendrils of unease crept into her body. She would be facing Maria Medici again. She looked at Alex, watched the way he meticulously cleaned up the kitchen. When had she known she was hopelessly in love with him? It was some time, she decided, between the first and second glass of wine at Mother's. Someday, she'd tell him.

"Maybe take a little afternoon nap," she added.

His hand stopped moving the cloth he used on the drainboard. "Definitely, we should plan on a nap."

"Maybe we should get a little exercise too."

Reading her mind, he asked, "Could you get away for a walk in the park? Maybe down to the waterfront?"

"I'd like that. Then, if I'm feeling brave, I'll call my mother and tell her I did something really crazy last night. That should be fun."

He raised a single eyebrow and gave her a smile filled with dimples. "That could be interesting."

"Maybe that can wait until we get back from Europe."

"Maybe a little longer. I have an idea I wanted to run by you. How about we go someplace after the parties? You know, why don't we have a real honeymoon."

A honeymoon. Like a normal couple. She didn't hesitate. "I'd love that. Where do you want to go?"

"I thought maybe you'd like to choose."

Their time in Paris, Rome, and London had been a dream honeymoon. "I think I'd like you to surprise me."

"I can do that," he said, showing a surprising amount of dimple. "I've already got a place in mind."

In the late afternoon, they walked through the lobby, Alex introducing her as Mrs. Stark to several members of the staff as they made their way out to the street.

They walked through the park, grabbed an early dinner at a little bistro not unlike Mother's, and returned to their suite in the early evening. Packing their bags side by side on the bed, they chatted easily, the simple act of domesticity not lost on Daisy.

"None of my dresses are very fancy," she said, feeling a bit inadequate. "I picked up a couple of new things this week. I hope they will be all right for the parties."

"You'll be beautiful, and they do have stores in Europe in case you feel you need something. Did you remember a mask for Carnival?" he asked, holding up his own mask, half black, half white. She thought the duality seemed appropriate. He was being her dream husband today, but she'd seen him be ruthless in business.

Reaching into her luggage, she pulled out her mask. It was just a simple face, pretty but unassuming. When she showed it to him, he smiled in approval.

One could only guess what Maria Medici would be wearing. At the increasingly prevalent thoughts of the other woman, her peace and contentment quietly vanished, a slight air of unease sliding in like a low-lying fog.

"It's perfect," he said and then picked up on her unease. "Are you nervous?"

"It's just different...now."

"We're married. What else?"

"People will treat me differently. It might be weird and if they figure out that you married me because I'm pregnant..." It was more than she wanted to say, but it hadn't stopped her.

"It just happened a little sooner than it might have, but you are my beautiful bride, and no one can deny that I'm a very lucky man," he said and gently brushed his fingertips along her cheek.

"I'm pleasant, but not beautiful."

"The term I've used to describe you to my cousin Adam is bombshell," he said softly as he went back to placing a second tux into a large garment bag.

"Wow," she said.

He dropped the shirt he was folding and kissed her until she was dizzy.

Her mind brooded in an emotional stew. She wanted to believe everything he said and did. She wanted to believe that when he made love to her, he was making love. She wanted to believe that somewhere, somehow, he didn't think of her as an inconvenience he was dealing with. Blinking back the emotion, she busied herself with her packing when he let her go.

Then she asked, "How is Adam?"

"A mess, but he is alive, and dealing with each day as it comes. I'm looking forward to having you meet him. It is too soon now, but in a few months, when the pain isn't so fresh, I think it will be better. I don't want to rub our happiness in his face. Do you know what I mean?"

"Yes," she said.

They went to bed early. Daisy dressed in a pale pink chiffon nightie she'd bought when she'd purchased her wedding dress. She hoped it would be off seconds after she got into bed. Sex was their great equalizer.

What she hadn't expected was to have Alex pull her into his arms and hold her close.

"You've been through a lot in the last few weeks," he said.

"That's an extreme understatement."

"Daisy, everything is going to be fine. We are going to get through the next week and then we are going to go off by ourselves... someplace where we can relax and forget about stupid barbeques and Carnival. We're going to focus on our future, our baby. When we feel like it, we'll come back. I'll meet your family and you'll meet mine and all this strangeness will start to feel normal. I promise."

Unable to answer, her voice trapped in a painful lump in her throat, she tightened her hold on him and began kissing any part of him she could reach. She wanted to believe him more than anything in the world, so for this moment, she did.

CHAPTER SIXTEEN

The next morning, as Daisy tried to calm her stomach with soda crackers, Alex stepped into the kitchen, cell phone to his ear. He kissed her cheek as he passed by her to get to the coffee pot. Her nightgown had been tossed off within minutes of going to bed, yet her appetite for Alex hadn't been satiated, but only fed. The last two days had been a dream. She couldn't wait for him to get off the phone so he could put his hands on her again.

"I don't want to do that, Gardot. If you don't have it together by now, how do you think Daisy can save you?"

Daisy dropped a cracker on the floor only to have Alex pick it up and toss it in the garbage can. Something was wrong in Paris, and she didn't like the sound of the call she could hear on her end.

"She's right here, I'll ask her." Alex turned to her, frowning in disapproval, "Your friend in Paris is panicking and wondering if you'd like to forgo the parties in Rome and London to help him with the final details."

"What do you want me to do?" she asked.

"As your boss, I'd send you to Paris to make sure we don't look like complete idiots, but as your husband, I want you with me. I don't want to be away from you, but I'm torn."

"You don't make it easy," she said, taking the offered phone. Ten minutes later, she'd reluctantly agreed to spend the time in Paris, while Alex would go to Rome and London without her.

"I'm sure you're doing the right thing," Alex said as they landed in Paris fourteen hours later. "But it sure doesn't feel like it. I'm not happy about this…not at all."

"I'm going to miss you," she said as she picked up her purse and carry-on bag.

"I'm glad. I'll miss you, too, but I'll see you in five days and then we'll have one hell of a reunion," he said, taking the carry-on bag off her shoulder. He walked her to the car Luis had sent. They watched silently as her luggage was transferred to the trunk of a large black sedan.

Opening the back door, he ordered, "Please take care of yourself. Don't let Gardot work you too hard. If you feel like taking a nap, take a nap. If you need anything, you call me."

"I'll be fine," she replied, wanting to caution him to stay away from Maria Medici.

Before Daisy got inside, Alex pulled her close and kissed her, once, twice, and a third time that made her heart race as his lips lingered for a long time. Leaning his forehead against hers, he let her in on a little secret. "After Paris, I'm taking you to St. Barts."

It would be heaven. Smiling up at him, she said, "I didn't think to pack a swimsuit."

"You won't need one. We have a house with a private beach, and I don't think you'll be wearing much if anything. But, if you insist, I'll buy you a dozen bathing suits."

"It sounds wonderful. Could we just go now?" she asked, rubbing against him.

"I wish," he said, kissing her a final time and stepping away, waving as he headed back to the plane. "I'll see you soon. Take care of yourself and the baby. I love you."

Stunned, she looked up at him and said the words she'd been holding in, "I love you, too."

They quietly stared at each other for a long moment, and then he pulled her to him again and kissed her as if were the last time they would ever touch.

And then without another word, he smiled broadly, and was gone.

Daisy did not remember the drive to the hotel. She was smiling like an idiot. *He loved her.* This changed everything. She'd see him in a few days, the longest few days of her life. They had things to say and plans to make. Everything had changed. For now, she was in the last place she wanted to be—away from him…

Luis was more nervous than unprepared, Daisy surmised after she arrived at the Hotel Imperial and took stock of the situation. In just a few weeks the hotel had transformed into a showplace.

It wasn't until after she'd rested—not sleeping but staring at the ceiling—that she began helping with the party and she understood why he'd called her. The ballroom looked like a set from *Urban Cowboy* complete with mechanical bull.

"Oh my god," she muttered as she stepped into the large space, looking at the hay-strewn floor completely obliterating the beautiful herringbone hardwoods. Bales of hay lined the walls smelling mildly of mold and barn. Naugahyde tablecloths resembling cow hides covered each tabletop.

"It's not exactly what I wanted," Luis admitted.

"Alex will fire you if he sees this."

"It's my fear," he said, his French accent thicker from the stress.

"Luis, damn it, you've got to get it together! Get rid of the hay and the fake cowhides. Air this place out and get rid of the smell. Get red and white gingham-checkered napkins on white linen tabletops. Move that mechanical bull out of here. Damn it, why does this damn bull keep reappearing? Haven't we already dealt with him?"

"He was very expensive."

"I. Don't. Care. I never want to see him again. Give me red, white, and blue. We want elegant barbeque, not roadside honky-tonk. These people are the richest, most famous clients we have. They will not appreciate the smell of moldy hay, neither do I for that matter," she said fanning the air in front of her face. The baby really didn't like it. "What did you do with the tumbleweeds?"

Luis looked up from the pad he was quickly making notes on. "I have them in the basement. I was going to have them brought up this afternoon. They are a bit dusty."

"Okay… Can you spray paint them gold and add twinkle lights? Make them look a bit more elegant?"

"That is a wonderful idea!" Luis exclaimed.

"We've got a lot of work to do," she said, wanting to throttle Luis and thinking for the hundredth time that he needed a keeper. "What did you decide on for the signature cocktail?"

"Well," he hesitated. "A large quantity of Budweiser beer had been arranged with an American distributor and I was unable to cancel the order."

"No!" she protested adamantly. "Absolutely not! I asked you to have the chef create something with liquor not wine or beer. What happened?"

"I might have forgotten to mention it. We lost another chef, the new one from Seattle, Paul."

"What?" she asked, flabbergasted. "When did this happen?"

"Yesterday."

"Yesterday? You've got to tell Alex. Right now."

She was reaching for her cell phone, but Luis placed his hand on her arm.

"We have it taken care of."

"Luis, how did this happen? Is there any way we can get him back?"

"He got a better offer from a restaurant in New York and quit. I believe he's already caught a flight back to America. Now Daisy, please, let me handle this myself."

"You make me want to beat my head against a wall."

"When it comes to the chef, I have it handled. Trust me."

"How do you have this handled? Convince me why I shouldn't call Alex right now."

"Jacques, our second in command, is very good and chose not to go with Paul to New York…You see? Everything is fine…you don't need to call your husband. Everything is handled. Jacques will step in. Well, you could help with the cocktails if you'd like."

"You really frustrate me," she said, wanting to punch him. "Why did you call Alex and request me if you wanted to handle it yourself?" *I could be with him right now. He told me he loves me!*

"Because you're my good luck charm. I wanted you to be here," he said simply.

She sighed with exasperation. She was going to kill this man.

"So, I've got a lot of good whiskey for party favors. I might've ordered too much. Can you work with that and create something for the party?"

"How much too much?" she asked, aware that he was trying to distract her.

"Maybe twenty cases too much."

"Well," she said, thinking of how many people were coming to the party. "That screw up is actually a good thing. We have a surplus of two hundred bottles."

"Two hundred and forty."

"Oh good, now you can do the math," she chided.

Luis had enough pride to look offended.

Reading his thoughts, she replied, "Don't start with me, Luis. My husband of two days, who I love and who loves me, is off partying in Rome without me because you wanted me here. Well, guess what? You're going to get my every thought, opinion, and criticism as I think of it! I can't believe you didn't tell Alex about losing another chef."

"I wanted to show you both that I could handle it. My pride is on the line."

"More than that. If this party isn't spectacular, he'll fire you for sure."

"Try not to sound so happy about it," Luis chuckled and wrapped an arm around her shoulder, "Thank you, Daisy, for coming early."

She stepped away from him with a disgruntled sigh and asked, "Do you have any fresh mint? Any cute little pewter cups?"

"We could get them."

"Good, I need like two hundred because every partygoer that comes in that door," she said, pointing to the large ballroom entrance, "will be greeted with a sweet mint julep. Google them and let's decide on the look I want for each drink. Then, I want big trays of them, and I want them sweet, so they go down smooth."

Luis just looked at her.

"It is an American drink they drink at the Kentucky Derby. Seriously, the goal is that we're going to get the party attendees stinking drunk. Maybe they won't notice how horrible everything is. In fact, get them drunk enough and they'll say this is the best damn party of the whole trip. Trust me, I know of what I speak of about the effects of alcohol."

"You know what, Daisy?"

"What now?" she asked angrily. "Did someone else quit?"

Luis shook his head and smiled. Then he admitted, "When Alex arrived in Paris the day you got lost well, how can I say this, I wasn't happy to see him. I can tell you this now, because you are married…"

"What? What are you trying to say?"

"We would be embarking on a sweet, passionate love affair. We would've discovered Paris together as lovers. I would have done everything in my power to show you how capable I am of giving sensual pleasure. I just know that we would have been very good together."

Alex had been right; Luis liked her. He liked her, a lot. Her anger all but evaporated. She playfully punched him in the shoulder and said, "Damn it, Luis! How can I stay mad when you say such sweet, yet inappropriate things to me?"

"You have the glow of love about you, the harmonies, they are messing with you."

"Hormones? I glow?" she asked pointing at herself.

"You are with child."

"You can tell I'm pregnant?" she asked, a little horrified. "We've told no one."

"I won't tell anyone, but I like to think that baby might have been conceived in my corporate suite. I take credit for providing the right, romantic ambiance, n'est-ce pas?"

"It was more likely Rome and my introduction to limoncello."

"I think what I want to think."

Over the next few days, the ballroom transformed into an elegant space, as elegant a high-end French fusion barbeque could get. Alex called Daisy every evening. At the end of every call, he told her he loved her, and she responded in kind. The freedom to say it was a gift she didn't know she wanted so badly until she got it.

As Alex wined and dined their elite VIPs in Rome, she arranged baskets of swag heavy with bottles of Jack Daniels and commemorative flasks to be waiting in the guest's rooms upon their arrival.

Taking a moment to relax in Luis's office the day before the party, she put her feet up and thought of everything they'd done. The party was finally coming together. The guests were due to start arriving that afternoon and would receive VIP treatment from start to finish. The valets, waiters, and housekeeping staff were on their best behavior. She had personally inspected all one hundred and eighty-three of the guestrooms the partygoers would be occupying.

Aside from the swag basket, each guest would receive a newly designed, claret red hotel robe made in a heavy silk satin with a large gold monogram on the left side of the chest. Additionally, they would be able to attend any of the special events provided by the hotel. Tomorrow night they'd enjoy an American-themed party after arriving back from their adventures to waiting trays of generous mint julips at every turn.

Alex would be with her soon, but it wasn't soon enough.

Alex had called that morning. He wouldn't be arriving until the day of the party. He needed to return to Italy to finalize his acquisition of the hotel in Positano. She couldn't wait to see him. She allowed a new confidence to creep into her subconscious. Alex was her husband now, she had the name and the rings to prove it, and they were in love. She was mad at herself for waiting as long as she had to feel happy.

"I heard the London party was a bit subdued last night, but Roma was fabulous," Luis offered as Daisy made a list of last-minute details.

"Rome always sounded like it was going to be decadent," she replied, thinking of the masks and costumes. Alex told her the guests had drunk way too much and partied until the next morning. He said more than one drink had been spilled on his tuxedo and he thought it was probably ruined.

"Photos from Roma were emailed this morning. I haven't had a chance to go through them yet, would you like to look?" Luis asked.

"Sure." She moved to look over his shoulder.

Frame after frame of elegant party dresses and flamboyant masks of Carnival slowly loaded and then filled the computer screen. "Everyone looks like they're having a good time," she said, noticing Maria Medici in a red costume accentuating her curves and cleavage. Leave it to her to leave little to the imagination.

A minute later, they were looking at Maria kissing a man in a black tux with a black and white mask in his hand. The face was obscured, but Daisy recognized the mask. Her husband of less than a week had his arms lovingly around another woman, one hand precariously close to her butt. Not just any woman. Maria Medici.

But Alex said he loved *her*. He'd said it. She'd said it.

"Print that one," she ordered sharply and then flicked the computer screen for emphasis.

"Why?"

"That's a photo of my husband."

For once, Luis seemed to feel the confusion of emotions coming from Daisy. "Daisy, you can't be serious…You can't be sure. You can't even see his face."

"Print it, please."

"Why do I feel that you are jealous of Maria?"

"Because, I am," Daisy said. "We have a bone of contention. His name is Alex."

"You know, I've seen them together many times. They aren't lovers. Look, she isn't kissing him on the lips. She is kissing his cheek. When she wants something, she kisses passionately. I know this for a fact."

"Really, Luis? I had no idea," Daisy said as something, some finger of doubt about Maria Medici started to take hold. "She's marking her territory and he's pawing her a little bit."

Luis scrutinized the photo and said, "I think he is keeping her from falling down."

Luis might actually be right, but Daisy still didn't like it.

"He doesn't look at her the way he looks at you. He never has," Luis said.

"How does he look at me?" she asked.

"Like he wants to be making love to you at that moment."

It was better than she'd expected. She kind of liked it.

"Daisy, he married you. The night you were lost in Paris, I thought he was going to strangle me for letting you out of my sight."

"That is good to hear. I'll take care of this. Print the photo."

There were two more photos of them together. In one, Maria and Alex were dancing, their bodies pressed tightly together and in the other, Maria was sitting on his lap. Each time their image filled the screen, she ordered Luis to hit the print key. He knew better than to argue with her.

Once she had the color prints in hand, she stormed out of his office and took refuge in her suite, but then she looked at the photos, really looked at Maria and Alex's faces.

What was it with Maria Medici? Why was she always tactile with Alex? Jealous? Angry? Or something else entirely? Yes, it was there all right. And now that she'd seen it, she couldn't get it out of her head.

When Alex called her that night, she tried to sound normal. She needed to talk to him but wouldn't have this discussion over the phone. He needed to look in her eyes and explain this to her. Then she would show him the photos. She hadn't sorted out what she would do from there, but it would come to her. Her intuition told her that Alex was being truthful, but she still wanted to get some answers about Maria. She wanted her conclusions confirmed because until they were, they were just the musings of a very, very hormonal woman who missed her husband and was thinking the worst.

"I miss you," Alex said simply.

"I miss you, too, but tonight, I'm tired," she replied with cool indifference. It was the truth.

"Get some rest," he instructed. Softly, he added, "I can't wait to see you. I can't wait to hold you and you know—"

"I want to hear you say it," she said, making her voice sound soft and low.

"I want to make love to you, I want you in my bed, my arms. I want you. Is that what you wanted to hear?" he asked.

"Yes."

"Most importantly, I love you," he said.

"Good, okay, I need to go."

"Are you all right? You sound, I don't know."

"I sound tired. I'm fine. I was on my feet a lot," she admitted, not adding that she'd been pacing with anger, while chiding herself for thinking that Maria had a chance with Alex. She couldn't believe she had been so stupid.

"Daisy, you need to take it easy."

"I'm fine," she repeated. "And I'll be rested tomorrow night for whatever you might have in mind."

"What I have in mind is making love with my wife."

"I want you to fuck my brains out like a hooker you picked up in Pigalle."

His silence had her smiling. That would give him something to think about until he got to her.

"I don't know what you did with my slightly shy wife, but I like it."

"I thought you would," she replied.

"What do people say when they find out they're meeting Mrs. Stark?"

"I haven't told them, but Luis knows, and he guessed I was pregnant. He thinks the baby was conceived in the executive suite."

"Remind me to punch him right in his loose-lipped mouth."

She didn't answer him right away, but instead she said, "You were right about him. He said if you hadn't shown up when you did, he'd have introduced me to his ability to give sensual pleasure and that we'd have experienced Paris as lovers."

She'd heard the term poking a stick at an angry dog, but she would never hurt an animal. Alex was a different kind of animal altogether.

At the other end of the phone line, she could hear him breathing, a bull seeing red.

Good. Let him be a little upset for a change. Let him wonder what she has been up to without him. Let him know that other men found her attractive.

He whispered, "If he said what you just told me, I'll kill him."

"No, relax, he knows we're married."

"I don't trust him, I never have."

"He knows that. He feels it. He really is a sweet man."

"He's a dead man walking."

"It is okay, he is very respectful. By the way, how did Maria take the news?"

"Since when did you care what Maria thinks? Daisy, what the hell is going on? Is this because we didn't have a big wedding? Because if you want a big wedding, I can make it happen. We'll have the biggest damn wedding you've ever seen. Everyone will know. I'll personally send out a press release."

"I'm just really, really tired. I want to be with you on our own private nude beach."

"I want that, too, just as long as you aren't mad at me for insisting we get married, just so you are glad you married me," he said, sounding disappointed.

There was a long silence as she considered his words, then, quietly, she answered, "I am."

"I don't quite believe you."

"Alex, I'm just tired. I made the gift baskets filled with bottles of booze. The sight of a bottle of Jack Daniels makes me want to throw up."

"I'm sorry," he said. "But you're not acting like the woman I left on Monday. I don't know what to think."

"Accept the fact that I'm tired and I'm worried about this stupid, stupid meaningless party. Maybe you should've fired Luis and we could've stayed home."

"Well, that's something we agree on," he said. "I need to have a talk with Luis."

"I told you all the lover and sensual stuff in confidence. Let it go."

"I'll think about it. And at this extremely ridiculous party, which is no doubt going to make our company look stupid, I'm going to introduce you as my wife, so be prepared."

"I'll wear my party dress," she replied and hung up on him.

CHAPTER SEVENTEEN

It came as no surprise to Daisy when Alex called and left a message that he would be late to the party. She'd let the call go to voicemail. The second time he called, she let it go to voicemail again. The game continued for two more calls, then she picked up for the fifth call.

No greeting.

"Are you all right?" he asked.

"Yes. Get here. I miss you," she said, and smiled at her directness.

"I want to be with you, you know that. I'm on my way as soon as we finish up here."

"Are you bringing the Italian?"

"Maria? She asked if she could get a ride on the company plane."

"She'd better not be staying in our suite."

"She's a Stark International Hotels executive and there is room in our suite. Where else can she stay?" he asked.

Daisy was ready for this. "Well, I didn't think you wanted her to hear us making love. Or maybe you do?"

"I see your point. I don't want you to feel inhibited because Maria is in the suite. The only reason I want her to have a nice room is that I like to be nice to people who make money for me. Now, for us."

"No one is staying with us. Luis is taking care of her accommodations," Daisy said.

"Just make sure she gets a good room. I don't care where she is as long as you are okay. And let's keep her away from Luis, I think they once had a thing."

"Really?" Daisy said. "Maria gets around a bit."

"Please don't say that, and let me reiterate, she is no threat to you."

"We will talk about it later, but I need to go."

"I'll get there as soon as I can," he said.

"Good," she said and hung up.

Daisy already knew the other woman had called and left word with Luis that she would be flying to Paris with Alex on his jet. Luis had reluctantly shared the information and then ducked for cover behind one of the arriving guests, but she let him know how she felt about it.

"Luis, find her a room. I don't want her in the corporate suite."

"But you have two bedrooms in your suite."

"I heard you, but listen to me, find her a room, give her a key when she arrives. And if you can't find her a room here, put her up in a different hotel. Got it?"

"Yes, Mrs. Stark."

"And never call me that again."

Daisy stayed in her room most of the day avoiding guests. If Luis needed her, he knew where to find her. She took a long time getting ready. The party would be a success. As for Alex, and their story, the ending had yet to be written, but if her hunch was right, she was feeling better than she ever had about her marriage. She played his words over and over in her mind, 'I love you.' *I love you, too.*

She slipped into her black dress and surveyed the result in the mirror of the pink marble bath. In a couple of weeks, she wouldn't be able to fit into it, her tummy was already a little tight from her expanding waistline where Alex's baby grew. She rubbed her stomach and smiled. *Their baby.*

Her off-the-shoulder gown defined elegance with black lace overlaying black silk taffeta. The dress showed a lot of cleavage and leg. It was the sexiest dress she owned. She hoped her husband liked it. She hoped he would be looking for the zipper sooner than later.

She liked the way she looked a bit dangerous, edgy, sexy, perfect for tonight. Okay, she thought, the gloves are off. She checked her lipstick one last time and looked down at the sparkling rings on her left hand. She was Alex's wife, and it was time she believed it and the world knew it. More than anything, he needed to know what it meant to her. She sounded more confident than she looked, but that is what she needed to get through the night.

She did place the intimate photos of Alex and Maria on the bedside table where she and Alex had first made love. She would ask him if her conclusions were right, but it was no longer the priority it had once been.

The party was in full swing by the time Daisy walked into the room. Everyone seemed to be having a wonderful time. She'd guessed the booze available on arrival that afternoon after the extravagant excursions had gone a long way to putting the group in a mood to celebrate. Happy partygoers boogied down to the band singing cover songs of Bruce Springsteen and Garth Brooks. And if she wasn't mistaken, they were partying like it was 1999.

"My beautiful Daisy, it is going well, yes?" a tuxedoed Luis asked.

"I would say it appears to be a success," she said and together they toasted, Luis with a julep, Daisy with sparkling water.

"And don't you look handsome," Daisy said.

"And you look sexy, dangerous. Mr. Alex Stark is one lucky bastard," he said.

"Bastard?" Daisy asked with a smile.

"I try to sound like a tough American, like Die Hard or Clint Eastwood."

She laughed and took his arm as she whispered, "You're not terrible, in fact, your American accent is pretty good."

They mingled together, working the crowd, and making sure that everyone was having a good time.

When two hands grasped her waist from behind, she stiffened until she saw Alex's wedding ring adorned hand reached for hers at the same moment his lips nuzzled her neck. A warm, sensual heat licked at her skin.

"Hello, Mrs. Stark," he whispered in her ear. "You look beautiful, but I can't wait to unwrap that dress."

She turned toward Alex, who was dressed in a black tux, black shirt, and black tie. She kissed him and he kissed her back and whispered in her ear, "Luis warned me that you saw some photos that upset you."

"I don't think I need to be as worried as I once would have been," she said. "A few words from you, earlier, like when we were in Rome, could have saved me a lot of grief and wondering. I've punished you and for that, I was justified."

Alex held her tighter, and he started to laugh. "Of course, you figured it out. I'm sorry I didn't tell you, but I couldn't break a promise."

"I'm your wife, we have no secrets," as she said the words her anger surged as she remembered her intense jealousy. Heck, she was still a little jealous until she heard him say it.

He steered her to a quiet corner away from the crowd.

"Relax for a minute. I hoped you were upset because I spent the first week of our married life away from you, but now I can tell it goes deeper, and for the role I've played that you perceive as deception, I'm very sorry. I should have told you the truth when we were in Rome."

"Just tell me there is nothing to worry about, tell me I'm right," she said. "I need to hear you say it."

"Wait a second, even if Maria was someone I could date, did you ever think that in the two years since my father died that I might have grown up? Maybe even become virtuous? Responsible? Fallen in love?" he asked, holding her still as he raised his hand to wave at someone.

"Have you fallen in love?" she asked.

"Yes, with you. You are everything to me," he said. "I love you, Daisy. I have since the moment I saw you in that café, even before I found the nerve to talk to you, I was already half in love with you," he said, his green eyes locked onto hers. "It hit me so hard, so fast…it kind of knocked the wind out of me. I should have told you that sooner, too."

"You are your own worst enemy," she said shaking her head.

"I'm coming to that conclusion, but you thought the worst as well. Look, I need to know that you love me. I need to know you feel about me the way that I feel about you," there was a pleading tone to his voice, a desperation that cut to her heart.

"For the record, I'm not just saying the words. I love you. I've been wanting to say that since our first day together. I love you, Alex. I am hopelessly, passionately in love with my husband."

He pulled her into the darkness and kissed her again and again. "Let's blow this party and go back to our suite and let me show you how much I love you."

"Don't you have something to tell me first? Something about Maria," she asked, enjoying the way he held her in his arms. He loved her and she loved him.

"I haven't been completely honest about Maria," he admitted.

"Bingo," she said.

"I also want to tell you something about Peter."

"I've only thrown up once today," she said. "I really don't want to be sick again. Thinking about how close of a friendship you had with Peter undermines the progress we've made here."

"Hold on," he said, raising his hand. "This is important. I want you to know I believed you from the moment you told me. Peter and I were friends for a long time, but now Peter is just the jerk who tried to seduce my wife and wouldn't take no for an answer. I never quite believed the story he told about his lawsuit, and Adam didn't either—Peter was always doing stupid shit like that, but I thought he'd grown out of it like the rest of us. And I certainly never thought he'd force himself upon someone I love, which is why once you told me you were the one he accosted—Daisy, you don't know what that does to me, I could just kill him. How dare he do that to anyone? How dare he do that to my beautiful wife?"

"Thank you," she said and quickly, almost shyly kissed him.

"With your permission, I'm thinking of strongly suggesting to a friend of mine in the media that they do a little investigation on Peter. I don't want him to get away with what he did to you. I'm guessing there are others, but I want to stop him from doing this to anyone else."

"You'd do that for me?" she asked.

"Anything for you, my darling."

He spoke softly among the raucous party noise around them, but she had no trouble hearing him. His eyes were luminescent in the darkened ballroom and full of honesty. The admission made her lean into his embrace.

Alex waved again to someone behind her. "I did lie to you about Maria. For that, I'm very sorry."

Maria Medici walked up to them, raising an eyebrow as she observed Daisy in Alex's grasp.

Alex focused on Daisy. "Do you remember when I told you I had a younger sister but wouldn't tell you her name?"

"Her name is Maria," Daisy said.

Maria nodded and gave a little laugh that wasn't all that funny.

"Oh good, she figured it out, finally," Maria said. "I told you she was too smart and would guess."

Alex said, "I'd like you to officially meet my sister, Maria."

The similarities were subtle, but they were there. It was the eyes that gave them away. And now that Daisy was in on the secret, she couldn't believe everyone else couldn't see it. "Your eyes are exactly the same shade of green…"

"And the nose, I'm afraid," he said, leaning toward Maria so Daisy could see them side-by-side. "We obviously have different coloring, but when you see us together and really look, it is easy to see."

"And she looks a little like Rebecca," Daisy said.

Alex smiled sadly, "She does."

"I just need one little thing cleared up," she said, gaining her composure. "In London, Peter told me that she was your girlfriend, and you were taking her to Dubai as a date. What gave him that idea?"

Alex shrugged, "I might have, I didn't want him too curious about my sister. Maybe I haven't trusted him in a long time. Besides, she speaks the language."

Maria merely shrugged with her perfected art of looking bored and said, "I speak English, French, German, Italian, and Arabic. Alex needed me to negotiate his deal, which I'm very good at. I'm his secret weapon. Other than that, I find him a bit annoying and clingy. He talks about you all the time, so much like a little boy with a new toy."

"Thanks, sis," Alex said and turned his attention back to his wife, "Daisy, now you know something that even my mother and sister don't. Maria works in the family business. Try to keep it our little secret."

"And she was very territorial of you in Rome," Daisy added, giving Maria a stern look.

"I didn't know how serious he was about you. I see the lovey-dovey looks between you and it makes me a bit sick," Maria demurred.

"You called me the flavor of the month," Daisy said.

"I think you need to apologize to my wife for that," Alex said.

"I am sorry, Daisy," Maria said very sincerely, "I'm very protective of my older brother. He's the only family I have." Then added with a wink, "Maybe, I helped to make sure you had the wrong idea because I was a bit bored, and you made it easy."

Daisy looked to Alex. "Glad I could alleviate some boredom. Blame my directness on the hormones, but I need to reiterate, I will not tolerate secrets between us. What else is there?"

"I think you know everything," he said, and bent to kiss her. She squirmed away and hit him on the shoulder, hard. It felt good to do so, but he just laughed.

"Alex, damn it! It's not funny…"

"I know, I'm sorry, but when you get all feisty…I lose my head and you're right, I should've told you. It would have saved us both a lot of unnecessary pain. Maria didn't want anyone to know, because my mother and Rebecca don't know she's the manager of the Villa Roma. They don't even know her last name. I'd like to bring it all out into the open, but she won't let me."

They both looked at Maria who seemed incredibly uncomfortable.

"I'm happy with one brother, I don't need the rest of the family," Maria said casually, but there was pain in the other woman's words.

Daisy looked at Maria, feeling sorry for the woman with whom she had more in common than she would have thought. She was the woman in Alex's arms and having his baby, so she could be a little generous.

"You have me, too. It might take a little time, but I think we can get past this. And now that I know you don't want Alex for the same reasons I do, I'm willing to share him. And we can flick him grief and gang up on him, like sisters do."

Maria looked a little confused and then, when the words sunk in, she smiled, the first genuine smile Daisy had ever seen on the other woman's face. "I think that I would like that."

The corner of Alex's mouth tilted into a half smile as he rocked Daisy in his arms.

"If I'm no longer needed, I will go mingle. I should be nicer to Luis, he looks a bit handsome in his tux and I might be wanting some sex later," Maria said, patting Alex on the shoulder and kissing Daisy on the cheek. "Welcome to my family, Daisy."

"Please don't mess with Luis," Alex warned.

"Relax, it won't be the first time," she said, and smiled as she turned and headed toward Luis.

"I really don't want to know," he said.

"You don't," Daisy said. "But they might be good for each other."

They didn't watch Maria walk away. Looking into Daisy's eyes, Alex said, "Now, about us…" His hands caressed their way along her sides, feeling every curve and dip. "I thought you might love me enough to trust me. Do you think you'll ever be able to trust me when I tell you that I love you?"

"Say it again," she demanded, softly pressing her body against him, seeking to get closer. "I need to hear you say it a few more times. Get used to saying it a lot."

"I love you," he replied and repeated it a dozen times between kisses. "I'm in love with you."

She heard the music in the background, felt other bodies bump against them as they passed, but everything but Alex faded to black. They both had their pasts that niggled their insecurities, but everyone does, she supposed. Fortunately, she was overcoming hers and saw the future with Alex and knew this would all work out.

Suddenly, a house and a white picket fence with children, a dog, and a cat all seemed possible. And she'd have them all with the man who rocked her world, Garrison Alexander Stark.

"I love you too," she said, reaching up to touch his cheek. "I'm in love with you."

He kissed her in a way that elicited catcalls and whistles from the happy partygoers around them.

"I've missed you, Daisy. I can't live without you in my life. Adam was right; when you know, you know. I know. I love you."

She smiled, allowing a tear to escape from the corner of her eye.

He said, "I've had enough of these people, when would you like to leave?"

"So soon?" she asked.

"They'll never miss us." He winked at her. "By the way…"

"Yes?" she asked impatiently, needing to be alone with him.

"Everyone appears to be drunk and dinner is an hour away. Is this your doing?"

She smiled, a Cheshire cat grin, "Maybe."

"Smart girl," he said, his arm encircling her waist.

They made their way through the crowd. Halfway to the door, the well-wishers broke into an acapella rendition of the song "'Born in the USA." The band joined in, and everyone began to dance. The "Paris Barbeque" as it would become to be known among the guests, was beyond a doubt, the best of all three parties.

Alex took Daisy's hand as they walked through the elegant and deserted lobby toward their elevator.

Once inside she asked, "How does this party compare to Rome and London?"

"Nothing will ever compare to this night," he replied and bent to kiss her. "You really love me."

"And you love me."

Later that night, as they watched the Eiffel Tower sparkle from the window of their suite, Alex asked, "What were your three wishes? Only tell me if they've come true."

Wrapped tightly in his arms as she was, Alex could feel as much as see her smile. Her lovely, soft blue eyes sparkled brighter than the light show outside as she looked up at him.

"I can tell you about two of the three," she said.

"I'll take what I can get and like it," he replied, eliciting laughter from his bride.

"That's right," she said, "And I think you will like it. Coin one, I asked if what I was feeling for you was real."

He whispered, "Check."

"Coin two was that I would be the only woman for you, like no one else that you've ever known."

Unable to resist, he kissed her, but he put his entire soul into the kiss. And when their lips parted, she had to grab onto him for support.

The first to recover, he asked, "What about number three? When do you think the big splash coin will come into play?"

"Not yet," she said, her breath a little shaky, "but in time, I hope." Her third coin wish was for Alex's cousin Adam who had lost so much. She wanted him to find peace, and finally to have love again when the time was right.

Alex made love to her that night as thoroughly as he could, erasing any doubt about his feelings for her once and for all.

Arms spooning her from behind, cradling her to him, he kissed her temple, her cheek, and wondered who their child would look like and whose personality he or she would favor. Either way, the kid would be a powerhouse.

Daisy turned toward him, her breast bumping against him pleasantly. Unable to resist, he reached out and touched the firm mound, stroking her nipple until it hardened.

"What about you?" she asked.

"Me?"

"Your coin at the fountain. Let me guess, it was for hotel world domination in the monopoly game of life? Or did you speculate on whether Luis would be employed after the party?"

"Oh that," he said, remembering that he'd asked her with the intent to reveal his own wish.

Now, after everything they'd shared, he felt a little, well, vulnerable. Building up his nerve, he kissed her shoulder, her neck, and then her cheek, before she stopped the tender assault and said, "I know it isn't about me and that is okay."

"Wrong," he said, clearly remembering his wish. "But it isn't easy for me to expose so much. This kind of vulnerability is relatively new for me."

"You're the strongest person I know," she said, running her finger along his cheek. "And I love every inch of you. Your secrets are safe with me."

He rolled her onto her back and kissed her as her legs encircled him.

"My wish," he whispered in her ear, "was for you to love me as much as I love you…"

EPILOGUE

Daisy cautiously opened the door to Alex's office as the dozen people sitting around the conference room table murmured their quiet greetings to the boss's wife.

She smiled back, noticing the docile tone in the room, and whispered, "Hello everyone, sorry to interrupt."

Alex smiled broadly from the end of the conference room table and gently stood, cradling a sleeping pink bundle in his arms. "No worries, darling. Alexandra, your mommy's here," he whispered and leaned toward Daisy, kissing her softly on the lips.

She took their daughter in her arms and said, "Thank you, darling. Everything okay?"

"Perfect," he replied with a wink, and she enjoyed the sparkle in his eyes that was just for her. The past few months had been the best of her life.

"Still on for lunch?"

"Yes," he said in a hushed tone, "Say, ten minutes?"

She nodded with a soft, knowing smile and walked carefully toward the door, Alex following behind her. Don waved him off and opened the door himself, whispering, "Eight weeks to go Mrs. Stark. Brigitte has already picked out her outfit."

Daisy smiled and blushed. She and Alex were getting married again, only this time it would be for love. They would declare their love in front of their families and friends on what would be their first anniversary. Her mother was ecstatic as were Alex's mother and his sister, Rebecca.

The wedding was the perfect venue to also introduce Maria to the family, but she was proving to be a reluctant guest. Over the past few months, they'd made a lot of progress laying the groundwork to integrate her into the family, but she was still hesitant to meet everyone.

Alex's cousin Adam was finding a way to deal with his new normal, but he had asked Alex for a change of scenery and Alex had taken the step to find something new for him within the company.

"There is a hotel that needs renovation along the California coastline. It is yours if you want it, your baby from the studs to the linens. You can oversee it as a gentleman in a suit or wear a t-shirt and jeans and get dirty with it with actual manual labor, your choice. You can stay at Tranquility, my friends' summer house just north of the site. You'll be gone three months at least and then if you want, we can discuss another hotel option for you. Dubai will be ready then and I'll need someone I trust to run it. I always secretly wanted you for it," Alex said.

Adam replied, "As long as it is far away from New York, I'll be thankful."

Little did he know what awaited him at Tranquility.

Precisely ten minutes after Daisy left Alex's board meeting, she heard the penthouse door open as Alex walked in and slipped out of his shoes as not to wake the baby sleeping in the nursery. By the time he joined her in the master bedroom, his jacket and tie were abandoned and he was unbuttoning his shirt. She was wearing a lacy black nightgown, one she had saved for this moment, the first time they would make love after the birth of their child.

He sat on the edge of the mattress just looking down at her. Slowly, he bent and kissed her as his fingertips gently stroked her cheek.

"You're fine?" he asked, as his hand moved down her body, touching her through gauzy lace.

"I'm perfect," she replied, meeting his emerald gaze.

"Yes, you are," he said between kisses. "And it's been a long six weeks, again."

"Yes, but this time we got a baby out of the deal," she replied.

"Let's practice for another," he replied, pulling her into his arms, and practice they did.

THE END

Mary loves to hear from her readers. If you'd like to send her an email, you may do so through her website: MaryOldham.com

Watch for the next book in the Hotel Baron's Series, *A Summer Affair*, Adam's story. Previously titled: *Laura Takes a Lover*, a Romance Writers of America Golden Heart Finalist.

"Fans of Kristan Higgins and Jill Shalvis will enjoy the witty writing of award-winning author Mary Oldham!"

SNEAK PEEK

A SUMMER AFFAIR

RELEASE DATE: DECEMBER 2021

CHAPTER ONE

Adam Stark would never allow himself to fall in love again. But, since he'd made the decision several months earlier, he'd felt better. The weight in his chest, where his heart once resided, seemed to lessen.

It was easy to be unemotional when he'd been sent away from every place which held memories of his once-happy life. He loved his cousin, Alex, for suggesting he get out of town, but he also hated his cousin for making sure that Adam might forget everything through hard work as in the most strenuous, hard physical labor he'd ever done in his life.

Did he miss an office where everyone called him Mr. Stark? No, he still missed his family.

Nothing was going to change that.

He was lonely. Lonelier than he'd ever been in his life. He needed something to believe in again. He needed, wanted to be close to another person. He wanted to be needed and not just to the Stark Corporation.

One quick glance to the shoulder of the road silenced every desolate thought as his jaded heart fluttered wildly to life and issued a warning that couldn't be ignored. Be careful what you ask for. You just might get it.

He laughed. How long had it been since he'd laughed? At least a year.

The woman was breathtaking as she kicked the bumper of an old, silver BMW with a flat tire. And by the dent she'd created, he suspected she'd been at it for a while. Then, with one last kick, she gave up and was now looking down at the raging ocean in the noto-riously evil cove known as Devil's Punchbowl. Her shoulder-length blonde hair whipped around her face in the warm wind, but she did nothing to stop it, just stared, perhaps mesmerized by the crashing waves as they hit the rocks below.

Or maybe she'd just broken her foot.

Either way, he had to stop. Damn it.

Pulling off the road, he coasted the old pickup with a faded Driftwood Shores logo to a stop a safe distance away.

Glancing toward him, she lowered her oversized, black sunglasses, her expression a mix of curiosity and apprehension. She was crying. Not a few tears, he realized, but a torrent. He surmised that this was about a lot more than a simple flat tire.

"Aw hell," he muttered, getting out of the pickup, and lifting his hand in a friendly greeting.

He knew how he looked. He'd spent the better part of the day digging up dead pine trees. As a result, a once clean white t-shirt and jeans were covered with a mixture of dirt and debris. But, on the other hand, she was elegant in a crisp white blouse and black wraparound skirt, which alluded to a lush, curvaceous figure.

"Hello," he greeted above the roar of the ocean. "Do you need some help with your tire?"

She nodded and held up a cell phone.

Her voice cracked as she said, "I can't get cell service in this fucking vortex, and the fucking tire won't come off the fucking car because the fucking tire guy used an air wrench to put the lug nuts on, and I can't fucking get them off because they are so tight."

"Wow, okay. Are you okay?" She was not okay, and he knew he probably should not have asked her.

"I'm fine, can't you tell? I'm peachy," she replied, with a sob she'd tried to stifle.

Adam's chest automatically tightened in empathy. "I can tell you're upset."

Bright blue eyes, rimmed in red, stared at him as her lower lip quivered.

Articulate by nature, he faltered. Best to get on with the business at hand. "I think I can help you. I'm stronger than I look. Do you know if you have a spare?"

"Of course, I have a spare. I tossed it over there," she said, lifting her hand, and he followed to where she pointed. The spare was leaning against a railing, a good hundred feet away. A little more spin, and it would be bouncing into The Pacific Ocean.

Adam walked slowly toward the tire. She must have been angry. The momentum wouldn't have sent it this far unless she had kicked it…hard.

He got to the tire, picked it up, and carried it back to where she was leaning against the disabled car.

"I hate that tire. Put it down, and I'll kick it some more," she murmured and started crying again.

Unsure of what to do, Adam set the tire down and gently laid a palm on her bare arm, just below the cuff of the white blouse.

"I think the tire has had enough for today. Now please, don't worry, I'm here, and I'll take care of this for you," he said, then added, "I've changed many flats, and I'm quite good at it." Well, he's changed a few but no need to worry her at this point.

She lifted her gaze to meet his. Beautiful cornflower blue irises seemed to glow as they searched his face. She'd been crying for a long time, her lids swollen, and he guessed, burning from the irritation.

He didn't expect what would happen next. She fell forward, and he opened his arms, her body supported by his own. He didn't judge, but he did understand. How many times in the last year had he wished for someone, anyone, to just hug him and offer comfort? He missed the touch of another person.

Trying not to think about the acutely feminine body in his arms, or the subtle perfume reminiscent of roses that infused the air between them, masking his scent of working male, he asked, "Would you like to talk about it?"

She blurted out, "My bastard husband left me for another woman, and the latest rumor is that she is pregnant. Didn't the wedding ring on his finger mean anything to either one of them? She's an idiot, and I hate him."

Adam said the first thing that entered his mind. "Your husband is an idiot."

She stepped away from him, and he felt the loss of her. But, he could have stayed the way they were for a very long time.

"Thank you. Thank you for saying that. He'd vacillate between wanting children and not wanting children. I've always wanted a baby, and he finally agreed. And then I couldn't get pregnant, and now he is having a baby with someone else. What the hell? Do you know what it feels like to gain weight and give yourself shots of hormones to get pregnant? It sucks, and it hurts. And that bastard told me I was gaining weight while he was having an affair with his legal assistant... meanwhile, I'm giving myself shots! Shots. I'm scared of needles, but I did it even though Dr. Mallory showed my husband how, but he was scared to do it, so I injected myself. In the stomach. Every fucking day. It was all for his baby, and she's the one who gets pregnant. I hate him," she answered softly.

"I'm sorry?" Adam said, not sure what to say. Apparently, she needed to get it all out, obviously pent up inside of her for a long time, and he just happened to be there.

The woman was lovely despite the grief and smeared makeup. He sighed, placing his hands on her shoulders, hoping she would believe him, when he said, "If your husband were here, right now, I'd punch him for making you feel so bad, for not being a man and giving you the shots, for messing around with someone else. You're beautiful, and he is an ass."

"Thank you, thank you for listening," she said and smiled, but he could tell she didn't quite believe him. Her gaze fell to the gold band he still wore on his left hand.

"Your wife is a very lucky woman. You'd help her with the shots."

"Absolutely, and I was the lucky one to have found her," he corrected. "Let me help you with this tire."

"You're very kind. I'm sorry about falling apart. I usually have my shit together, but this tire, this fucking tire, and all the hormones. The doctor said it would take a while for them to get out of my system," she said, smiling a little and stepping aside as he reached for her trunk latch. "I don't think they are out yet."

"Don't worry about it. Let me have a look in the trunk."

"The jack and lug wrench are over there," she said. However, it was evident that she'd thrown them in frustration as they were a good ten feet away from her car.

He retrieved them and said, "Don't go back to him, whatever he says. You deserve someone who adores you. He sounds like a real bastard." His tone conveyed it was more of an order than a suggestion as he began to loosen the nuts on her wheel. He had no respect for men who cheated on their wives. He and his cousin, Alex, had disowned one of their closest friends from school after forgetting his marriage vows and hitting on Alex's new wife.

"I'll never talk to him again. As of 8 a.m. this morning, I'm divorced," she said, and he thought she might start crying again.

"Good. He wasn't worthy of you, and life is too short."

He jacked up the car, removing the nuts and hefted on the new tire, then tightened the nuts back on again. Then he opened the spare tire well, and placed the damaged tire in the open space, replacing her luggage.

Looking down at her white blouse, he cringed. He couldn't help but notice the lacy outline of her bra through the once pristine fabric.

Guiltily, he stepped back and apologized, "I'm sorry, but it seems I've covered you in dirt."

"It's a fair trade. You're covered in my tears and lipstick," she said, pointing to his t-shirt where a perfect red lip print was emblazoned next to several damp spots.

They both smiled tentatively, and she reached out, her small hand gently touching his arm, "Thank you," she said with heartfelt sincerity. "I'm so glad you stopped, not only for the tire but what you said. Thank you. I want to pay you for fixing my tire."

Placing his hand on hers, he shook his head and said, "It was no trouble. Of course, I won't accept anything from you, but will you be okay?"

"Yes," she replied.

"I'm not far from home."

He smiled one last time and turned away, walking swiftly back to his pickup. It was more complicated than he thought, leaving this woman he'd only known for a few minutes, but he'd served his purpose, and it was time to move on. The pain he usually felt thinking about his family and what he'd lost subsided for those few minutes and all because of her. Getting back in the truck, he gave her one last smile and was rewarded with a wave, which he returned, before driving away.

OTHER BOOKS BY MARY

Don't miss any of Mary Oldham's exceptional stories:

The Silver Linings Wedding Dress Auction
(stand-alone) October 2021

The Hotel Baron's Series:
A Paris Affair, November 2021
A Summer Affair, December 2021
A Roma Affair, 2022
A London Affair, 2022

ABOUT THE AUTHOR

Mary Oldham is a multi-award-winning author, and three-time Golden Heart Finalist with the Romance Writers of America in the areas of Contemporary Romance and Romantic Suspense. Mary resides in Portland, Oregon when she is not writing by the Pacific Ocean in scenic Yachats, The Gem of the Oregon Coast.

ACKNOWLEDGEMENTS

I first wrote this story on an airplane to Atlanta when I found out *Laura Takes a Lover* had finaled in the Maggies, the first contest I'd entered. *Laura* went on to be a Romance Writers of America Golden Heart finalist and is now the book that will follow this one, entitled, *A Summer Affair*. This story, *A Paris Affair*, was originally titled: *The Hotel Baron's Mistress* and received 1st Place two years in a row with the Spring Into Romance Contest. It is the first book in the Hotel Baron series, the cornerstone to the foundation of this series, and also really a love story about two people who fall in love and can't believe the other person loves feels the same way.

I couldn't have done this without a strong team behind me, Sue Grimshaw, my dream editor and Mama Bear Protector, thank you. To Lynn Andreozzi, who designed another beautiful cover, you get my style. To the Deliberate Pen, Tamara Cribley for making my baby shine and Chris Knight for flawless grammatical editing, thank you.

To Leslie, Suzie, Trudy, and Valerie, my supportive family, thank you for handing out my books to friends and introducing them to venues where you think they belong. Your belief in me brings tears to my eyes. To my financial planner, Good Shane, thanking you for encouraging me to live this dream and calming me down when I freak out, which I do on a regular basis.